FRANNIE
and
TRU

FRANNIE

and

TRU

Karen Hattrup

An Imprint of HarperCollinsPublishers

HarperTeen is an imprint of HarperCollins Publishers.

Frannie and Tru

Copyright © 2016 by Karen Hattrup

All rights reserved. Printed in the United States of America.

No part of this book may be used or reproduced in any manner
whatsoever without written permission except in the case of brief
quotations embodied in critical articles and reviews. For information
address HarperCollins Children's Books, a division of HarperCollins
Publishers, 195 Broadway, New York, NY 10007.

www.epicreads.com

Library of Congress Control Number: 2015951378
ISBN 978-0-06-241020-7 (trade bdg.)

Typography by Ray Shappell
16 17 18 19 20   PC/RRDH   10 9 8 7 6 5 4 3 2 1

First Edition

To Kevin, who always believed

O N E

The summer sky was dark outside my window when the phone rang. Not a tinny version of a pop song from somebody's cell—the hard jangle of the landline. Almost no one called that number. Mostly telemarketers, sometimes ladies from church looking for volunteers, donations to the bake sale. But they never called this late.

Opening my bedroom door a crack, I listened as Mom picked up the receiver in the kitchen and gave a little "Oh" of surprise. Seconds later she was rushing up the steps and into her room. She didn't look in my direction, just closed her door with a click. Before she did I heard two soft words. "Oh, Deb."

Deborah. Her sister. The two of them were just a year apart, but hardly ever spoke. My room shared a wall with my parents' room, so I leaned against it and tried to hear, thinking about everything on the other end of the line. Aunt Deborah with the perfect hair. Uncle Richard who worked at some sort of firm, the kind of place with three names. Somebody, somebody, and somebody else.

And then there was my cousin Truman. Tru for short.

Minutes passed, and Mom kept talking. Dad came up the stairs and disappeared into the room with her, staying silent as her voice murmured on. If it had been a year ago, I might have barely noticed, barely cared about some strange phone call from Aunt Deb, but right now I needed a distraction. Summer was here, but for me it promised to be a long and terrible slog. School had let out three weeks earlier, and I'd hardly left the house or spoken to anyone. Wrapped in gloom, I was practicing a kind of stillness—like a tightrope walker who looked straight ahead and thought only of keeping her balance.

But now . . . now something about this secret conversation stirred me. Leaning closer to the wall, I felt a twinge of excitement. I had a sense that *things* were happening. I made myself flat, pressed my ear to the fading purple paint. Most of my mother's words were indistinguishable, but one soft note sounded over and over, until finally I knew what it was.

Tru.

I woke just after midnight, tangled up in sweaty sheets, a dream slipping away before I could catch it. Minutes ticked by, and I couldn't sleep. I couldn't stop wondering about the phone call. About Truman.

He was two years older than me, the same age as my brothers, twins Jimmy and Kieran, which meant he was now seventeen. We almost never saw him, just a couple of Christmases or Easters here and there, and that was years and years ago. There in the dark, an old memory came to me. His family was with mine at our dinner table. Tru, hair nicely combed, fork and knife delicately in hand, was asking for something to be passed. Mom complimented his manners, but there was something off about it all, something in his practiced, smooth politeness. . . . Later I overheard Dad tell Mom, "That kid's got a shit-eating grin."

His words had jolted through me. I was little, maybe eight, and swearing was a serious offense in our house. But then Dad chuckled, and I realized that he wasn't mad. Not exactly. I thought about what he'd said, and even though I'd never heard that phrase before, I was pretty sure I knew what he meant.

Tru was bad, but people liked him.

Years passed when I didn't see him at all. I knew practically nothing about him except that he lived in Connecticut and went to prep school, which I understood was fancier and more expensive than the Catholic schools we went to in Baltimore. He had slipped from my life so completely that I might barely have remembered him at all—but then there'd been that one amazing day. When I was eleven and he was thirteen, Tru made it to the big spelling bee, the one they show on ESPN. We'd had a family party, my brothers, my parents, and me crowding in front of the television with Coke and microwave popcorn. The camera panned over the kids onstage, and there was Tru. I could hardly believe it. We all cheered and clapped, and Dad called him "the great white hope, treading water in a sea of Indians and Asians." Mom said that was inappropriate, while Jimmy and Kieran laughed so hard they fell off the couch.

My heart fluttered like a little bird every time he approached the microphone, his name appearing in bold letters on the screen: Truman Teller. Lots of kids used their fingers to trace the words out on their palms, but Tru never did. Instead, he put his hands in his pockets and stared at some point off in the distance. He seemed to spell without effort, like he was pulling letters down from the sky.

I was sure he was invincible, but in the end he fell. It was the end of round five. About half the kids were left.

"The word is *corpuscle.*" "Repeat it, please?" "Corpuscle." "Language of origin?" "Latin." "Definition?" "An unattached cell, especially the kind that floats freely, a blood or lymph cell." "Use it in a sentence?" "Red corpuscles have a biconcave shape, allowing for the rapid absorption of oxygen."

Tru missed the second *c.*

When the bell dinged to signal his mistake, my parents and brothers groaned and shouted in disappointment, while I sank off the couch, landing in a heap on the floor. A sympathetic burn of embarrassment and disappointment filled my chest. I was someone who felt all my failures—bad grades, dropped balls—as little scorches of shame, and I couldn't imagine what it was to fail so publicly, so enormously. As he came down from the stage, the camera caught his face for the briefest moment. His head was ducked, but I could see the hint of a hooked little smile.

We turned off the TV after that, but I kept picturing Tru, that look on his face. I remembered my father's words, "a shit-eating grin," and a strange tingle came over me. A flash of understanding.

Tru didn't care about the spelling bee. He didn't care at all.

Somehow I knew that I was right. I'd seen it in the flare of his right lip when he thought the cameras weren't looking. The idea amazed me, almost scared me. How could someone not care about something this grand, this important? I tried to imagine how that would feel, but it was impossible. I'd always been a good girl who followed rules and wanted to please. Still was today.

When I was eleven I couldn't have explained why that smirk mattered so much, why it affected me. But now, as I lay in in bed, staring out into the darkness, I found the words for what had struck me so.

Tru was a person not afraid of the world.

I woke up groggy, sunlight cracking through the crooked blinds. The morning was hot and sticky. Mom was banging around in the kitchen, so the boys had woken up, too, even though it was early for them. We settled around the dining room table for breakfast, because that's what my parents liked us to do. We ate meals together, at a table, as a family. It was one of their big rules, like no back talk and no cell phones after eight p.m. Most of our friends thought we were freaks, and we didn't blame them. But this morning something was wrong. I could tell right away. Our bowls were filled with dry cereal, and we were waiting for the milk, but Mom was holding it and wouldn't let go. Dad put a hand to his mouth and coughed awkwardly.

"Your cousin Truman is coming to stay with us. For the rest of the summer."

At first, we all just stared at him. He might have said the president was coming for all the sense it made. But then Mom told Jimmy that he would have to move out of the basement bedroom and back in with Kieran upstairs, like when they were little. That snapped everyone awake. Kieran gave a heavy sigh and leaned back in his chair, while Jimmy went red in the face.

"Are you kidding me?" Jimmy asked. "Seriously. You're kidding me, right?"

Dad told him to deal with it. Jimmy opened his mouth again, but Dad gave him one of his looks that stop a person dead, then crossed his arms over his chest, swelling up like a gorilla. Jimmy shut up. I knew Dad was pissed, really pissed, because his cheeks were all mottled. He told us he was picking Tru up that night from the train station and would like for someone to come with him. To welcome our cousin. He glared at my brothers, who looked away and stayed silent.

Seconds went by. Tick.Tick.Tick. Then I opened my mouth. Shut it. Opened it again and took a breath.

"I'll go," I told him. "I want to go."

TWO

An hour later, Mom and Dad had disappeared on errands unknown, while the twins were busy moving Jimmy's stuff back upstairs and squeezing it into the too-small room. I was cleaning the kitchen, but as soon as I was alone, I started sifting through the junk drawer, pushing aside old rubber bands and stray birthday candles until I found what I was looking for: an old school portrait of Tru.

He was just twelve or thirteen in it, still a little baby-faced, not smiling exactly, but cocking an eyebrow. This was the same Truman I remembered from the spelling bee, except here he was wearing his school uniform: navy blazer with an embroidered crest; crisp, white shirt; red tie. He was dark-haired and dark-eyed, nothing like my brothers and me. Like my dad, we were red-haired, fair, freckled, and tall. Impossibly tall. They were both six three. I was five ten and still going.

I searched the photo like it could tell me why he was coming. Kieran had eventually asked Mom, once things had calmed down a little, but all she would say was that we hadn't see him in forever and were overdue to spend some time together. There was no way that was all there was to it, but the picture, of course, told me nothing. All it did was remind me that I had no idea what he looked like now. The more I stared at his face, the more he seemed like some kind of ghost boy, frozen in time and full of secrets.

Before I knew what was happening, Jimmy snatched the picture from my hand.

"Oh god—he's worse than I remember."

Kieran came loping up the stairs and into the kitchen as Jimmy held up the little wallet print. I glared at both of them, but they didn't seem to notice.

"Can you believe we have to put up with The Blazer here all summer?" Jimmy asked.

Kieran grinned. "But don't forget he has to put up with us."

"Good point," Jimmy said as the two of them headed back down the stairs. "I mean, look around. Does he know we're living in the dark ages here?"

This summer was the Dark Ages because we had just given up our internet and cable and would only be running the air conditioners when we were absolutely dying. These were just the latest blows in a series, all of which had begun in the fall when Dad started running low on work. He was a marine welder, which meant he went underwater and worked on things like submarines and bridges. Sometimes he had to travel, leaving for weeks at a time, and while it could be dangerous, it paid pretty well. But then his long-steady contracts had started to slow, and since December, they'd gone dry almost completely. Now he made almost nothing but spare cash through random jobs he picked up here and there—light plumbing and handyman chores, fixing the cars of friends and neighbors. When things first got bad, we'd pretended everything could stay the same, but as winter wound down, we kept cutting back, spending less and less. Finally, Mom had decided to double her shifts at the hospital. She worked there as a medical transcriptionist, listening to recordings that doctors made and typing out what they said. Whenever she talked about work over dinner, Jimmy would pretend to fall asleep.

And now we had a hot, cramped house with no internet, no cable. I was sweating as I scrubbed a cluster of old, angry coffee cup rings that had set near the sink. For the first time I wondered what Tru would think of where we lived, our situation. I leaned into the sponge and scrubbed harder. The twins had left the photo of him on the counter, slightly crumpled now, and my eyes kept flitting toward it.

Jimmy reemerged from the basement into the kitchen carrying an armload of T-shirts.

"Frannie," he asked, "do you think The Blazer knows that Baltimore is a cesspool of drugs and STDs? I don't think the kids around here are going to be *his type*."

Kieran shuffled in behind him lugging two big dumbbells in

his hands, two smaller ones tucked under his armpits. "Dude," he said, "chill with the Blazer talk." He tried to sound serious but was grinning. Jimmy acted like he hadn't heard.

"Do you think The Blazer really understands the concept of a row house?" Jimmy asked, looking pointedly at me. "I mean, does he even remember that all we have is a skinny little house that is *connected to other houses*? I don't think he's going to like the accommodations here at all."

"Well, shit," Kieran said, now giving up and laughing, "you might be right about that."

"I mean, think about it," said Jimmy, plucking the photo from the counter and waving it around. "This kid wants *us* to feed *him*?"

Kieran rolled his eyes. "Uncle Richard must be giving them some cash. You know he must be."

"Shit," Jimmy said. "Sometimes you're not an idiot. I hadn't thought of that."

I hadn't thought of it either, but now the idea made me blush, embarrassed for Dad. Embarrassed for all of us.

The twins turned in unison to look at me. Jimmy had shaved his head down to the faintest fuzz on the last day of school, and Kieran had been letting his grow for months into a great mass of clown curls. They were actually fraternal, though everyone found that hard to believe—they were practically mirror images. And right now I was sick and tired of both of them. I didn't want to hear their jokes about Tru, because all the reasons that they couldn't stand our cousin were the same reasons that I thought he was interesting. I kind of liked his school uniform, which was better than the stupid, shapeless sweaters we had to wear. I liked that he seemed too smart for his own good.

And to be honest, what I really liked was that he was so different from my family.

Jimmy sighed. "Frannie doesn't seem concerned about how we're going to make The Blazer comfortable. She doesn't seem concerned at all."

Kieran shook his head at me, *tsk-tsk*ing, and then the two of them headed back downstairs to carry up another load, voices trailing behind.

"Do you think he prefers squash or tennis?"

"I'm guessing polo. Or fox hunting. You know—anything with a horse."

I looked up at the ceiling and sighed. In that moment I was glad that I was the only one going to the train station with my dad. It might be my only chance to make some kind of impression on Tru before he met the twins and decided we were all a bunch of loudmouthed idiots. I needed that chance; I knew I did. Because while I couldn't say why exactly—maybe just because I had so little else to hope for—I thought that Tru might be able to lead me out of this sad and lonely summer.

He was different from my family, so he might notice that I was kind of different from them, too.

On the twins' next pass by the kitchen, I turned my back, ready to ignore them, but then Kieran came over and put a sweaty arm around me, wrestling my neck into a gentle sort of sleeper hold. Some of my anger dissolved. It had been ages since he'd done something like that and, instead of yelping or fighting, I just went limp. I let myself be held. Kieran told me that my wrestling skills sucked as he gave me an extra squeeze that was almost a hug. He let me go with a pat on the head and a final thought.

"I was going to suggest that the kid bring a sleeping bag and ride out the summer on the floor in your room, but I just couldn't do that to you, Frannie. 'Cause as far as I remember, Truman is kind of a dick."

As I put the cleaning supplies back under the sink, I got a little rush of nerves. There was something hiding here—a secret treasure, tipped on its side, wedged far back in the dark and dirty cabinet. I pushed past the trash bags and mousetraps and some old jars of oil. I moved aside the avalanche of cleaning supplies. And there it was.

A small but almost full bottle of vodka.

I'd been cleaning the kitchen for months now, ever since Mom had started working more, but still, I'd only noticed the bottle a few weeks ago. That's how far it was shoved into the sticky recesses. And whoever left it here, Mom or Dad, had clearly completely forgotten—I was sure about that, because its disappearance had been the source of a major blowup just last week.

Dad had been looking for it the other night, had ransacked the kitchen, in fact. When he couldn't find it, he totally freaked out on the twins. A truly epic screaming match, apparently. I missed the whole thing, and when I finally heard about it, I knew I should tell everyone, but . . . I didn't want to. If I told them where it was, it would be like admitting that I'd never need it. That I really was that profoundly uncool.

Now, alone here in front of the cabinet, I liked the idea of having the bottle when Tru got here. I had no friends, no life, but I could offer this up, like it was no big deal. It wasn't much, but it was something.

I knew Dad might go looking for it again, might eventually find it—so if I really wanted it, I should hide it away. Hide it somewhere extra safe.

The boys were loud and busy upstairs. No one else was around, but that wouldn't last long. If I was going to move it, I had to move it now.

Grabbing the bottle, I leaped to my feet and ran through the vertical stretch of our house, the three rooms lined up in a neat column—kitchen, dining room, living room. I burst out of the front door with a squeak and a slam, flying across the street into the dog park. Rushing down the steep hill, I dodged rocks and trees until I reached the big, grassy basin at the bottom.

I was standing in a valley the size of a football field, and there was no one there but me. A sharp bark came from somewhere in the thick trees, far off ahead of me and to the right. Slower, more cautiously, I jogged across the expanse of the park until I reached the creek. I turned left, following its rocky edge, looking over my shoulder every few seconds. Still no one. This was the most exciting thing I'd done in weeks, which was ridiculous, but I was just happy to feel my heart pumping as I ran. I was glad for this bit of danger, small as it was.

The creek led into a huge cement cavern, cars roaring by on the bridge overhead. White walls arched over me, a story and a half high. Every footstep echoed. I made my legs pump faster, faster, faster, carrying me along the thin walkway, the creek trickling alongside. Grafitti screamed from the walls. *EVA IS A SLUT 4EVA. BOBBY SNORTS CRACK.* (*For reals?* someone asked just below.)

I burst out the other end, into the outer edge of the park. Turning toward the trees, I quickly found the one I was searching for, the old beech tree with a knot in the center. I stood at the proper place in front of it, took a right, and walked until I reached a thick covering of what looked like poison ivy but was just a harmless patch of sumac.

This was it, our perfect hiding spot. Years ago, Jimmy and Kieran had buried an old toolbox here in the dirt. I had stood lookout while they dug, working for what seemed like forever to hollow out a big enough hole. They called it the safe, and they used it to hide fireworks and cigarettes. Plus things I never even knew about, I'm sure. Now here I was, being the bad one. Or at least trying to be. I tilted the bottle back and forth, watching the liquid slide, feeling excited, hopeful. I might actually have a reason to drink this before the summer was out. It might end up being the key to some perfect summer night.

I tiptoed into the sumac, which I hadn't dug through in—what? Three years? More? It was insane to think the safe would be still be here, but I pushed aside the leaves and looked. The pyramid of rocks they used to pile up on top was gone, but something was sticking up from the dirt. I kneeled down to look closer, poking it.

It was the red plastic handle of the toolbox.

My hands reached into the cracked, dry dirt, and I started to dig.

With the bottle hidden, I walked slowly back through the tunnel and cut across the length of the park, following a dirt path up and out, back onto the sidewalk.

I was a block and a half from home, but didn't want to be there, not yet, not with the twins stomping up and down the stairs, yelling stupid jokes about Tru. Instead, I walked down the sidewalk in the opposite direction. I listened to birds, watched squirrels, kicked an old can. Head down, I circled around and went back a different way than I'd come, taking the alley that ran behind our row of houses. There were backyards on either side, and I peeked over short fences or in between the planks of tall ones, spying on the barbecue grills, sandboxes, and tiny vegetable gardens of our neighbors.

I was almost home, and I was grimy. I tried to brush the dirt off my knees and hands. I was scraping it from underneath my fingernails when I heard Dad's voice. He was in the backyard with Mom.

"Christ, Barb. He's not my kid. What do I care what he's into? You think I need a lecture on being nice to my freaking nephew?"

Mom whispered angrily back at him, spitting each word too low for me to hear.

Silence. Dad sighed.

"Well, yeah. It's bad. It's a bad situation. It's a lot to deal with. Your sister needs time. They both need time."

Her voice came back softer. Dad cut her off.

"Look, let's talk about this later. I don't want the kids to hear."

Another mumble from Mom.

"No, no! I mean, god. I don't think we should tell them."

The smallest hush, which must have been Mom again.

"No, don't tell them any of it. Right? How would we even begin? This is all so, so . . . personal. And what good would it do? The kid's here for the summer, not forever. You think he's going to prance home with some new boy toy every night?"

Boy toy?

At first I didn't understand. It was like listening to my Spanish teacher—the words had a hint of meaning, but I had to roll them around to make the connection. . . .

And then suddenly I did.

The sun glared down, and I waited to hear more, but they said nothing. Their footsteps moved across the little plot of grass that was our backyard, and the screen door slammed behind them. For several beats, I didn't move. I stood there in perfect stillness, thinking of the only Truman I could clearly picture—the ghost boy in the school photo.

He was cocking his eyebrow as if to say, *What?*

THREE

The train station was big and beautiful, with old wooden benches like church pews and soaring stone walls like a castle. Standing at its center, I hoped that Tru would be impressed, that he would think Baltimore was somewhere special. Somewhere beautiful, even.

Then I imagined telling Jimmy and Kieran that, how they would fall over laughing.

Dad and I waited together, not saying much. He checked his phone repeatedly, looking at who knows what, while I stared at the glowing arrival board and thought of nothing but the conversation I'd overheard in the backyard.

When I watched TV, it seemed like there were gay people everywhere, in every high school and law office and hospital, but I'd hardly met any at all. There was my old gymnastics coach,

Miss Ann, but I hadn't even known she was gay, not until just last year, when I saw her picture in a slide show online, getting married at the courthouse after Maryland made it legal. She was waving a bouquet over her head, and her new wife was crying, and that made me want to cry, too, even though I hadn't seen or thought about her in ages.

So there was her, and then of course there was the only kid who was actually officially out at our little Catholic school. The gorgeous, the quiet, Jeremy Bell. But he was older than me. I'd had class with him once, but never really talked to him. I just knew about him, like everybody did. I knew that he was only really friends with girls, and that last year they ate in the art room together, to avoid the cafeteria and some group of asshole senior guys. I knew that he used to play baseball, but that he quit the same year he started telling people he was gay.

And I knew he still went to all the big parties at Beau Womack's house, just like my brothers did, but I'd also heard Jimmy tell a story about how every time Jeremy walked in the door, Beau would say, "No date tonight? Good." Then he would laugh like that was hilarious. Jimmy clearly thought it was hilarious, too.

Technically, as Catholics, my parents were supposed to care, were supposed to think it was a sin, though who knows if they actually did. The two of them couldn't even sign my sex-ed permission slip without blushing, so it wasn't exactly the kind of thing we'd talk about over dinner. Now that I thought about it, I did remember my mom getting really upset when there were all those stories about bullying and suicides, but she got upset at the news a lot. And I guess she liked that show about the hairdressers, but whenever it was on Dad would say, "My god, not this," and leave the room.

Still . . . earlier today in the backyard, when he'd said he didn't care, even though he'd said it roughly, harshly, I was pretty sure he'd meant it.

I looked up at him then, watching as he rubbed his eyes with his hand. There was something backward and buttoned-up about the way they whispered in the backyard, but at least it seemed like they could handle that Tru was gay. So why couldn't Aunt Deb and Uncle Richard do the same? What had Dad said—that they "needed time"? The more I thought about it, the angrier I got. I wanted badly to tell Tru how sorry I was. I wanted him to know that I wasn't like that, not at all, and I wasn't like my parents either—he could talk to me. I sat there writing righteous little speeches in my head, imagining how relieved he would be to hear me say it, how impressed he'd be by me, how eager he'd be for us to be friends . . .

The PA system came on, and a crackling voice announced that his train from Bridgeport had arrived. Passengers were already rushing up the stairs from the platform, hurrying and scurrying along.

There was a big crowd of people, but I saw him right away. He pulled a small suitcase behind him and had a messenger bag slung over his shoulder. Other people were fumbling and straining beneath their loads, but Tru walked easily, as if his bags weighed nothing. He was wearing jeans and a black T-shirt, with a pair of Converse sneakers exactly like the ones Jimmy and Kieran had.

Wouldn't they be surprised.

He stopped a slightly awkward distance away, removed from us but smiling. His face was much leaner than in the old picture in the drawer. He had bright eyes, dark but shining, and the kind of perfect skin I wanted for myself. His hair was thick and straight, worn longish but unfussy. And I knew it was kind of weird, but I tried to imagine what the girls I knew would say about him.

Hot. They would definitely say he was hot.

He greeted Dad first. They said empty words to each other— *hello*s and *how are you*s and "How was the train ride?" and "Thank you, Uncle Patrick, for picking me up."

My father towered over him, as he towered over almost everyone. He was absolutely enormous—a great big man with the last name Little, which always made people laugh. His hand was a paw, and it swallowed Tru's hand whole when the two of them shook. His grip could crush, but I noticed that Tru didn't flinch, didn't seem to even blink, and I wasn't sure if Dad was going easy on him or if Truman simply wasn't rattled by it.

I told myself it was stupid to be nervous, but I couldn't help the blush that rose to my cheeks. I hated that I had to stand here, on display for someone who hadn't seen me in years. He turned to me, and I was ready for all the obvious comments about how tall I was, how he barely recognized me. I realized too late that I should have been prepared, should have thought of something clever to say. . . .

"Hi, Frannie."

His face was expressionless. He hardly seemed to see me at all.

I started to say hello back to him, but my mouth was dry, and I practically choked on the words. He looked at me like I was some sort of unfamiliar creature, a bug that he was not particularly happy to have stumbled upon. After that he clucked his tongue. Checked his watch.

Dad shifted his feet and cleared his throat in a way that seemed loud and unnecessary. He asked about carrying Tru's bags. There was a pause, and Tru shrugged. It was pretty clear he didn't need our help.

We left the train station through the fancy glass doors, heading toward the garage where our car was parked. My mind was a jumble of thoughts, stray puzzle pieces that I couldn't make fit together. Shit-eating grins. Corpuscles. Boy toys. An echo of Kieran's voice: *Truman is kind of a dick.*

Why had I ever thought he would make my summer better?

We walked in a straight line: Dad, then me, then Tru. I could hear his suitcase rolling behind him, hitting a seam in the sidewalk every few feet. Then the sound stopped. I turned to see what had happened, and there was Tru, paused in his tracks, caught in a streetlamp's glow as distant skyscrapers sparkled behind him. He was looking straight up into the air.

"What *is* that?" he asked no one in particular.

The question caught Dad, who glanced back, too. He followed Tru's gaze and began to giggle.

My father looked like he should have some deep, echoing belly laugh, but no. He had a high-pitched little giggle. Like a girl, really. I'd seen people jump at the sound, it was so unexpected. Right then he couldn't seem to stop. He was going like a motor.

When he'd gotten control, he crossed his arms over the expanse of his chest and looked at Tru. "It's art!" he said. "Fine art. Can't you tell?"

Tru looked again at the object in question, neck craned to see it in full. Seconds passed and then he laughed, too.

"No, actually. I'm not sure that I can."

Dad and I had seen the sculpture a million times, but we came to stand beside Tru so we could look along with him. Two colossal figures, one a man and one a woman, were towering up from the roundabout in front of the train station. Their stiff, paper-doll-like bodies intersected to form an X. They were silver, constructed of shiny, rippling aluminum, and where their chests met, they shared a single heart made of soft lights that changed colors. They were fifty feet tall, a part of the skyline, and the bulbs at their center acted as a strange lighthouse that glowed gently over the city.

People hated the thing.

The sculpture had been up for years, and everyone still complained about it—how much it'd cost, the way it clashed with all the old buildings around it. Just last year the newspaper had printed a letter to the editor about how even with some time and perspective, it was still a monstrosity. Dad had read it out loud to us, giggling until there were tears in his eyes. Whenever we drove by it, he rolled down his window and screamed, "CULTURE!"

Now, after months of being so much quieter than usual, Dad was positively lit up. Devilish-looking. He stepped forward and put a hand on my shoulder.

"Ask Frannie what it means. Her social studies teacher had her class debate the thing last year—it was the tenth anniversary or something. She knows all about it."

Tru half looked at me, his eyes already bored. My throat dried up again. There were things I could have said, if I'd wanted to. We'd had to come up with a list of pros and cons and then pick a side, and I'd taken the pro-sculpture side, with just a few other people. I knew the thing was weird, but I kind of liked that it was weird. I liked that it bothered people and maybe even made them think. Plus, at the right time of night, from certain angles, I swear it was actually pretty.

So, sure, I could have told Tru about how the artist was a big deal and had his work all over the country and the world. And I could have explained how a lot of his pieces were these giant paper-doll people, and they were supposed to be superhuman and spiritual and symbolic.

Instead, I said none of these things, because I knew with a deep and sure instinct that Truman didn't give a damn. He wanted to laugh at this thing, not hear a thesis on it.

I looked for a way to escape this conversation. I opened my mouth to say, *Nobody cares, Dad*, but wasn't able to do it. This was my father, he'd lost his job, and he was fragile now in a way that he hadn't been before. I stewed in a fierce silence, as none of us made a move to leave. Dad turned to me.

"C'mon, Frannie. You don't want to school your cousin on the finer points?"

Next to me, Tru's indifference was a great invisible wall, a force field between us. I looked at the sculpture through his eyes, and there, in that moment, I started to hate it a little bit, too. The thing was a joke, the silly dream of some stuck-up artist who thought he was deep and smart. As I watched the heart's muted glow turn from magenta to lilac, it seemed uglier to me than ever before. Ugly and embarrassing, just like everything here, everything in my life that Truman was about to see. For the first time, it struck me that the whole idea was childish and simple—the two figures, male and female, joined together like it meant something.

So when I finally spoke, I spoke as sarcastically as I possibly could.

"It's a man and a woman made into one thing," I said, waving an arm in its direction. "So it's superugly, but it's a superbrilliant commentary on, you know, *gender* or whatever. Very subtle."

In that moment, something happened to Tru's posture. He straightened a bit and glanced in my direction. He started to grin, *really* grin, his face transforming into something delighted and wicked, like a handsome version of the Grinch.

He looked . . . pleasantly surprised.

He cocked an eyebrow, just like in the photo, and turned his gaze back skyward.

"Yes, Frannie," he said. "Very subtle indeed."

FOUR

We'd been in the house only minutes, but Tru seemed to have already defused the anger and sarcasm bomb that was Jimmy and Kieran. It happened right in front of me, and I still couldn't explain how he did it.

On seeing them, he had nodded instead of shaking their hands, and stood in front of his suitcase, seeming to take up very little room. He refused offers of a drink, didn't make a move to sit, and didn't ask where he would be sleeping. His eyes had connected with a lacrosse stick in the corner and he'd made an offhand comment about how Connecticut kids couldn't play lacrosse for shit.

He'd actually said those words. *For shit*. He'd then sent an embarrassed, apologetic, totally charming smile in my mother's direction.

To my amazement she'd smiled back and said nothing.

Over the course of the next few minutes, everyone talked a little more, Jimmy's face relaxing a bit and Kieran's growing almost warm. They actually asked Tru if he wanted to come with them to the basketball courts down the street for a pickup game. He seemed to consider before declining by saying he was "kind of beat." With that, the two of them were out the door, and Dad disappeared after them, saying he needed a beer, would be home soon.

Then it was just the three of us. Mom had been scrubbing the bathrooms and picking up the basement, and she was still wearing her cleaning getup: an old pair of the twins' gym shorts and an Orioles jersey. One of those dumb pink ones they make for ladies. Her hair was swept into a wild mess of a bun that leaned awkwardly to the side. I was afraid she was going to say something corny about how happy we were to have him and how much family means, blah blah blah. But she didn't say anything. She just walked over to Tru, put her hands on her hips, and let out a sigh. Then, with a pained, stiff motion, she reached her arms out and gave him a hug.

After swearing that he'd eaten a perfectly fine sandwich on the train, Tru was allowed to escape to Jimmy's old room and begin moving in. He'd been down there now for half an hour, and I'd been sitting on the living room couch, trying to begin the first book of my summer reading. I couldn't get through one paragraph. My whole body was on alert, aware of the presence rumbling in the basement. Like a dragon was shifting its bulk and whipping its tail, searching for room in the confines below.

Tru had his own bathroom and shower down there, and I started to think he'd stay there indefinitely. Not just tonight but all summer. He would never come out; he would just lurk underneath us, doing whatever he did.

As I was thinking this, Mom came down from upstairs, and I ducked my head toward the unread pages. She walked right over and dropped a pile of towels on my lap, accidentally knocking the book to the floor.

"Take them down, please."

I knew it should have been the most normal thing in the world, but the idea of taking those towels to him sent my heart racing. This was it. This was my chance. A chance at *what* exactly I wasn't really sure, I just knew I wanted to talk to Tru, to get him to smile at me like he had outside the station.

Yes, Frannie. Very subtle indeed.

Arms full, I walked carefully down into the basement. The bedroom was straight ahead at the bottom of the stairs. The lock had been broken for as long as I could remember, but the door was shut tight.

I knocked lightly, then waited. One second. Two seconds. Three.

"Come in."

Tru was in Jimmy's bed, sitting up against the headboard, his legs stretched out and crossed at the ankle. His things were invisible, either still in the suitcase or tucked completely away in drawers. There was a book next to him on the bed. *The Great Gatsby*. In his right hand there was . . . something. Something that he was flipping around and around in his fingers, deftly as a magician, making the object appear and disappear from sight. I wondered if it was a little pencil, a golf pencil, when suddenly it was gone, tucked into his T-shirt pocket with a single motion.

He sat up and turned toward me, sitting cross-legged, hands folded neatly in front of him.

"Towels," I said.

"Thank you," he said.

I placed them on a desk chair just to my right, realizing that once again I had nothing to say. Seconds passed in silence, each moment humiliating, but I felt madly compelled to stay. I had to. Just yesterday, I'd been sure the summer would be long, miserable, pointless. Now Tru was here, with all his charm and his jokes and his shit-eating grin, and there was a chance that he could give some life to the coming weeks.

So I stood and stood and stood but did not leave.

Tru broke the silence.

"So your dad was saying something in the car right before we pulled up to the house. Something about a new school for you? A magnet school?"

"It's . . . yes. It's because . . . Do you know that my dad's been out of work?"

Tru nodded like he knew, but still, I felt like this was some kind of betrayal. I got defensive.

"Jimmy and Kieran are seniors, so it makes sense for them

to finish at St. Sebastian's, but I have three more years, and we can't...ah...well. You know. It makes sense for me to go to public school. So I applied and got in. To the public magnet school."

"In the city?" he asked.

"In the city," I answered.

Jimmy had been the one to pull me aside, months ago, and ask if I knew what that meant. That most of the kids would be black. "So what?" I'd snapped. "They're just a bunch of dorks like me." But the week before Mom and Dad pulled the plug on our internet, I'd hunched over the computer to look up the student breakdown and seen that he was right. I felt ashamed for looking it up, and yet I knew without the slightest doubt what Jimmy had been trying to convey: that I'd be some freakish redheaded refugee from Catholic school. That I wouldn't make any friends.

But . . . that wasn't how the world worked anymore. Was it?

The pathetic thing was, I didn't actually know.

For the first time ever, I tried to imagine what it was like for black students at St. Sebastian's, and realized I had no clue. There were about eight hundred kids altogether, and there were, what, maybe a hundred who were black? I wasn't really friends with any of them, even though they hung out with plenty of white kids— sat with them in class and joked with them in the locker rooms and dated them sometimes. But at lunch, most of the black guys and girls sat together, and I had no idea why, if they wanted to or felt pressured to or some combination. All these questions had gotten tangled in my mind with my worries about next year at my new school, the whole mess of it consuming me when I was trying to sleep. Eventually I'd started calming myself down with an elaborate fantasy.

It went like this: I would arrive at the magnet school and immediately start dating a boy on the JV basketball team. We would take the world's most beautiful homecoming photo, the dark skin of his arms circling my snow-white shoulders. He would have an older sister, who would hover over me with great affection, and the two of them would come to my house, and my parents and my brothers wouldn't know what to do. They would look in awe at the new person I had become, and they would feel proud but also distant from me, because of how much I had changed. *Can you believe*, they would ask each other, *that we ever worried about sending her to that school?* This would be my new, beautiful life, and my boyfriend would never know I was the kind of person who had done secret racist searches on the internet.

I had constructed this drama months ago, reliving it again and again until it grew warm and familiar. Now, as I talked to Tru, the whole of the fantasy flashed through my mind like a movie on fast-forward. He seemed on the verge of asking me more about school, but didn't, and I sensed something in that hesitation. There was understanding in the look he gave me, as if he knew how serious this change was, what it meant. We met each other's eyes, and then he cracked his knuckles, tilted his head, and let out a sharp sigh.

"Frannie, do you know a place called Siren?"

Siren was less than a mile from our house, a dark little restaurant and bar where local bands played at night. I nodded, and my heart began a trill. I told him it was close, and he said that he knew that. He had looked it up.

"I have a friend, Frannie. She just started as a waitress there. She was a year ahead of me in school, and she's down here for the summer, before she goes off to college, taking some special class at MICA. Do you know MICA?"

MICA was the art college off Route 83. Or as Dad called it, "the planet's single greatest concentration of white kids with dreadlocks."

I told Tru that I knew MICA.

"Well, then you're probably imagining that she's some kind of artsy nightmare. She's not really that bad, but I make sure to tease her about it mercilessly, just to keep her in line. Anyway, she's just finished up her shift, but she's sticking around to watch a show tonight." He paused and waved his phone in my direction, a text lighting the screen. "Now, you and I are too young for after hours, but here's the thing. My friend can get us in, and from there we should be fine. I, for one, am agonizingly close to eighteen, and while you are not so close to eighteen, you *are* very, very tall, and I think that will work to our advantage."

He paused and looked at me. "That would be fun, yes?"

All the blood in my body seemed to be surging up, up, up, as if I were standing on my head, rerouting my insides, looking at the world upside down. I wanted to go to Siren with Tru. I couldn't remember wanting anything more than this in my entire life.

I nodded, and Tru looked pleased.

"All right," he said. "Now here's the thing, Frances Little. I don't imagine your parents will be very thrilled with this plan. So this is the all-important question. Is there anywhere acceptable we could possibly pretend to be walking to at nine thirty at night?"

Happiness swelled inside me like a physical force. For once I knew exactly what to say.

"Yes," I said. "We can tell them that we're going to Stix for Chix."

He blinked at me several times, as if I were blurry and he was trying to make me come clear. He put his head down and did a quick cough, looked back.

"Well, I can't say we have that in Connecticut. By all means, please tell me more."

FIVE

For ages, I'd dreamed about the Sophomore Summer Retreat. SSR, to all of us at St. Sebastian's. I dreamed about it the same way I dreamed about kissing and prom dresses and being a grown-up with my own place. Yes, on some level I knew that unless I became some sort of freakish hermit cat lady, those things would happen to me eventually. They had to. It's just that right now they seemed as distant as the moon. The stars. Magic glowing monuments that I would never ever reach.

And when it came to SSR, I suppose I'd been right to be worried. That dream was never coming true.

For kids at St. Sebastian's, the retreat was huge, epic, this one special weekend before sophomore year when the boys and girls were carted off to neighboring cabins, where everybody did spiritual exercises and talked about feelings. For years, I'd heard older girls whispering about things that had been said during those weekends in the woods, about the intense talks and tears as everyone sat in a circle. Who knows what went on with the boys—Jimmy and Kieran still gave each other these stupid, knowing looks whenever somebody mentioned it. But the circle part was only kind of important, anyway. What really mattered was that kids always snuck in beer and met each other in the woods late at night. I'd been sure that I was going to have my first drink. My first kiss. I just had to make it to that cabin, into those trees, and my real high school life would finally begin.

Except now, of course, that dream was over. There was no St. Sebastian's for me. No summer retreat full of spilled feelings, secret booze.

I'd planned to bunk with my three best friends: Mary Beth, Dawn, and Marissa. They must have picked another roommate by now, but I had no idea who. I hadn't spoken to any of them since school let out, had actually been pulling away from them for months, ever since they found out about my dad, about my new school. When I first told them, their eyes had gone all big, and afterward they'd begun to tiptoe around me as if I were dying. First I resented them and then I began to think of them as silly. Pathetic, even. Pathetic little girls who lived sheltered little lives.

And then had come that morning in the hallway.

It was the end of winter, an icy March day. I was running late. My hair was knotted, and I was wearing last year's uniform sweater, the only one I could find in the mess of my closet, the polyester stretched and worn, the sleeves too short. Rushing to my locker, I turned a corner and was surprised to see the three of them clustered around Kat Deveraux. She towered over them, slender, polished, and cold, not one of us. Their voices were hushed but thrilled, and I heard my name, a breathy whisper about my father and my new school.

I couldn't figure out why they would be telling her this, why she would care, but there was something in their voices that was a little nasty, and I started to suspect that I was being used. That my life was a hard flint of gossip, a way to strike a flame that would impress this witchy blonde.

I tried to brush the thought away—I didn't want it to be true—but then I caught a final hiss from Mary Beth.

"She'll be, like, one of the only white girls."

Just then the bell rang, sending everyone in different directions. At the same moment they spotted me and mumbled embarrassed *hello*s before rushing to class. I'd wanted to run away before they saw me, but I was frozen there, struck dumb not only by Mary Beth's words, but the way she'd said them. With just a little too much eagerness, that desire to shock.

Her voice, that closing thought, had echoed in my mind all morning. I'd never really thought of myself in those terms before, as a white girl. At least, I'd never felt that being a white girl actually meant something or mattered. But in that hallway that morning it suddenly did, and I got a flash of complicated feelings, a fleeting sense of what it would be like to be labeled like that. The words were a cold burn, harsh as snow on skin.

When I saw the girls again at lunch, I was too big a coward to confront them, pretending, as they did, that nothing had happened. But things changed after that. I started ignoring their calls. I made excuses not to go places with them.

Which was exactly why I'd had no plans to go tonight to Stix for Chix, this silly charity field hockey tournament that benefited a local women's shelter. Girls came from all over the city to play little scrimmages in goofy costumes, while pop music blasted in the background. It went all night, like Relay for Life, so parents hated it, and kids loved it. Mary Beth, Dawn, and Marissa all played field hockey, so they'd be there, wearing ugly old prom dresses they'd bought at a thrift store about a month ago, one of the last times I'd really hung out with them.

That day, I met them at the thrift store counter ready to buy some clothes of my own. Not joke clothes. Real clothes. Clothes I could actually afford with my babysitting money. Dawn noticed first, then poked Mary Beth who gave a little *whoa* of surprise and stifled a noise that might have been a laugh. Marissa sort of turned away, like she was trying not to see.

The most painful part about it was that, in a way, they were just pretending. Acting. They weren't that snobby, not really. Pushing me away had become a game, a power play, the kind of thing we'd done to other girls in middle school for no real reason except that we could. And we could, of course, because those girls were weak and scared. They didn't speak up. And now that was me.

As I counted out my cash and grabbed my bag of secondhand shirts and jeans, I decided that I wanted absolutely nothing to do with them. Not ever, ever again. They could have their stupid dresses and stupid all-night fun fest and stupid mean-girl games, all the more stupid because they weren't even that cool. They didn't party, didn't have boyfriends. And who knows? Maybe that's why they needed to push somebody around.

I'd tried hard to forget that day, but now I was all tangled up in the memory as I told Tru what Stix for Chix was in a confused rush. I started to explain that my friends were there, only they weren't really my friends anymore, but all I could do was trip in and out of an unfinished sentence. I finally just shut my mouth. Tru's face grew supremely amused. He paused, considering me, and I could see he was fighting a smile.

"Did you . . . want to go to this thing?" he asked.

There was a level of politeness to this question. He seemed genuinely interested in what I would say. To be honest, before things had changed with the girls, I absolutely would have gone. It was the perfect excuse to be out late, and I would have loved any chance to run into boys from school, or better yet, new boys from different schools. But after everything that had happened, I didn't want to go. Not at all. So I was happy, then, to answer with a roll of my eyes, giving the kind of opinion that I was pretty sure he'd appreciate.

"I would rather die."

When I told my mother we were going to watch Stix for Chix, and that I wanted to say hi to Mary Beth, Dawn, and Marissa, she became a happy wreck. She knew I hadn't really been speaking to them, and now there were tears in the corners of her eyes.

Hot guilt coursed through my body but didn't stop me.

She offered to drive us three separate times, until finally I yelled, "My god, it's a ten-minute walk! Ten minutes! Tru *likes* to walk. It's one of his favorite things!"

And with that we were finally out the door. I told him that we'd have to make an awkward loop so that it would seem like we were moving in the right direction, in case Mom was watching. We moved temporarily toward the shining stadium lights.

"So that's where your little friends are, with their little sticks? What college is that?"

"Johns Hopkins," I said. "It's a smart kids' school. Science and premed and stuff."

Just a few weeks ago, I'd heard my Dad call it "loserville, land of the unlaid" when he was talking to my mom, not realizing the twins and I could hear him from the other room. "Yeah," Jimmy had yelled with a snort, "I bet Frannie will go there."

Dad sort of huffed around, face red, caught between being embarrassed and pissed. Not Mom. She'd come over and slapped Jimmy on the back of the head. She had a way of doing that where it was light but still shocking, not so much a physical thing but the surest, fastest way to make you feel like crap.

After a couple of blocks, I turned left and Tru followed, as we moved toward our real destination. The two of us arranged ourselves side by side on the sidewalk. I watched him watching the houses. We lived in what people called a working-class neighborhood, which I was pretty sure meant kind of poor, but not really poor. Still, our street was on the outer edge, the part closest to the university, where things were nicer. People on our block sent their kids to some of the cheapest private schools, just like my parents did. And our neighbors cared for their lawns and planted flowers.

Things changed quickly, though, on the way to Siren. Soon Tru and I were passing yards that had rusty chain-link fences and tacky plastic flamingos perched in the ground. The cars were dented or duct-taped and the dogs, staring at us from side yards and front windows, were uglier. Meaner. We were quiet for a while, and when Tru finally spoke, I thought for sure it would be a joke about where we lived.

"You know what's funny?" he said. "I actually do like walking. It really is one of my favorite things."

The mysterious item was back in his fingers, flitting between them and hiding from view. I tried to look without making it obvious. For a second, he paused the elliptical motion and simply held the item in his fingers—a cigarette, I finally saw.

No, not a cigarette. Something hand-rolled, tapered at the end.

He resumed his magic trick and chuckled.

"We're almost there," I told Tru as we turned down a busy little street, its sidewalks crowded and storefronts lit up.

Two boys in short-sleeved hoodies whizzed by us on their skateboards, almost knocking over an older couple dressed nicely for a date. Tru took in the scene and asked where exactly we were, what kind of neighborhood. I explained that lots of people thought the houses around here were dumps and the residents were trashy, but they also thought the stores and restaurants were cool. Rich folks came here for shopping and dinner.

"This area is gentrifying," I added.

That was something I'd heard my mom say. I didn't really know what it meant, and had no idea why I'd repeated it, except as some lame attempt to sound smart. I prayed that Tru wouldn't ask me more, and he didn't, we just moved quietly down the block past the fancy shoe store and the antique gallery. We began to see packs of young people. Young people with tattoos, young people wearing boxy glasses, young people in tight jeans and band T-shirts. Tru whistled.

"Didn't know you lived so close to hipsterville," he said, giving me a side-eye.

I struggled to say something clever, settled on the simple truth.

"You told me to take you to Siren. It's hipster ground zero."

Tru laughed. "Touché. I didn't realize it was that kind of place, but I'll take your word for it."

I looked away, not wanting him to see me smile.

We arrived at Siren, a brick building with a black awning and big windows littered with fliers. Half a dozen people were taking a smoke break out front. I felt about eight years old, but Tru looked as cool and calm as could be. He took out his phone and texted his friend to come get us. I peeked in the windows and saw a small stage. A girl with a blunt, purple bob was singing while a nerdy-looking guy hunched over the keyboard behind her.

It was madness, the idea of trying to get in there. Total madness.

Tru tapped one of the fliers, an advertisement for tonight's show. The photo showed the two people on stage, sitting in a pile of black feathers. Their band was called Nevermore.

"Get it, Frannie? Like what the raven says in the Edgar Allan Poe poem? It's very subtle, right?"

"Very." I tried to sound casual while desperately hoping that none of the people around us were friends with the band.

Tru turned around to lean against the window. "Baltimore is really into its Poe references."

"Well," I said with a shrug, "he lived here."

"Mostly he *died* here. In a gutter. Probably from syphilis."

To this I had nothing to say, but I was saved, because right then the door opened and a girl came out—a girl so beautiful I may have actually sucked in my breath. She put her arms around Tru and kissed him on the cheek and I could actually see guys on the sidewalk turning jealously in our direction.

"Frannie," Tru said. "This is my friend Sparrow. Sparrow Jones."

He hadn't said her name until this moment, a delay I could tell was on purpose. A little game of surprise he was playing with me, revealing her all at once.

Sparrow was tall and elegant. We met each other exactly eye to eye, and for some reason that made me happy, as if we were two kids who'd met on the playground and realized that we were the same age. Her hair flared out into a little afro, like a halo around her face. She wore bright pink eye shadow and a black-and-white-striped dress, perfect and simple.

"Did you know," Tru asked me in a whisper, "that we have black people in Connecticut, too?"

Sparrow covered his face with her hand, pushing him away, inspiring him to fake-stumble backward. He somehow looked cool when he did this, falling with a kind of grace.

She stepped toward me then, and gave me a hug, a vanilla scent radiating so strongly from her skin I could almost taste cookies. Pulling back, she kept an arm around me and fingered the ends of my hair.

"Gorgeous. Isn't this gorgeous, Tru? You can always tell a natural redhead."

Tru rolled his eyes and asked when we could go in. She did a come-hither gesture with her fingers, and we followed her through the front doors.

Inside the skinny entryway to Siren there was a bouncer waiting on a chair. He had a sad blond mustache and scrawny arms. My whole body stiffened at the sight of him.

"Cool?" Sparrow asked him, indicating Tru and me.

He shrugged and nodded, but I could tell by the way he was shifting around that it wasn't cool at all. I knew, too, that he couldn't say no to this girl.

"We'll stand in the back," she promised, gliding past him. "No booze."

"Actually, I would like booze," Tru said, but she yanked on his arm, whispering to sad-mustache man that her friend was only joking.

I ducked my head as I walked by, letting my hair shield my face.

And that was it. Like a miracle, we were inside.

For some reason I'd expected punk music, maybe because of

the purple hair, but this was nothing like that. This was dreamy water music, the girl's voice the voice of a fairy, light and tender over the waving, bubbling sound of the keyboard. Still, though, it was loud, loud, loud. Fifty people or so were gathered around the stage, swaying and clinging to cocktails and wineglasses and pints of beer, plus some college-age-looking kids with sodas and these cones full of fries. Sparrow herded us to the back where we leaned against the wall, and I knew it would be almost impossible to talk, which was perfect, because I had nothing interesting or smart or relevant to say. I wanted only to stand against this wall with Truman and Sparrow, drowning in the sound of the music.

I got my wish. Soon after we settled in, Tru rolled his eyes toward the stage and I knew that he hated the band. He leaned over toward Sparrow, speaking directly into her ear, which was the only way they could possibly have a conversation. She was doing lots of head shaking and eye widening and kept mouthing, *Oh my god.* More than once she looked at him with disapproval.

I tried not to watch too closely, not wanting to seem like a spy. A new fantasy formed in my mind. Sparrow would drop me off on my first day of school and everyone would see me get out of her car. She would yell, *Bye, Frannie, you be good now,* and we would laugh and wink at each other and everyone would love me because everyone would love her because how could you not?

With this beautiful, completely illogical picture in my head, I watched the purple-haired singer. Her voice swallowed me whole, but I couldn't hear the actual words—it was all just a sweet, pretty mumble run together with the underwater melody.

At the end of the song she began to chant, and finally I caught something she was saying.

"I am here now, waiting."

She sang that line again and again.

"Hey there, Ginger."

I looked up and felt sick, physically sick. The man was gross, and he was ancient. Ten years older than me at least. The beginnings of a beer belly pushed against his thin T-shirt, and his dirty hair was shoved into a ponytail. An unidentifiable tattoo crept from his collar up his neck.

In a single instant I was filled with regret, deep and paralyzing. I shouldn't be here. I'd done something very bad by coming to this place, and now I was paying for it.

It was intermission and the room was quieter, music from the radio playing faintly out of a distant speaker. Tru had wandered off. Sparrow was talking to her coworker, some guy who was messing with the sound equipment. I was parked against the back wall, alone.

The man tried again.

"You look awfully young to be in here, but I won't tell anybody."

I refused to look at him. I was sure if I said nothing, he would creep away, go back to whatever hole he'd crawled out of.

"I love redheads, you know. Always have."

He leaned against the wall next to me *and lifted a strand of my hair.* My face and palms got hot and sweaty. I thought the word *help*, over and over again, but couldn't say it. I couldn't say a thing, my voice paralyzed. The strand of hair was still in his grip, and he started to wind it around his finger, tighter and tighter.

"You live around here, right? I feel like I've seen you. Walking around. Maybe by the park?"

And then Tru was there, suddenly, fiercely. He put his hand against the wall, so that his arm was between me and the man, who dropped my hair. A beer sloshed in Tru's other hand, and anger radiated from his whole body. I sensed it from the strain in his neck, the thrust of his chin.

"Seriously?" he asked, and I flinched at how loud his voice was. "Thanks but no thanks, pervert."

The guy put his hands in the air like Tru had waved a gun, then slowly backed away. Tru held his position, and I held mine, tucked behind him, Tru's eyes trailing the man as he snaked away through the crowd. He seemed ready to yell something after him, but then Sparrow was there, looking angry and grabbing us each by a wrist. She pulled us toward the back door.

"That's it for tonight. No scenes allowed. I do work here, you know."

As we hurried toward the exit, she let go of us and plucked the beer from Tru's hand. None of us had the little plastic bracelets for people over twenty-one, of course, so where and how he'd gotten the drink I had no idea, but now Sparrow left it on the bar as we hustled out the back entrance and into the alley.

The door shut with a slam, and the three of us were left in the stagnant summer air, the streetlamp giving off a dim light. We stood in a circle and looked at one another.

"I'm sorry," Tru said to Sparrow. "Seriously, I am. But some old guy was hitting on Frannie. He was touching her fucking hair."

"Oh god," Sparrow said. "I didn't see! Are you okay?"

I wasn't sure how to answer, because I wasn't sure if I was okay. I didn't want to overreact, but my hands were a little shaky. Everything had happened so fast. I hadn't had time to think.

I almost told them all of it, but then I couldn't imagine standing there and repeating the words he'd said. About how I looked young, how he liked redheads. There was a lump in my throat, but I forced it down.

"It's fine," I finally said, and my voice came out steady. I even managed a casual shrug.

"Are you sure?" Sparrow asked.

I nodded, and she patted me on the shoulder, mumbled something about how men were repulsive.

"Hey, hey," Tru said with a grin. "Not all men. But I am sorry, Frannie. I shouldn't have left you alone."

He turned ever so slightly away from us, and I heard a click and an inhale. The lighter was gone before I even saw it.

Sparrow smiled and motioned for us to walk down the dark alley. I stayed two steps behind, watching the two of them pass the joint back and forth as Sparrow told Tru and me about her summer plans.

She was staying with her aunt Regina and her cousin Devon, working at Siren for spending money and taking graphic design courses at MICA, prepping for when she'd start her undergrad at Carnegie Mellon in the fall. She said that Baltimore was smaller than she'd expected and so *pedestrian*, and I knew she was using that word in a way that I didn't understand.

Sparrow sucked deeply on the joint and told Tru that despite it all she didn't miss home, not one little bit. She was ready for something new.

Tru turned, walking backward to look at me.

"Sparrow's mother is an ex–ballet dancer and her dad is a big shot at a credit card company," he said. "That's why she's the perfect woman. Beautiful and rich."

She shoved him again and he spun back around, kept sauntering along. She dropped back to walk beside me.

"Tru said you're at a magnet school—is it the one for the arts? Devon's at the one for the arts."

I told her no, I was at the math and science one. She just smiled, so I stuttered out a little more. "I'm . . . I don't know, into science I guess. I like science."

Tru called to us over his shoulder. "Way to make her feel like a dork."

Sparrow ignored him and told me that her aunt was a scientist of sorts, and that we should meet. Then she went on and on about Devon and how he played the violin all day and all night. She said I should meet him and his friends, too—she was pretty sure one of them went to my new school.

Sparrow handed the joint back to Tru, and asked for a piggyback ride. She was taller than him by about an inch, and the two of them arranged their bodies awkwardly, almost falling, laughing, then righting themselves at the last moment. He carried her for a couple of blocks, her arms wrapped tightly around his neck. I trailed behind them quietly, wishing that someday I might have that kind of easy affection.

We dropped Sparrow at her car, which was sporty and red. Tru made promises to see her soon, and we headed for home.

I convinced Tru that we should stray at least to the outer edge of the lacrosse field, as if giving it a passing glance would somehow lend truth to our lie. We moved toward the lights and came just close enough to see the impression of the girls on the field. From where we stood, they were blurs of colors, nothing more than birds swooping and tittering in the distance. I said that was good enough and we turned around.

We walked quietly for a while side by side. As we came to the edge of the park by my house, Tru stopped and turned to me.

"I was trying to be good, Frannie. I was trying really hard. But if you want . . ."

He was extending the end of the joint in my direction.

I had tried a cigarette before. Three times. No—maybe four? But as I took this from him I felt right away that it was different. The paper was delicate. I handled it like a buttercup, the kind we used to hold under our chins to look for the yellow shadow. I did a quick scan and we were alone, still a couple of minutes' walk from home. I stared at the nub and couldn't quite bring it to my lips—it didn't seem right. Not yet, at least. I'd been trying so hard to be cool, but there in the dark, I said the only thing I could think of. The truth.

"I haven't even had a drink," I said. "It seems wrong to do this first. Like I should do things in order?"

He laughed, and I tried to laugh, too.

"Must be the scientist in you," Tru said, and I was more embarrassed than ever, because I wasn't a scientist. I just liked nature. I knew the names of trees and plants, and I'd aced freshman biology, winning a prize for my poster about photosynthesis. I guess it looked nice—a maze of green and brown, showing all the structures and systems, the parts that had to teem and whirl just to keep things alive. But it was a dumb science fair project that somehow became this thing that defined me, made me into someone in people's minds. A science girl. I tried to find a way to say all that to Tru, but ended up keeping my mouth shut.

I waited for him to keep walking, but he was staring at the moon. I squinted into the darkness of the park and thought of my trip to the safe, imagining that one night we might drink the vodka with Sparrow and her cousin and his friends. I could tell Tru about it now, but I was worried it might seem weird and silly that I'd buried it in the woods. Instead, I kept quiet, thinking again that I would save it for something special, some big moment when I could produce it like magic. . . .

"Frannie?" He said my name cautiously. "Do you know why I'm here?"

Cicadas chirped. A distant roar came from the lacrosse field.

I tried to gather myself, searching for the little speeches I'd been writing in my head all day, but I couldn't remember the words that had seemed so right at the time. I wished I could just tell him in some simple, graceful way that I didn't care, of course I didn't care. I didn't think it was wrong or weird and I wanted to him to know that, but I didn't know how to say it. I managed to mumble something about having overheard my parents in the yard.

"I'm not supposed to know, I guess, but I do. I know that you're ... um ..."

The rest got caught in my throat.

"You know that I'm ... ?" Tru let the sentence trail off, just as I had. When I still said nothing, he saved me by filling in the blank.

"You know that I like boys?"

At first I opened and closed my mouth like a fish. Finally, I found some words.

"And I heard them say that your parents sent you here, because they needed some time—because they found out? And I think that it's awful. Your mom and dad, I mean. I just think it's awful. They shouldn't care. No one should care."

I'd said it all with my head down, but now I looked up and saw him hesitate. There was a flash of darkness that came over his face, quickly replaced by a smirk.

"So you're one of the more progressive Catholic schoolgirls, huh?"

I was afraid for a moment that I'd lost him for good, that I'd become a kid to him, like I'd been at the train station when he first saw me. But then his face resettled into a friendly look. I was still holding the end of the joint, and he motioned to me that I should drop it in the grass. I did, and he stepped on it, put an arm around me.

"Sorry, Frannie. Only kidding. I'm glad you said that. I really am. Now let's go home."

SIX

There was a loud snap, and I flinched awake.

Mom had opened the blinds and was hovering over my bed. As I blinked her into focus, the entirety of last night returned to me in a flash.

She's here because of what you did. She knows everything.

Panic rang through me like an alarm. I squirmed and kicked the sheets, trying to sit up. Already, half-formed lies were perched and waiting on my lips. My eyes met hers.

"We're going to the beach," she said. "Be ready in twenty."

Moments later she was down the hall, fist pounding against Jimmy and Kieran's door as she told them what she'd just told me. I looked at the clock—nine thirty a.m.

Voices rose from the dining room below. Tru was talking to my father, and the two of them were laughing. I heard Dad ask Tru if he wanted the sports section. Creeping out of bed and toward my bedroom door, I hoped I might catch more, but then Mom was yelling from the hallway, telling me to move, move, move. I scrambled, yanking at drawers and digging out my swim clothes and flip-flops. I started to grab my chemistry workbook, which had arrived in the mail yesterday and was supposed to prepare me for next year. But then I thought about how ridiculous that was—what kind of loser brings homework to the beach? I shoved it under the bed and went in search of my sunglasses. Nothing was where I remembered, and I was completely distracted. Scenes from yesterday were looping through my head. The train station. The sculpture. Sparrow. Siren. Coming back home.

It was almost midnight when we'd climbed the porch steps. As I'd fumbled for my key, Tru had told me to wait a second. He'd coached me in a soothing whisper.

"If they have questions about tonight, just roll your eyes and act like whatever they asked is stupid and you don't feel like answering. That's what grown-ups expect from teenagers anyway. And the less you say, the less likely you'll be caught in a lie."

I'd gone inside and done exactly that. We'd hardly had to say a word to anyone.

Watching Tru get into our rusty old minivan was strange. He was cheerful this morning, popping into one of the middle seats and buckling up with a little too much enthusiasm. He looked like a kid at the fair, amused by a ride he'd grown too big for.

Kieran grabbed the seat next to him, so Jimmy and I took the back. As the van grumbled to life, Dad told Truman he was in charge of the music. The van was beyond ancient, no hookup for an iPod or phone or whatever, so he gave Tru the only three choices he ever gave anyone, the only CDs he kept in the car: U2, The Rolling Stones, or Bruce Springsteen.

Tru surprised me by picking Bruce.

"Um, have we explained to Tru where we're going?" Jimmy asked, leaning forward to yell over the first strains of "Born in the U.S.A." "Because if he's expecting, you know, an actual *beach*, he's going to be pretty pissed."

Kieran snorted. "C'mon, man. A crappy swimming hole in a crappy park is almost like the real beach!"

Jimmy leaned forward farther, straining his seat belt, putting a hand on Tru's shoulder. "Don't worry. The people are cool. It's all, like, rednecks swimming in jean shorts and insane packs of wild children from the nature camp."

Dad told them to shut up. Mom yelled at them for exaggerating. Angry shouts filled the car until Tru broke in.

"Look, I'm just happy that I'm not in the car with my mother and father, sitting in hours of stop-and-go traffic so we can go to *the Hamptons* along with half the social-climbing assholes in New York City."

Next to me, Jimmy tried to stifle a laugh and practically choked. Mom turned around and glared at him, which made him explode, setting off Kieran, who set off me. Tru was wearing his best attempt at a sheepish grin, but I was pretty sure he was pleased with himself.

"Uncle Pat, Aunt Barb, I'm sorry. Really I am," he said, hands clasped in a kind of mock prayer. "But you have to believe me. There's no other way to describe the place. It's just a total asshole convention."

Mom cried out Truman's name in admonishment, but she didn't really sound that mad, and besides, Dad was giggling now—and Tru was still going.

"I don't know what's worse, the ten-year-old girls texting in their bikinis or the moms all Botoxed to hell. No, wait, scratch that. The dads are the worst by far," Tru said, and now he adjusted his voice, taking it down a notch, talking in a baritone that was somehow how both peevish and gruff. "Coming here is a privilege, boy! This is what success looks like. These are some of the most expensive residential properties in the nation."

Jimmy and Kieran kept snickering, but I sensed an undercurrent of nervousness from Mom and Dad. The car grew quiet after that. For most of the remaining ride, we disappeared into our own worlds, watching the landscape rush by, listening to Bruce's rasp.

Huddled in the backseat, I nursed a suspicion. As the houses and strip malls and billboards passed, I became more and more sure of it, for Tru's little bit of showmanship had shaken loose some old, vague memories I had of his family. What he'd just done was not the voice of some random social-climbing jerk. It was a dead-on imitation of his father.

I said little to anyone the whole time we were in the van. Tru said nothing to me.

* * *

The parking lot was almost empty. It was supposed to rain today, though right now the sun was blazing. The six of us gathered our things and headed down to the water.

We were the only family I knew who called this place the beach. I liked it here, always had, even if it maybe wasn't much. The water stretched about as far as a neighborhood pool and was edged by the smallest ring of fine white sand. Beyond that was a collection of splintery picnic benches and crusted-over grills. A wooden signpost explained how the swimming hole was once a quarry. They had mined iron ore here for decades, and when the work was done, the hole filled naturally with spring water. The deepest points went fifty feet down.

A few makeshift paper signs warned that the lifeguards weren't on duty for another week. Looking around I saw a mom with her toddler, an elderly couple hiding under an umbrella, a few scattered families like ours. We settled on a picnic bench that was tattooed with pen marks and pockmarked with old gum. Mom and Dad said they were going on a hike, and headed immediately toward one of the paths off in the trees. The four of us watched their retreat.

"So, wait," Jimmy asked as soon as they were out of earshot. "We came all the way here, and they're not even going to swim in the shitty hole?"

Tru took off for the little pavilion that had the bathrooms and soda machines. The twins stretched out on the benches and put on their sunglasses, looking ready to fall asleep.

With no one paying attention, I stripped down to my suit and went straight for the quarry. I flew across the grass and through the sand, but came up short as my toes touched water. From there I walked in gently, feet clinging to the gritty land as it sloped away. I hung on until the last moment, standing on the very tips of my toes, chin just above the water line. Then I dove.

The water was fresh, clean, ice-cold. The butterfly was my best stroke, and that's what I practiced, keeping close to the surface and moving in circles. Sucking in my breath, I forced my body to sink down under, but didn't open my eyes. I never opened my eyes here because there were fish and turtles, sometimes snakes. I didn't like to think about them. Still, I used to like hiding down there in the darkness. I liked how alone it made me feel, even if it was a little scary.

Today, though, I couldn't find the magic in it. I only felt chilled, annoyed by this odd little place, which looked dumpier today than ever before. Maybe Jimmy and Kieran were right about it. And even if Tru acted happy to be here, I was sure he probably agreed.

Breaking the surface, I began to tread and turned back to look for everyone.

Jimmy and Kieran hadn't moved. Mom and Dad were nowhere to be seen. And Tru . . . Tru was still at the pavilion. He was leaning against the soda machine, talking to a couple of girls. They looked about my age, maybe older, and were barefoot, wearing loose little dresses over their bikinis. Both of them seemed to be posing, and one kept playing with her hair. Jealousy took over before I could stop it, even though I knew that was ridiculous—if anything I should be laughing at them, their clueless flirting. I told myself not to be stupid, but I couldn't stop thinking about last night at Siren, hoping that more nights like that were waiting.

I hadn't thought of the possibility that someone else might come along, take my place.

Now Tru was gesturing toward the water, and the three of them turned in my direction. I leaned back, gently floating. I assumed this position would show just how little I cared.

I stayed in until I was cold and wrinkly. When I finally emerged, I came back to our picnic bench to find it empty. Mom and Dad were still hiking. Jimmy and Kieran had been pulled into a volleyball game on the little sand court off by the trees. Tru was still talking to the girls—although now they were leaving the pavilion. For a minute I thought he was bringing them over, but then I realized the girls were just headed for the parking lot.

The three of them looked over at me again as they talked. Annoyed and embarrassed, I pretended not to notice, turning my back to them as I dug through my backpack for a T-shirt.

By the time Tru arrived, I'd managed to hide behind a magazine. He held out a Coke. Gave it a little shake.

"Bought an extra. If you want."

I took the can from him and it froze my fingers. Tru sat down on the bench and leaned back against the table, so I was left staring at the back of his head.

"Making new friends?" I asked him.

"Oh yes. Have to introduce myself to the Baltimore social scene."

I almost let it go at that, but I couldn't.

"What were they saying? When you guys were looking over here?"

"They liked your bathing suit. One of them was going to ask where you got it, but they were in a rush to get somewhere. Don't worry, she gave me her number, so I can be sure to text her this vital piece of information."

"Oh," I said. "Well, actually I don't even know. My mom bought it."

I immediately regretted how childish that sounded. At the same time, I was trying to make sense of why Tru would have this girl's number. Was he messing with her? Did she offer it and he took it to be polite? Or was he genuinely looking for some company to fill the coming weeks? That is, company that was more interesting than me.

"Well, your mom knows clothes," he said, still staring off into the trees. "At least, that's what my mom always says. That Barbie knows clothes."

That was true. My mother was heavy like half the moms I knew, but she hid it better. Around the house she was a mess, but whenever she went out she looked put-together. She wore skirts and sweaters to work when she could have worn jeans. She had junk jewelry that looked like the real thing.

"Your mom used to make prom dresses for both of them, did you know that?" he asked, still not turning back to look at me.

"No," I said, shivering. "She doesn't talk about your mom much."

I sat down and cracked the Coke, hoping that he'd say more, maybe offer some insight, some information, at least a reaction that I could read. But his head didn't move. The breeze ruffled his hair.

I watched Tru watching the distance and tried to think of the last time I'd seen Aunt Deborah. Nothing came to me. What I remembered were her birthday cards. Pink or lavender with flowers or rainbows. She wrote nice notes in careful script, things like *I saw your school photo and you look beautiful. I know you'll have an amazing year.* They always had a crisp fifty-dollar bill inside, which seemed amazing and extravagant. I hated breaking them and would carry them around in my wallet or leave them in my nightstand drawer for weeks.

"I know I haven't seen them in forever," I said. "But your mom always seemed kinda nice."

"Kinda nice?" he said, turning finally to look at me. "That's high praise."

"I just . . . I don't know. Maybe she'll realize she's wrong and apologize. Before you go back home? Are you going to talk to them at all?"

He turned his back on me again. "Yes, I'm going to talk to them. I think we'll avoid deep philosophical debates about the relative wrongness of things that I've done, but we'll need to discuss other items of note. You know, like how much I can put on their credit card while I'm here."

He turned back to me now, looking serious. "Have you been talking about this with your parents?"

"No!" I said, embarrassed and blushing. "I mean, I don't really talk to them about, you know . . . things like that. I haven't said anything."

"It's probably better that way." He relaxed a bit, even started to smile. A smile that made me feel happy and nervous all at once.

"Do you know about Prettyboy?" he asked.

Goose bumps erupted all over my skin. I tried to play it cool.

"Everyone knows about Prettyboy."

I attempted to sit casually but couldn't find the right way to arrange my body. My elbows and knees bent awkwardly, pointing everywhere.

"You look concerned," he said.

I wiggled the tab off my can, trying to buy some time.

"Well," I said finally. "I know what you're thinking."

He raised his eyebrows and waited.

"You want to go to the jump-off," I said.

He laughed again. "It sounds like a good time."

I asked where he'd heard about Prettyboy, and he rolled his eyes.

"My two new lady friends. Did I tell you they were headed to their first day of cheerleading camp? They're captains of their team, even though they're only juniors." He made his eyes go wide and reached a hand toward me. "Try not to faint from amazement, okay? Though if it's all right with you, I think we'll skip hanging out with them." Now he went down to a whisper. *"I don't think they're really our type."*

I smiled, feeling a little bit better, starting to think that last night wasn't a fluke, and that I did have reason to hope this summer wouldn't be a miserable bust. Tru was here, and Sparrow, too. And there was her cousin who played the violin. His friends. The coming weeks didn't have to be a dead end. They were wide-open with possibility—I just had to make sure that Tru remembered I was here, that I was the kind of girl who said clever things about sculptures and helped him sneak into bars. A girl worth knowing.

He had turned to the trees again, leaning against the table.

"We should go to the jump-off," he said, his back still to me. "We should go before the summer is out."

"Okay," I said. "We'll do it."

But even as the words came out of my mouth, I was hoping the day would never come.

We were quiet on the ride home, all of us rubbed a bit raw by our first real day of summer. Skin was tinged red, hair damp and matted, feet gritty with sand and soil and broken blades of grass. I leaned against the window and watched as clouds moved in. Drained by the sun, I drifted in and out of sleep, falling into half dreams about the Prettyboy Reservoir.

I'm not sure I could have found it on a map, but I knew it was north of the city, somewhere down a lonely county road, tucked away in a thicket of wood. Prettyboy was a twisting snake of deep water, the currents swift and dangerous. Swimming there was forbidden, which was exactly why people went. There was a special spot where a rock ledge jutted out over the water, the perfect diving board. Next to it a rope hung from a high branch, always pulled down by park rangers, always replaced. From that rope, kids would fling themselves like stones into the reservoir below. That was the jump-off. We used to whisper about it during middle school sleepovers, making stupid dares about going there, dares we couldn't possibly fulfill for years, not until we had cars and boyfriends and ways to get beer. Always when we talked about it, we talked of the two boys who'd died there, years and years ago. St. Sebastian's boys, I was pretty sure.

And that was why I'd never really wanted to go to Prettyboy. Not then and not now.

I didn't want to go, because I knew that I'd freeze there on the edge, unable to jump at all. I was always the one who chickened out in line for roller coasters and water slides. Those were things that I actually knew were safe. The jump-off was the opposite.

Half-awake in the back of the car, I tried to think exactly what I knew about the boys who had died, but couldn't remember a thing. Eyelids heavy, mind floating again toward sleep, I kept seeing the two boys leaping, then flailing, the pair of them faceless as they sank down below.

That evening we ate hot dogs and corn on the cob at the plastic table in the backyard. Afterward we gathered in the dining room to sort out our work hours for the coming week, fighting over who got the new-ish sedan, who got the ancient minivan.

Just the night before, as I'd walked back from Siren with Tru, the coming weeks of summer had seemed like they might be one long stretch of magic nights, music and bars and who knows what. Now reality crowded back in. I was babysitting Duncan Hart three doors down. Kieran was a counselor at a sports camp. Jimmy was working a regular weekday shift at the gas station a few blocks away. That afternoon, Tru had received word from his parents that they'd had him squeezed at the last minute into an intensive, five-days-a-week Latin course at Loyola, the Catholic college about a mile and a half down the road, the one his father had gone to.

I wondered if my parents would let him have a car and how that would go over with the twins, but then Tru jumped in and said that he would walk. It would take twenty minutes or so each way, but he insisted he didn't mind, and frankly that was easier on everybody.

Meanwhile Jimmy was trying and failing to control the look on his face. His mouth puckered in amusement.

"Intensive Latin?" he asked. "Sounds . . . intense."

Tru just laughed.

"My dad's idea. Or rather, his command. I've been taking Spanish for the last three years, which makes sense to me since half the country speaks it. But who cares about that when you can conjugate a bunch of verbs that only matter to dead guys?"

My father seemed to take a strange delight in this, giggling loudly. Mom shot him a disapproving look as she started cleaning up the plates.

That night, we all half watched a movie in the living room, a goofy comedy about mistaken identities, miscommunication. Mom folded laundry and Dad slept in his chair. The twins texted and cruised the internet on their phones. I had nobody to text and no phone to play with either, because I'd dropped mine down a sewer grate three weeks ago. I couldn't get a new one until I had enough babysitting money or until my contract renewal kicked in at the end of the summer. So far I didn't really miss it, since I barely heard from the girls anymore—not having the phone meant I didn't have to look at my empty inbox. Instead, I sat flipping through magazines, hardly seeing what was on the pages. Truman was sitting in the corner under the floor lamp reading *The Great Gatsby*, looking absorbed and content.

"Ugh," Jimmy said when he saw it. "We were supposed to read that last year. Couldn't do it."

Kieran threw a pillow at his head. "Dude, you're seriously pathetic. It's short and the whole thing's just drinking and car wrecks."

Jimmy did his well-worn act of pretending to fall asleep.

I thought I might get a chance to talk to Tru before bed, to ask him when we might see Sparrow, and to feel out how serious he was about Prettyboy. But he slipped downstairs early when his dad called his cell, and he never came back up.

I eventually gave up on him and went to my room. I turned off the light, but for a long time couldn't sleep. I kept imagining the reservoir, what it would be like to grab the rope and swing out over the void.

SEVEN

I woke up Monday with time to kill, as usual. I watched Duncan five days a week, but just for a few hours in the middle of the day. His father was some kind of foreman at a plant and worked long shifts, but his mother was a part-time librarian who was only gone from about eleven in the morning until three in the afternoon. Duncan was on summer vacation from school like the rest of us and needed somebody to be with, so I was it.

To be honest, watching Duncan barely felt like work at all. He was twelve and autistic, with very personal, intricate ways to entertain himself. I'd never said this out loud to anyone, but sometimes I really liked being with him. He was sweet and gentle and possibly the only human being who I never felt awkward or shy around. If I said something dumb or embarrassing, I knew he wouldn't care. I'd babysat for him here and there this whole past year before I'd gotten the regular job this summer. He couldn't really express himself or tell me what he needed, and that used to break my heart, make me feel helpless. But the more we were together, the more I understood all his likes and dislikes. Now I could almost always make him happy.

That morning everyone was on their typical schedule, Mom and Kieran leaving early, and Dad gone soon after. He almost always found somewhere to be during the day. Today he was doing handyman-type stuff for people a few blocks over. Our house was empty by nine thirty, after Tru had left for Latin class and Jimmy for the gas station. Once everyone was gone, I took a never-ending, scalding shower, singing the whole time. I dressed slowly, switching one shirt for another and another when nothing looked right, as if it even mattered what I wore to babysit. Then I went downstairs and turned on the television. Back when we had cable I used to watch MTV for hours sometimes, lulled by bad music and shameless people doing shameless things. Now there was no MTV, and not much to pick from. I just clicked nonstop, moving from local news to soap operas to courtroom shows. People squabbling over a few hundred dollars. I guess I knew how they felt.

By the time I walked over to the Harts' place, the street was pretty empty of cars, people having gone off to work. It gave me the feeling that I was late even though I knew I wasn't. As usual, Mrs. Hart was dressed and ready to go as soon as I got there. She left with a breezy good-bye, in a cloud of perfume. On the table was the day's memo, which always told me what to make for lunch. Today it was microwave macaroni and cheese. Underneath, just like every other day, she wrote a Bible passage for the two of us.

I always read the passages out loud to Duncan, even though I didn't think he cared. Today's was a classic: "Blessed are the meek, for they shall inherit the earth."

I stared at it for a moment, wondering if it could possibly be true. Then I looked up at Duncan.

"Let's skip the Bible today, all right?"

He gave me a half smile, soft and sweet.

After that, like always, I told him what we were having for lunch and that we'd eat in an hour. And then, just like every other day, he asked me his standard set of questions. I answered them the same way I always did.

"What's your name?"

"Frannie."

"How old are you?"

"Fifteen."

"Where do you go to school?"

"St. Sebastian's."

He'd heard the answers from me so many times, starting last fall, the very first time I babysat him, that I'd decided not to change the last answer. I was afraid I'd upset him if I said something else. And to be honest, the name of my new school didn't sound right to me yet either.

After that, we passed the day like we did most others. He built a beautiful block tower that he didn't want me to help with. He leaned protectively over a sheet of paper and drew his own mazes. I stole a few moments on their computer, unable to keep myself from looking at some of the photos that Mary Beth, Dawn, and Marissa had posted from Stix for Chix. In the afternoon, Duncan and I went down into the basement and played with his train set.

The train set was beautiful. Not a kid's toy but an antique, his grandfather's. Duncan could spend hours rearranging the cars and the tracks and all the pieces of the town. I watched from a little way off or sometimes helped a bit. My favorite part was the farmhouse and barn with all the miniature animals, cows and pigs and a chicken.

Duncan hated the chicken.

"The chicken is too big," he said, holding it up for my inspection.

In the months I'd known him, he'd probably told me that hundreds of times, but I didn't mind hearing it again. It always made me smile, because Duncan was right. It *was* too big, although it actually wasn't a chicken. It was a rooster. A monster red rooster with a scarlet crest flaming from its head and one foot scraping the ground with fierce talons. It must have come from some different set from all the other pieces because it was completely out of scale, towering over the animals, half as big as the farmhouse.

It had no business being there at all.

The six of us reconvened at dinner, hungry, tired, and impatient. Kieran sweaty from camp, blowing his whistle to drive everyone crazy. Jimmy complaining about customers and sucking down the free slushie he got at the end of every shift. Mom clomping around in her heels, work ID still dangling from around her neck as she started to cook. Dad huffing through the door, disheveled and dirty and lugging a toolbox.

Tru came in last, with his messenger bag full of Latin books and neatly organized papers. The class lasted all morning, and afternoons he said he planned to stay in the library or at the coffee place on campus, doing homework and surfing the web.

We ate dinner together at the table, per Mom and Dad's command. Then we watched whatever we could find on the five or six stations that still came in on the TV. The twins texted. Tru read. I flipped through magazines.

When a call came through on his cell, Tru left his book on the arm of the couch, and I grabbed it as soon as he was gone, opening to the first pages. There was a little poem in the beginning, something about a gold-hatted, high-bouncing lover. I had no idea what that meant—was it supposed to be silly or sexy?—but it made me blush just the same. Then I read the first couple of paragraphs, where a dad gives advice to his son. He told him not to criticize others, because they don't come from families with as many advantages. I wondered if it was the kind of thing Uncle Richard would say to Tru, and I decided to stop reading, putting the book back exactly as I'd found it.

Tuesday came, and I kept waiting for Tru to invite me somewhere, to tell me we were meeting Sparrow again. Or maybe he would talk to me more about Prettyboy. About *anything.* But he didn't. He went out with the twins instead—going to play video games at their friend Drew Pipkin's house. Wednesday they went to swim in Michael Donovan's backyard pool, and Tru went with them again.

I was quickly going from disappointed to depressed, so on Thursday I finally caught Tru alone in his room and asked him how Sparrow was doing, but he just made some joke about how she was busy trying to set the world on fire with her digital artscapes. I even brought up Prettyboy, because I thought it would get his attention. But when I asked if he was really serious about going, he just said "deadly serious," then took out his phone, ignoring me completely.

That night I didn't sleep well, and I woke up early, too early, on Friday morning, chasing the tail end of a bad dream.

I couldn't remember much of it, only that I was back at Siren alone, and the man was behind me, holding fistfuls of my hair.

I wondered again if it was a big deal, what he'd said, about my age, my hair, seeing me around. I was pretty sure that the guy was full of it. He didn't say what park, and there were a million around here.

I rolled out of bed and looked out my window, convinced the weekend would bring better things.

After dinner that night, I went and sat on the front porch alone, my summer reading ignored in my lap as I stared at the sky. I'd been hoping to see the sunset or the first glint of stars, but all of that was lost behind a shifting mass of thunderheads, the rain starting to come down in big, fat beads that burst on the road. It was the Fourth of July, and Mom had been planning to drag us all out to watch the fireworks together at the house of someone she worked with, a lady who lived downtown and had a roof deck. Of course the twins had moaned and whined that they weren't twelve, that they had better things to do, and couldn't she just take Frannie and leave them out of it. Then this storm crept in, so much worse than expected, and the city had to postpone the show until tomorrow. Jimmy and Kieran were freed. I was freed, too, but of course, I had nothing else to do. Lightning cut the sky overhead, and instead of counting until I heard the boom, I turned and ran inside.

I had to go see Tru.

Tiptoeing down the stairs, I saw the door was closed tight. He answered my knock with a loud, happy "Come in!" and I found him dressed in his standard plain T-shirt and jeans. He pointed at his watch.

"Leaving in a minute," he said. "Going to a party with Jimmy and Kieran."

An "Oh" escaped my lips, sounding pathetic, and he looked at me, amused. He explained that he was fairly certain Jimmy and Kieran didn't want me around while they chugged beer and tried to make out with girls.

"Well, yeah. I know."

"Jimmy kept saying that the party is at 'The Mack's,' like that was something I should be able to understand. Can you translate?"

He wasn't even looking at me, too busy instead clicking around on his phone.

"Beau Womack," I said. "He's a big, dumb football player. His parents are never home. He's The Mack."

"How charming!" Tru said, pulling his sneakers from under the bed. "Frankly, I was a little surprised they've been inviting me out so much, but then I overheard Jimmy telling Kieran that I'm excellent girl bait, which I suppose means he wants my scraps and rejects? I think I should be flattered, don't you?"

I said nothing, tried to force a smile. I now had a vivid picture of Tru with all the St. Sebastian's upperclassmen. He was handing out carefully rolled joints. He was pumping the keg perfectly. He was standing there, smiling, at the center of everything.

And Jimmy was right. He would be girl bait: handsome and funny and, best of all, he was new. A mystery. Watching as he pulled on his socks and his shoes, I got some small pleasure from thinking of the dumb, drunk twits who would flirt with him and have no idea. . . .

And that's when I thought of Jeremy Bell.

"There's, um, there's a guy who will probably be there," I said.

Tru was tying his laces, but paused to look up at me.

"Jeremy. Jeremy Bell. He's, ah. He's just . . . He's cute. You might . . . I just thought you might want to talk to him."

Turning back to his shoes, Tru snorted dismissively.

"Well, thanks so much," he said. "Maybe the two of us can go for ice cream and hold hands."

A blush hit my face like a slap.

"Yeah, sorry," I said. "That was stupid."

I fled up both flights of stairs and buried myself in my bed. I was sure now that Tru and I would never do anything all summer. I'd either have to crawl back to Mary Beth, Dawn, and Marissa, or suffer through the coming months completely by myself. I'd been okay, I'd been getting by before Tru got here. Then I'd said that thing in front of the sculpture, and suddenly everything was different. I'd felt smart and funny again. I'd met Sparrow, who actually seemed to like me. I thought she was going to introduce me to her cousin, his friends.

Now that was all starting to seem like a hopeless dream.

Scrunched in a ball, sheets pulled up over my head, I tried to remember how I'd been surviving just a week ago, back when I was a tightrope walker, alone and focused, keeping my balance by blocking everything out. I couldn't get that feeling back. I wanted something else now.

I wanted to fall.

I heard the twins tell my mother that they were taking Tru to play video games at Drew's house again. There was a long pause, and I could practically feel her looking at them. With suspicion hard and heavy in her voice, she told them when to be home. She told them they better behave. After they left, she yelled up and asked if I wanted to watch a movie with her and Dad.

Part of me did. Part of me wanted to be with people, to laugh or cry at something imaginary, or to look at perfect faces on a screen and just not think. But I yelled back, "No," in a snotty voice. I shut the door loudly. Sitting at my vanity, I confronted my angry, blotchy face in the mirror. Then I found the most melancholy music I could and turned it up high, attempting to reach a whole new state of misery.

I thought if I sank low enough, my sadness might achieve a kind of grace.

EIGHT

Lying a certain way on the corner of my bed, tilting my head back just so, I couldn't see the brick of any houses or the dull gray metal of any streetlamps. Not one hint of the city. There was only the crisscross of branches, leaves twitching in the wind. Beech leaves, I knew. I always knew which trees were which.

Maybe that explained why it was the weekend and I had nothing to do.

It was now seven days since Tru arrived and we went to Siren. Six since we'd been to the quarry. I was back to being alone. Breathing quietly, I tried to focus on the leaves and only the leaves. My seventh-grade health teacher had taught us to meditate, which everybody mocked and hated, no one really trying, the boys falling asleep or pretending to, the girls peeking at each other through eyes that were supposed to be closed. But like always, I'd listened and done what I was told. The lesson had stuck with me. I went home and tried it on my own, and years later, I still did it—at least my own version, here on the edge of the bed. I always kept my eyes open, losing myself in the green, and on good days I could almost forget where I was.

But today, instead of trying to drift away, I was writing a simple speech. I would tell Tru that I wanted to see Sparrow again. Not wanted to, needed to. I had to meet her cousin and his friend who went to my school, because otherwise—come September—I'd be walking into the building a hopeless nobody who knew no one. I'd add something at the end about needing Tru's help, maybe point out that he'd been a little mean to me. But I'd make that part quick. Nothing desperate.

I got up and hurried down to the basement.

It was just past noon. The twins were stirring, but not actually up, since on the weekends, we weren't forced to eat breakfast together. Tru I found wide-awake. He was in his room, making his bed, and his hair was still wet from the shower, slicked back, like an actor from some old movie. I was ready to blurt out my whole canned speech, but as soon as he saw me, he smiled and pulled a set of keys from his back pocket. My mom's keys. He gave them a jingle.

"You need to get dressed," he said. "We've been invited to band practice, and I've even been given permission to drive. While you were sleeping the morning away, your mom and I did a test run around the block."

I stared at him, uncomprehending. "What do you mean, band practice?"

"Remember Sparrow's cousin, Devon? Kid who plays the violin all day? Guess he has a little rock band, too, with a couple of his friends. They're doing a show soon, and they need to practice for an audience. I already told your mom that Devon's friend goes to your new school, and she's very excited for you to make friends at your new school, Frannie. *Very excited.*"

This was exactly what I'd wanted, but I was still sort of annoyed. I had things to say about what I needed, about how he'd been treating me. But even as I tried to hold on to my anger, I felt it receding. I now suspected that when it came to this summer, to Truman, I had two distinct choices. I could choose my dignity, or I could choose Tru's world.

"Are we leaving now?" I asked.

Tru raised the keys again, jingled a "yes."

We got into the minivan and Tru looked through the CDs in the glove compartment, this time picking U2. As soon as the van was out of the neighborhood, he rolled down the windows and turned on the music. He made some *ugh* noises, flipping past a few tracks, finally settling on "Bad."

"So I saw the famous Jeremy Bell last night."

I waited for him to say more, but he said nothing. As he pressed on the gas, the van became an unbearable wind tunnel, warm air whipping our faces and tangling my hair. The bass bumped brokenly from the old speakers, creating a humming under my skin.

"He was at the party?" I asked dumbly.

"Yes, he was."

The car rolled on. The wind blew on.

"So did you talk to him?" I asked. "What happened?"

"What happened?" Tru got that sneaky look, the one that was all in his eyebrows. *"Veni, vidi, vici."*

I was pretty sure I should know what that meant, but I couldn't remember, and when he offered nothing else, I finally had to ask.

"Was that—was that Latin? From class? How did you learn that so fast?"

Tru looked out his window and laughed.

"Well, that was some Latin I already knew. It's a famous quote? *Julius Caesar*? It means 'I came, I saw, I conquered.'"

"Oh, right."

And I *had* known that. I'd heard it somewhere, I was sure, I'd just forgotten. I looked out the window, feeling stupid and trying now to commit the phrase to memory. *Veni, vidi, vici. Veni, vidi, vici.* The words tumbled around in my head, poetic and sharp. A whole minute passed before I actually thought about what he meant.

When I finally did, my head swiveled back to him in an instant.

"You and Jeremy . . . ?"

He rested an elbow on the open window, the fingertips of just one hand delicately directing the wheel.

"Does that surprise you?" he asked.

"No. I guess not. I just thought you said . . ."

He cut me off with a laugh.

"I'm kidding, Frannie. I didn't do anything with Jeremy. I

didn't even talk to him. But you're right. He's cute. I might keep my eye on him."

He turned the volume up high, higher, all the way to the max, as we drove north. We were headed for a nice part of town, just on the city's border. We sped along, lashed by the wind, deaf from rock 'n' roll, while I admired how easily he piloted our beast of a car.

Tru drove fast, took turns smoothly.

Sparrow's aunt lived in a pretty but tiny stand-alone house with pink and white flowers out front, plus a newly planted tree, held up by splints. A Bartlett pear. The car in the driveway was shiny clean, a hybrid with bumper stickers about peace and recycling.

"My god," Tru said, as we pulled in. "They're hippies. Frannie, this woman is going to serve us kale chips and soy milk."

In fact, she offered us hummus with pita and diet soda. She wasn't beautiful exactly, but striking, with hair sheared close to her scalp.

She introduced herself as Regina, not Mrs. Jewell, and asked sweet, thoughtful questions about us. When she heard that I was going to the science and engineering school, she put out her fist for me to bump. She told me she was a public-health professor who did research and fieldwork with water. I longed for something intelligent to ask, but could only nod, impressed.

She told us we could go on downstairs, and as we headed in that direction I heard a guitar being plucked, a cymbal shimmering. Tru went first and I followed. We walked slowly down creaky steps into a half-finished basement. The walls were rough stone, the floor painted an industrial gray. One half of it was filled with a soaring set of shelves stuffed to the bursting point with textbooks. There was a desk with a computer and papers stacked to dangerous heights. A photo on the wall showed Regina somewhere stark and dusty. She stood next to a well and was surrounded by children with big smiles and dingy clothes.

In the other half of the basement was the band.

I had expected a minicrowd that I could disappear into, but it looked like we were the crowd. Or rather, us and Sparrow. She bounded over and greeted both of us with hugs. Her hair was under a handkerchief and she wore thick black glasses, yoga pants, and a too-big T-shirt that hung off her shoulder. Looking at her, I could imagine for a moment what it would be like to be in love—to be bewitched by someone in all their forms.

Sparrow led us over to the other side of the basement. A busted couch and pilled carpet sat in front of the band's practice space: a ten-foot-by-ten-foot square that was a tangle of microphones, amps, instruments, and boys.

There were three of them. Sparrow introduced each with a flourish.

Winston was the drummer, a pudgy beanbag of a kid with a shaved head and glasses, sweet brown eyes, and light brown skin. His gaze tended downward, shyly. He was the one who went to my school.

On bass was P.J. Tall and gawky and white, with overly styled emo hair, twitchy fingers, and a manic grin. I felt his eyes on me, assessing. His hands began to work more nervously on the strings.

And then finally Sparrow's cousin, Devon. Oh my god, Devon. Yes, he was kind of short, shorter than me for sure, but he had this white, white smile against dark, dark skin, set inside a perfect face. The kind of face that belonged on the front of a college brochure. Fresh and all-American. His hair was done in those little twisty things that probably had a name, but one I didn't know. What I did know was that he was cool. I could tell just by the way he was standing, the easy way his instrument hung down from his shoulders. He played guitar and was the singer, too, of course.

"So this is definitely a dry run, you know?" Devon told us. "We're not, like, *ready* ready yet."

"Devon," Sparrow said. "They don't mind."

"We don't mind," Tru echoed and elbowed me.

"We don't mind," I agreed, voice squeaking.

P.J. was still looking at me, and his grin was now practically exploding.

Tru took a seat in the middle of the couch and patted either side. Sparrow and I squeezed in. It was more of a love seat, not really big enough, and the three of us wove ourselves into a cocoon, bare arms warm against one another. I huddled down, feeling heated and alive as Winston beat a four count with his drumsticks and the music began.

NINE

As we walked with the boys to a nearby park, my ears were still ringing from the hour we'd spent in the basement. Their set wasn't at all what I'd expected. They played a bunch of old songs converted into throbbing, happy pop-punk. They did the Beatles and a bunch of Motown, but they played everything fast, hard, hopped up with energy, beat pounding. Winston's pudgy arms flew in the background, almost a blur. P.J. ran all over the place, climbing speakers, dropping to his knees. Devon stayed planted under the microphone, belting from somewhere deep down inside. . . .

I loved it. I loved every single song.

We walked down a gravel path that ran through the trees, passing a fancy playground. The equipment was bright and looked brand-new, the ground covered with some kind of high-tech, cushiony foam. It was mostly empty, probably since dinnertime was fast approaching. There was just one dad with his two toddlers and a big, woolly dog.

Devon was in front, and he took us farther down the path, to a shadier corner of the park, where the old, unused equipment lingered. A rusty graveyard of abandoned playthings. This was apparently where the band came after practice to smoke their cigarettes.

The three of them took seats on a group of rocking animals: a sea horse, a dolphin, and a killer whale. The springs were squeaky and the dolphin was missing a fin. I leaned against the ladder for the monkey bars. Tru and Sparrow took side-by-side swings.

I was keenly aware of being the youngest person there, having discovered on the walk that the three boys were all a year ahead of me. Meanwhile, my fear of being the new white girl at school had temporarily vanished, pounded into oblivion by the music in the basement, by watching Devon and P.J. and Winston. I told myself that Jimmy was wrong. Mary Beth and the other girls were wrong. They were backward and behind, stuck at small-minded St. Sebastian's, where everyone was alike. I started to think that next year, among the smart and sophisticated, things would be different. Come September I'd be laughing that I ever did that Google search. I'd scoff that I'd spent nights worrying.

When the pack of cigarettes came to me, I passed it on without taking one, too afraid of coughing and looking like a loser. With nothing to occupy my hands, I looked nervously down at my feet, tracing circles in the wood chips with the tips of my sneakers.

"So why haven't you told us your band name?" Tru asked.

Sparrow laughed. "Probably because they don't have one yet."

"Whoa, now!" P.J. said. "We have *ideas*. Good ideas." He started an antsy rocking on the sea horse. His fingers tapped nonstop against the handles.

Tru leaned forward expectantly. "And those ideas are . . . ?"

P.J. took a deep breath and his eyes got wide, but Devon, looking slightly embarrassed, jumped in first.

"Well, we have three that we're thinking about. The first one is The Penny Dreadfuls. The second one is Chuck Darwin. The third one is Thunderface."

Tru choked on a puff of smoke.

"The last one," he said. "You gotta go with the last one."

Sparrow pushed her swing to the side, knocking into Tru's.

"Don't listen to him," she said. "He's too cool to like anything."

"Hey, hey," Tru said, acting offended. "I was impressed. Look, I know music, and you guys are good musicians."

Devon gave a little nod in thanks, while P.J. performed an exaggerated and awkward bow from where he sat hunched over on the sea horse.

"Tru does know music," Sparrow chimed in. "He sings like an angel."

"An angel?" Tru almost choked again. "No one has ever, ever said that. Ever. But these guys are good. I like them."

He hopped out of the swing, took a drag, exhaled dramatically.

"So," he said with a smile, "I'm *not* too cool to like anything. Suck it, Sparrow."

The boys snickered, and Sparrow stuck out her tongue. As it grew quiet, Tru's words echoed in my mind.

"That would be an okay band name," I said.

Now everyone was looking at me. The monkey-bar ladder pressed hard stripes into my back, and I grabbed one of the rungs until my hands hurt. I hadn't really meant to say that. It just tumbled out.

"What would?" Tru asked, crossing his arms, looking amused.

My face burned. Why had I opened my mouth? Saying nothing was safe, and safe was always better. Always. But everyone was still staring at me, so I had to explain.

"Suck It, Sparrow?" I said it lamely, like a question.

P.J.'s mindless rocking on the sea horse stopped. He looked at Devon. Devon grinned and looked at Winston, who'd said even less than I had all afternoon. From his timid perch on the killer whale, he grinned, too. All three of them looked at me.

"That's good," Devon said. "That's really good."

He was still smiling, and I could not stop looking at his perfect, perfect teeth.

Tru tapped Sparrow's shoulder, then pointed at his chest. "You know, technically I came up with it."

She ignored him and stood up from the swing. Cigarette dangling from her lips, she gave me a long, slow, heartfelt clap.

The clouds charged back in as Tru and I drove home for dinner, and then came the lightning, the thunder, the rain. Another night of canceled fireworks, delivering us from family time. The twins had taken off in the new car, and Mom and Dad were settled on the couch for the evening, eating microwave popcorn and watching baseball. Tru got on his phone, and the next thing I knew we were back in the van, headed to the movies to meet Sparrow and the band.

Someone had gotten the time wrong, so we were a few minutes late. We scrambled into the theater as the previews were ending, and the lights went out before we could sit. As we slinked in the dark to an empty row, there was an awkward shuffle, some shifting and hesitation that would determine who sat next to who. The boys kept tripping over one another, stalling. There was a tense second . . . two . . . three . . . and then Tru elbowed his way around everyone, made a show of pushing me gently in front of him, guiding me down the aisle to the seat at the end. He settled in next to me, threw a friendly arm across the back of my chair.

"So sorry," he whispered, almost gleefully, "but I sensed that one of those young men might be trying to sit next to you, and I just didn't feel that was appropriate."

I felt my face go hot and was thankful for the dark. Everyone else started filing in, and as they dropped into their seats and clicked off their phones, I whispered back to Tru as quietly as possible.

"Thanks so much. You're an A-plus chaperone."

He laughed so hard that Sparrow told him to shut up. The standard message blared about walking, not running, in case of an emergency. The screen turned bright, and music came in over the first scene, but I barely saw or heard anything. All I could think about was what Tru had just said and what it meant.

He could tell that someone liked me.

Tru put out an empty hand, demanding some of my Sno-Caps.

I poured a pile into his waiting palm as my mind raced through everything that had happened that afternoon. I reviewed every passing look, every expression, every nervous motion that I could remember, but I'd known even before I started who it had to be.

P.J. It must be P.J.

And yes, P.J. was a little hyper and only kind of cute, but in that moment I was flush with the knowledge that somebody wanted me. Somebody who was a year older. Somebody who was in a band.

Nestled in my seat, hidden in the dark, I kept thinking about him. I began to like his hair. I remembered that he had nice eyes. Greenish-brown ones. My head buzzed with happiness and fear. My body glowed.

I felt like I owned some small piece of the world.

The movie was silly and went by fast. When it was over, we converged outside on the sidewalk to chart our next move, only to realize it was time to split up and go home. People had curfews, and Sparrow said she didn't misbehave when she was in charge of Devon, which made both Devon and Tru roll their eyes.

Sparrow popped back inside to use the bathroom, and Winston wandered down the sidewalk to look at the movie posters hanging on the wall outside. That left the four of us. Me, Tru, Devon, and P.J. Tru took out his cell to get Devon's and P.J.'s numbers, making a little jab about how I'd sacrificed my phone to the sewer gods of Baltimore.

"It's cool. I had a supercrappy one until last year," P.J. said, waving his, dropping it, and then squatting down to pick it up with a goofy laugh.

"Well," Tru said, "if you need to get in touch with Frannie, you can always just call me. I'll be happy to find her and put her on the line, or convey any important messages you may have for her, plans you might want to make. Didn't you say something about repeating a science class this summer, P.J.? Because Frannie is *fantastic* at science. Aren't you, Frannie?"

In my head I was screaming at Tru that he was absolutely unbelievable. In reality, all I did was mumble, "Sure," and then slink away without looking at P.J., escaping before anybody could say anything else. I took a place next to Winston, pretending to care passionately about what movies were coming next month.

We stared at the posters in mutual silence, and behind me, I heard Tru addressing Devon and P.J. in a new hushed tone, saying something about the jump-off that I couldn't quite catch. Then Winston cleared his throat. He spoke a whole sentence for the first time since I met him.

"I don't know if you know anybody at school, since, uh, you're new. So if we have the same lunch next year, you can come find me and my friends. If you want to."

For a moment I thought I had it wrong, that it wasn't P.J., it was Winston. But no, I peeked at him and could tell right away he wasn't flirting. He was just being kind.

My throat tightened, but I managed a very soft thank-you.

After that it was time to go. The boys and Sparrow piled into her sporty car on one side of the street. Tru and I got into my parents' van, which was parked on the other side. Our car passed theirs in front of the theater as we headed off in opposite directions. Everyone had their windows down and we shared glances and small waves. Tru put on the Stones, spun the volume high on "You Can't Always Get What You Want."

"This is a great song, but a terrible message," Tru told me. "You should always try to get exactly what you want. That's what I do."

I thought about what I wanted. Or maybe what I needed. This morning, I'd missed my chance to tell Tru what I was thinking. I reached over and turned the music down a little.

"You can't abandon me this summer. I know you're not going to hang out with me every night or whatever, but you can't just abandon me."

He turned the sound down completely and went into his actor mode, pretending to be shocked and offended.

"Abandon you? Who's abandoning you?"

"You did! At least kind of. You needed help getting into Siren, and then you ignored me until Sparrow happened to call. You can't do that to me. I thought next year was going to be terrible. And now I already met somebody who goes to my school. Don't laugh at me, but that's really important. Today was important."

"So you need me because I hook you up with cool girls and supercute boys who are in *an actual band*?" He pretended to pout, but he was loving this. "And here I thought you enjoyed my company and scintillating conversation."

"I do. When you're not being a dick."

The light in front of us turned yellow and he slammed

unnecessarily hard on the brakes, jerking both of us forward and bringing an angry honk from behind.

"Frannie!" He looked at me like he was appalled. "That's very harsh. But, frankly, it comes as part of my whole package, so I don't really know what to tell you."

I thought for a couple of seconds, then shrugged.

"Fine," I said. "Be a dick. Just don't, you know, ditch me. Please."

"I won't—I promise. I pinky swear, if that's what you're into. In fact, I was just going to ask you to run an errand with me tomorrow."

I wondered if I should push him, try to make him be serious, but I decided that this was good enough. At least for now.

"Okay," I said. "What's the errand?"

"It's a surprise. You'll just have to wait and see. And I promise, I won't abandon you. Who's going to get you into trouble if not me?"

The light turned green, and Tru hit the gas, spun the dial until the Stones were blasting again. He was grinning, and it was one of those times when he looked genuinely happy, not just pleased with himself. I was happy, too. More than that, for the first time in months, I started to think that maybe I was going to be okay. Not just today, but tomorrow, the next day, the next week. Maybe even when I entered the abyss that was the next school year, although I didn't really want to think about that yet. Couldn't even imagine it.

The only thing that mattered now, the only thing that was real, was this summer.

TEN

Late the next afternoon, Sunday sunlight streaming in the window, Tru fetched me from my room. After two nights of canceled fireworks, the city had delayed them until later this month, some night when they wouldn't interfere with an Orioles game, so once again we were freed from family obligations. The two of us went to find Mom, and he told her he'd forgotten his running shoes at home, and needed a new pair anyway. He asked if we could take the van to the mall, offering to get me dinner afterward, his treat. A few minutes later, as we were buckling our seat belts, I asked him where we were really going.

"Sneakers? I need sneakers? You may want to get your hearing checked."

He turned up Bruce until it was too loud for us to talk, then whistled the entire ride to the mall. After we pulled into the parking lot, he hustled inside, while I practically ran to keep up with him. We came in through Macy's at the shoe department, where he immediately pointed at a pair of blue-and-white Nikes and bought them without trying them on. Then I chased him out of there to the food court, where he ordered us two chicken sandwiches with fries and Cokes, not even asking what I wanted, and then practically sprinted back to the car. We shut the doors, and he revved the sad, old engine, looking over at me as he did.

"Just enough time to make it to Prettyboy."

In fact, there wasn't enough time. Not really. It was going to be twenty-five minutes to get there, followed by what Tru had assured me was a "very fast, very stealth recon mission," and then forty minutes home.

"It's like we took a long time at the mall, followed by a leisurely sit-down dinner at some disgusting chain restaurant of your choice," he said, one hand holding his sandwich, one hand on the wheel. "No biggie. Tell them I'm exceedingly fussy about my shoes. A real queen. I tried on a million pairs. It'll be fine. We're going to be fine."

"But why did we even go the mall? We should have just skipped it!"

Tru looked at me like I was possibly the stupidest person he'd ever met. "Because I needed new athletic footwear, Frannie. Trying to stay in tip-top shape for the coming season."

"You play sports?"

"No, I do ballet."

"Shut up—you know that's not what I mean. I just . . . can't picture you on a team. Listening to the coach. High-fiving. Caring."

I could tell he was trying not to laugh.

"Track, Frannie. I do track. So not as much of all that."

"Are you good?"

"Nothing special. Short distances are my thing. I'm a pretty good sprinter. Actually, I've become an unexpected star at this new event they started last year—Devil Take the Hindmost. You just keeping running around the track, and at the end of every lap, they pull off the last person. You go and go and go until there's only one person left."

"Whoa. That's kind of awesome."

He gave me a very specific smile of his, one he reserved for when I sounded extra dopey.

"Yeah, it actually *is* 'kind of awesome.' You have no idea what's going to happen, how fast you should run. The smartest thing is to stay in the middle of the pack for the first half or so. But I never do that. I like to stay out front, run too fast, set the pace. I can run until I puke, no problem. I'm used to it."

"Why are you used to running until you puke?"

He didn't answer at first, and then his phone conveniently beeped with an incoming text. He gave it a glance.

"Sparrow. She says thanks for coming yesterday. The boys are grateful."

"Oh, cool." My voice was high and ridiculous, and I saw his Grinchy grin come out.

"Frannie, have you ever had a boyfriend?"

"Oh, sure," I said, as sarcastically as I could. "I've had tons."

"Just asking, just asking."

"Have *you* ever had a boyfriend?"

He laughed loudly at that, which warmed me to the core. I always felt like my laughs from Truman were hard-earned, special.

"Nobody worth writing home about, I guess you'd say. Not really interested in being tied down. You should never have a significant other in high school. That's a complete waste of your best make-out years."

I finally saw an opening to ask him all the million questions I'd been wondering about, but, as usual, couldn't find the words that came so easily when I was alone.

"How, um . . . how is it where you are? Is it, you know, liberal?"

"Well, it's not Iran. Or Oklahoma. But it's not San Francisco either. It's a smallish town, but pretty close to New York City. A very tiny, exclusive, stuck-up school. No LGBT club or anything. But I don't care about that shit. You've probably noticed that the tide of the world is flowing in my direction. I'm going to be fine."

If it were somebody else, I'd think they were putting on a bit of a brave face or whatever. With Tru, I thought I might believe him.

"But what about your parents?" I asked. "I mean, they must be super-Catholic. Mine used to be, but the older we get, the less they seem to care. Now they're only pretty Catholic."

"What makes a Catholic only 'pretty Catholic'?"

"I don't know. We never say grace anymore. A few years ago we started taking the summer off from church."

"Ha! So that's why we haven't been. Well, my family goes to church all year long. They're hard-core like that. Richard grew up in New Jersey, in a little Irish neighborhood. Everybody was Catholic. So on the one hand, he got away and left all that behind to be a rich, WASPy asshole, and on the other hand, he still clings to it. I don't think he really cares in some deep way. I mean, ask him how he feels about money or war or the death penalty, I promise you none of it actually aligns into some kind of structured view of the world. Certainly not a Jesus-y one. Going to church is just a good excuse to make me do something I don't want to do. He's a real dick about it."

"How did they find out?" I asked quietly. "About you?"

There was a small hum from the CD player, the pause between songs amplifying the silence.

"Let's just say I told them and leave it at that."

The sun was beginning to fade, and I watched it a little desperately, hoping we'd make it to Prettyboy before dark.

"Do you always call your dad Richard?" I asked.

"Not to his face," Tru said, and he gave me a little half smile.

Then he turned the volume up until Bruce was screaming in our ears, and I knew it was time to stop asking questions.

"So you've never been here?"

"No!" I said. "When would I come here? You're not allowed to come here!"

"Not exactly. I think you've been hearing some trumped-up stories. According to the most basic of internet searches, you can hike and boat and fish here, not to mention hunt birds with a bow? Not sure what that's all about, but look out for stray arrows flying at our heads. I mean, the place has a freaking parking lot. There's definitely no swimming, but it's not quite as mysterious as everyone likes to make it sound."

"So why did we have to lie? Why did we sneak off to do it right now?"

"I don't know, I just really felt like coming tonight. And because it's fun, Frannie! Aren't you having fun?"

I was, a little bit, even if I was still kind of nervous, but I didn't want to tell him that.

"If it's no big deal to be here, then why are we parking on this random street in the middle of nowhere?"

"Well," Tru said, "it is going to be dark soon, at which point we are *not* supposed to be here. Plus, I've been looking at maps. The jump-off is just a quarter mile that way."

He hopped out of the van and headed for the trees, leaving me to lock the doors before I caught up.

"So nobody died here or whatever?"

"Oh no," he said. "That part's true. Seems like every five years or so it happens again. Swimming here is a terrible idea."

We entered the woods, no path for us to follow, just me darting after Tru as he clomped through the trees, following the GPS on his phone while the daylight began to dwindle. At first I could still hear cars off in the distance, but as we got a little farther, those noises died away, replaced by birds chirping, squirrels rustling. I named the trees to myself as we passed. Ash. Pine. Oak. Truman was a few steps ahead, on a singular mission, plowing right through the debris of the forest, the tangle of vine and stick and bush. A leaf fluttered down and stuck in his hair without him feeling it.

Just as I was wondering how close we were, I caught a new sound—the sound of water falling. Falling and churning. Tru must have heard it, too, because he looked back and gave a little twitch of his head, telling me to catch up. I hopped my way over to him, reaching up to pluck the leaf from his hair as I did.

We pushed on, ducking under low-hanging branches, dodging roots and saplings, the gushing getting louder. Another few feet and we could see a rocky outcropping, jutting off into the sky. Tru and I started to jog toward it. We hit the edge of the tree line, took our last steps slow and measured.

Prettyboy gaped and gleamed below us, the water pristine. The reservoir stretched for ages in both directions, a dam surging to the left, a metal bridge arching to the right. No sign of any fishermen or hikers or bird hunters. No boats. I wondered how cold the water was, how deep. Tru pointed to the right, and there was the rope, wound tightly around a high branch, hanging perfectly still.

We moved forward, a little closer to the edge than I would have liked, and sat on the flat, gray rocks, still faintly warm from the sun. Tru flipped onto his stomach and kept inching forward, until he was right at the lip, peering down. For a few minutes we said nothing. Tru flicked tiny pebbles off the edge and watched them fall.

"Gatsby spends a lot of time staring out across the water.

Looking at a green light. Dreaming about a girl across the way, who he's still in love with. Does that seem romantic?" he asked.

"Of course," I said. "Don't you think so?"

"I do. Well, I'm pretty sure I do. All this tragic shit happens in the book, and it's because Gatsby and Daisy get together, even though she's married. So, yeah, they create all this turmoil, but there's a madness at the heart of what they're doing that's beautiful. Or maybe not beautiful, but real. Or powerful or something. I don't know. The first time I thought that's what it was all about. The romance. But the second time I read it, part of me wasn't so sure."

A hawk swooped in front of us, and Tru propped himself up on his elbows, watching it descend to the water. I got down on my stomach, too, and shimmied forward until I was next to him, looking down the fifty-foot drop to the reservoir below. The surface was glistening, threatening. Shining like diamonds.

"It's always a little romantic, looking at the water," I said. "It has that forever feeling. It fills you up."

"Does it?" Tru asked. "Water reminds me that I'm small. It's like this soulless void that's bigger and older than me. Part of an endless cycle. So I get that infinite feeling, but only because it goes on forever and I won't. It's weird, but that's the forever feeling I like. Standing there helplessly makes me feel kind of powerful. On a good day, I can look down and will myself not to care."

I shifted forward a bit, peering over the edge and letting the water swallow my thoughts. I felt a little scared, but for once it wasn't about any of the real things in my life. I was scared of the view, the swirling currents below.

"I like looking at water because it makes me forget," I told Tru.

"Yeah," he said. "Me too."

The hawk rose back into the sky, curving to the left and gliding away until it was a blur, a dot, nothing. We sat there for several more minutes in silence, the day dimming down. With only a few rays left to guide us, Tru stood up and headed back toward the car. Again he moved almost too quickly for me to keep up, some secret urgency fueling him on.

ELEVEN

The weekend was over, and Monday reared its head.

I was back with Duncan, reading a new Bible passage, watching him do mazes, frying up some grilled cheese. As usual, I ate twice as fast as he did, and as soon as I was done I hopped on the laptop they kept in the kitchen. At the beginning of the summer, I'd lurked around a lot on Facebook and Twitter and Instagram, scrolling through the immature jokes and cat videos and bikini pics of my old classmates, thinking how stupid it all was, but still feeling lonelier than ever. Today I hovered for a minute over the keyboard, wanting at first to look up Truman and all the boys in the band, then deciding not to. I didn't want to find them on there. Or that wasn't completely true. Part of me was desperate to find them, to excavate their online lives, looking for pictures of their exes and seeing how many followers they had. But a bigger part of me didn't want to see all that, the one-off comments they made and never thought about again. I liked them right now just the way I knew them. If I saw or read too much, it might ruin all that.

Instead, I started searching other things. I looked up and memorized the lyrics to a couple of the songs that Devon sang. I read about Gatsby. I Googled "marine welders new careers," which was so idiotic I closed it out before I even saw what came up.

After that, Duncan and I went down to the basement as usual. He played with his train set, and I tried to focus on my summer reading, wanting to get as excited about it as Tru was about Fitzgerald.

After a while I gave up and went to play with Duncan, but again I couldn't seem to relax. Usually I only got a little bored hanging out here, but today I felt restless. I couldn't stop thinking about the band. The way Devon sang. P.J. smiling at me. Winston's promise about lunch next year. When I might see them all again.

I went to stand by the little basement window—it was one of those skinny ones up near the ceiling that only show a patch of grass and hint of light. I suddenly felt a little trapped, wanting to be somewhere else. Almost anywhere else. I thought about Tru in a college classroom, learning Latin. Sparrow making art. The boys playing music.

From down on the floor, Duncan told me that the chicken was too big. I found it harder than usual to smile and say, "I know."

* * *

Our family was not its best at dinnertime. We were still living without air-conditioning, and the back of the house got unbearably hot whenever anybody cooked. Chores fell behind with Mom working more, and there were never enough clean plates and silverware. Some key ingredient was always missing from the pantry. We were grumpy and tired and hungry by the time we sat down, and while the table fit five people okay, with six, we were crowded, bumping elbows. Mom tried too hard to make everyone talk. Dad didn't try enough.

That's how things were on Wednesday night, as we settled in our chairs, a heaping mound of pasta steaming at the center of the table. The bowl was too big to pass, so we all had to lean awkwardly over or give our plates to Dad to spoon some on. Two minutes in, marinara was splattered all over the tablecloth. Jimmy muttered something about who eats spaghetti in the dead of summer. Everyone looked annoyed and sweaty, except for Tru, who I'd never seen sweat in my life. Mom handed me the basket of rolls and tried to break the quiet.

"How was Duncan today? Busy with his trains?"

I shrugged. Nodded.

Silence descended, and Mom turned to Tru, who was sitting next to her. She put a hand on his arm.

"Has Frannie told you much about Duncan?"

Tru looked up, smiling, fork paused in the air.

"Yes, she's told me a little."

In fact, I'd barely told him anything at all.

"Well," Mom said, "you probably know that Duncan is autistic.

He's a very nice boy, very sweet, but he does repeat himself a lot. Some people would get impatient, but Frannie is so good with him. She has the right temperament for it."

Of course Mom would think that was a compliment, and not something that made me sound like the world's most boring person. I stared at her, hoping she'd let it go at that, but she just went on and on about what a good job I did, how nice and even-keeled I was. Tru kept smiling.

"I'm sure Frannie is really good with him," he said. "I certainly couldn't do it."

I stabbed at my spaghetti, irritation boiling over. Mom was about to start talking again, but I cut her off.

"It's barely a job. He plays with his trains, and I sit there. It's lame."

Mom looked at me in surprise.

"Frannie! It's not lame. Watching someone else's children is a huge responsibility. You're very important to their family."

I just kept stirring my pasta, not in the mood to eat, definitely not in the mood to talk about this anymore.

"We have an autistic kid at camp," Kieran said. "It can be really hard some days. You work hard, Frannie."

I still said nothing, while next to me, Jimmy sighed and rubbed his shaved head, which had become a kind of angry habit of his in recent weeks.

"They don't even pay you that much," he said. "If I had to put up with that kid every day, I'd be pissed I wasn't making more money."

Mom put her fork down and frowned at him.

"What?" He raised his hands, palms turned up, looking back and forth as though trying to locate the problem.

"Don't be rude. And don't say *pissed*."

Jimmy rolled his eyes again, this time harder.

"So sorry, Mom! I'll never do it again!"

He said the words with a lisp and flopped his wrist.

I shouldn't have been surprised. It's not like Jimmy hadn't made that kind of joke before. Or Kieran, for that matter. Or Dad. Still—I was mortified. I told myself not to react, not even to turn my head. *Don't look at Tru. Don't look at Tru. Don't look at Tru. . . .*

I couldn't help it. My eyes flashed to him, and there he was. Expression smooth as porcelain. I searched for cracks and saw none.

I turned to the twins, who were shoveling noodles into their mouths, oblivious. Mom wore a certain distant look, the masterfully detached expression that she used when pretending not to have heard something. Dad remained as he had through almost every meal that summer. Not his giggly self. The other side of him. The angry, silent side. He was a mountain rising from the end of the table, cold and unchanging.

Kieran tried his best to keep dinner from tanking completely, talking a little bit more about the autistic kid they had at camp. But now everyone was irritated, and nobody was really listening.

Then Tru spoke.

"I met a kid like that when I used to do spelling bees."

There was a barely noticeable pause all around the table. Tru didn't usually say much at dinner, just did a bullshit routine of eating, listening, and laughing politely. I always thought it was kind of funny, especially because I felt like the only one who really knew when he was full of it, which was—well—most of the time. Now, though, we were all at attention.

"His name was Spencer Todd. He grew up one town over from me, so I'd seen him at other competitions, before the big ones, kind of got to know him. He was a savant, really amazing. Memorized people's birthdays, did math without a calculator, that kind of thing. Before we competed, when all the other kids were pacing around or cramming at the last minute, like that was going to help, I'd just sit next to him and feed him equations. You know, something to pass the time."

He started to twirl more spaghetti, then paused.

"And, yes, I realize I just outed myself." He sent the faintest wink in my direction. "As a kid who did spelling bees."

My fork clattered against my plate. The wink had been a thing of beauty, the faintest of movements. So swift it was deniable.

"Oh, dude," Jimmy said, head down, consumed by eating, "we already knew about the spelling bees."

"Well, of course we knew!" Mom said. "We all watched you on TV. Oh my gosh, we were so excited. When you finally missed one, poor Frannie! I thought she was going to cry."

This time my fork fell all the way to the floor, and I was able to disappear beneath the table. When I came back up I shot her a death stare that she didn't even notice, but Tru—Tru was looking at me with a kind of delight.

"Well," he said, turning to address the whole table, "blame my dad for all of it. He had this dream of me as a chess champion, but when I wasn't so hot at that, he turned to *spelling*. Because apparently it was also his dream for me to be socially crippled."

At the mention of Uncle Richard, my father broke his quiet spell with a giggle.

It was a long, loud giggle, one that he tried to but could not restrain.

That night Jimmy and Kieran asked Tru if he wanted to head over to Michael Donovan's place again, to his backyard pool, but Tru begged off. I couldn't stop wondering why—if it was because he was mad at the twins, or Jimmy at least, or if he was just starting to think that their friends and their parties weren't that cool.

I tried to imagine what his life was like at home in Connecticut, with his prep school friends and his rich, angry parents. All I could conjure was a ridiculous picture of him and Sparrow, drinking cocktails in fancy clothes while a disco ball twirled overhead.

Agitated, I went downstairs to see him. Ever since our day and night hanging out with the band, I didn't feel so bad bothering him. Tonight his door was open, and he was sitting on the bed with *Gatsby*, which apparently he'd started again.

"Hey, sport," he said, resting the book in his lap but not closing it.

For once I didn't fumble around for words. I just asked him what I wanted to know.

"Why didn't you want to go out to Michael's? I mean . . . I was just wondering. If it was because you don't feel like hanging out with the twins. Or just Jimmy or whatever."

Now he set the book aside.

"Well, Frannie. Here's the thing. My mom and Richard wanted me kept on a pretty tight leash this summer. Sort of semi-grounded. Very little fraternizing. And that's a lot to ask of Barb and Pat, don't you think? The responsibility of keeping me caged up? Anyway, I try to lie low here and there, because your mom's let me out way more than she's supposed to. She's not so bad, you know. You're lucky."

I felt a little bad then, remembering how I'd kind of snapped at her. I was still annoyed with her, but I also realized that I'd never bothered to wonder what she'd been going through this summer, how she felt about having Tru here and what it might mean for her relationship with her sister. There was too much there to think about right now, and I pushed those worries aside, not wanting to deal with them yet. Besides, I was confused by what Tru had just said.

"But why are you grounded?" I asked. "For being . . . ? You know. For *that*?"

He sighed, picking the book back up and flipping through it, shutting me off. I was afraid I might not be welcome much longer, so I changed the subject as quickly as I could.

"Did you decide yet, if it's romantic?" I asked. "When Gatsby's looking at the water?"

He looked at me like he was the teacher, and I was his smartest student.

"You're a very good listener, Frannie. I'm still thinking about it. I'll let you know."

"Is that why you're reading it again? To figure it out?"

"You could say that. This is the great American novel, you know. I've decided it's all I'll read this summer, until I know it inside and out. F. Scott Fitzgerald and I are becoming very good friends."

I shuffled my feet a bit, thinking about what I'd Googled that week.

"I, um, I was reading about it online? Some people think that the main character is gay? The Nick Carraway guy?"

I could tell right away this was not the right thing to say. Not because it was off-limits, just because it was dumb.

"Right, and that must be why I'm so into it!" Tru gave a girly little shrug. "I love things that are gay. Like me."

A week ago I would've been completely embarrassed, but now I could read him a little better. I knew he was just screwing with me.

"But is it true?" I asked.

He laughed, gave another shrug. A real one this time. "Actually, I don't know. He might be. It's definitely possible. But I don't know how important that is. I'm still figuring out what's really important. What Fitzgerald is trying to say. I haven't looked up anything about it. I don't want to know what Wikipedia or SparkNotes says. I want to figure it out for myself. And it's pretty damn complicated."

"But you always seem happy when you're reading it. Why does it make you so happy if you don't even know what it's about?"

He scoffed. "Jesus, Frannie, you make me sound like a moron.

I get it on some level. It's about power and greed and money and secrets. And dreams. Stupid, stupid dreams. But I don't want to know the themes or whatever. Any idiot can figure those out. I want to know it more deeply. I want to know what it says about the human condition. Then someday I can speak of it very eloquently at a pretentious party or in a college lecture hall, and lots of attractive people will want to sleep with me. The men *and* the women, of course."

I tried to kill my laugh and ended up snorting, which pleased him to no end.

"Besides, that's not why I like reading it. The words make me happy. The way it sounds. All of it sounds so beautiful."

He tossed me the book.

"Read something out loud," he said.

I opened to a random page.

"'Every one suspects himself of at least one of the cardinal virtues, and this is mine: I am one of the few honest people that I have known.'"

I looked up. "I didn't know there were cardinal virtues. I've only heard of cardinal sins."

He laughed at this, not his normal short snickers or self-satisfied chuckles, but a real laugh, long and loud.

"Well, that's the Catholic in you. Always focused on the guilt. I was raised that way, too, but I've tried very hard to reject it."

He motioned for me to toss the book back, and I did.

"It's true, by the way," he said. "There aren't many honest people. I think you might be one of them."

At first I felt warmed by the compliment, but then it gave me pause. It *was* a compliment, wasn't it? Being honest was a good thing; everyone thought so.

Or did they?

Maybe Tru thought honesty was boring. Maybe he thought my "good temperament" was boring.

I searched for a way to break the silence.

"What are you doing this weekend?" I finally asked.

He interlocked his fingers, furrowed his brow.

"Well, not this weekend, but next weekend—assuming you're free, of course—you and I are going to see Suck It, Sparrow at the South City Rec Center. It's their big debut. Part of some high school battle of the bands."

"Oh!" My body tensed and warmed. "That's . . . wow."

"Did you have something better in mind?" he asked. "Because if you do, I can be persuaded. More field hockey charity events?"

"No, I . . . No."

"Well, this weekend I'm not sure about Friday or Saturday, but Sparrow wants us to go to a baseball game with her and whoever is around tomorrow. Speaking of honesty, I should say that I think her whole sporty side is a bit of an act she puts on, because it's so very cute and unexpected. The hot, arty girl likes sports! Isn't she just the best? But whatever. We can try to have fun. Fresh air, hot dogs made from spare animal parts. Overpriced beer we can't even buy. Why the hell not?"

I picked at my nails, looked down at the stained carpet. "So who's going exactly?"

"Well, I don't know," he said. "But I can text her and tell her you need to know."

He whipped out his phone and scrolled around for a minute, while I stood there praying this was a bluff.

"I have the boys' numbers in here, too. It would probably be easier to ask them directly."

Now he was genuinely typing. He was typing something long. I tried to wait it out, but then I caved.

"Don't! Okay? Just don't. Please."

He giggled almost like my dad as he put the phone away. Then he picked his book back up, and I took the hint. I closed the door behind me and was just starting back upstairs when he called my name. Turning back, I poked my head inside his room. He had somehow produced a notebook and pen without seeming to move.

"So you're a science person and all. I was just wondering—do you, by any chance, know how to spell *corpuscle*? I can't seem to remember."

I told him to shut up, then turned and pounded up the stairs, listening to him laugh behind me.

TWELVE

Before the game I lingered in the kitchen, nothing to do but will the clock to move, while stuffing Oreos into my mouth and trying to eavesdrop on Tru and Dad in the backyard. They were drinking coffee together, and Dad asked if Tru rooted for the Yankees.

"God, no," Tru said. "The only thing worse than the Yankees are people who like the Yankees."

My dad giggled, and I marveled that Tru could make him laugh. For the past few months, his quiet side had won over his jolly side again and again, but Tru always seemed to bring out the scheming glint in his eye. I hardly ever did, which made me wonder if I ever tried.

Tru came inside then, and I went to the backyard, brought my dad the cookies. His face lit up, and I suddenly felt awful, hollow, thinking of everything I hadn't done these last long months.

"Did you take the price tag off that yet?"

Tru flicked the bill of Sparrow's Orioles hat, which did look brand-new. It was perched, adorably and perfectly, on top of her hair, so he almost knocked it off. She caught it, adjusted it, gave him a look.

He'd already made fun of my giant, faded O's T-shirt, which had once belonged to the twins. Sparrow told him that oversized tops hung perfectly on my frame, to which he said, "I'm sure that's what she was going for," to which she'd told him to shove it. At first I thought they were actually kind of fighting, but this was just how they talked to each other. Already, they were laughing again, leaning over a program together, saying yes, no, or maybe to all of the players.

"Yummy," Sparrow said, pointing to the perfect-looking one with the jaw and the long hair.

"Boring," Tru said, then raised his eyebrows and tapped his finger on someone else—I couldn't quite see who.

"Eh," Sparrow said, flipping the page. "Oooh. That one. I saw him on TV last night."

"Well, yeah," Tru said. "Everyone likes that one."

"That one" was the guy with the scruff and the smile and the attitude. Left fielder. He said ridiculous things in interviews, never really answered the questions he was asked. He wasn't a superstar, but he made big plays. He was fast as hell. And he definitely wasn't handsome.

"Do you like him, Frannie?" She turned the program in my

direction, and I looked at his face, trying to understand what it was about him that got everybody going. I wrinkled my nose and shrugged.

"Yeah, it doesn't really make sense," Sparrow said, holding the page out in front of her, turning it this way and that. "I mean, why? What is it?"

"Self-possession," Tru said.

"Self-possession," Sparrow echoed. "You mean confidence? Sure, confidence is sexy. Everyone knows that."

"Nah," Tru said. "This is different. Confidence is an attitude. Self-possession is deeper. More complete. It's owning yourself." He grabbed my box of Cracker Jack, dumped a huge pile into this hand.

Sparrow shook her head in disgust. "You could ask first, pig."

"What?" he said. "Frannie only wants the toy anyway."

I snatched the box back and he grinned at me, cramming a fistful of popcorn into his face, spilling some on his shirt. I was starting to notice that he was different around Sparrow. A little sillier. Not quite so perfectly smooth.

Sparrow was on her phone, texting and scanning the stands around us. We'd been hoping to find some empty seats together where we could sit with P.J. and Devon, but it was beautiful out, and the O's were doing well this season. The stadium was packed. The only free seat around us was a lone one next to me.

"Nothing's clear near them either," she reported. "I told them they can pop over one at a time and say hi, if they want. They can get down here without a ticket, right?"

"Um, yeah," Tru said, gesturing at the distant field. "These seats aren't exactly worth policing."

I tried to focus on the game, willing myself not to chew my fingernails, not to turn around every five seconds to see who might be coming down the steps. It was the third inning. Two outs, batter up. The Os' biggest hitter. A burly guy who had elicited a firm "no" from both Sparrow and Tru. On the first pitch a crack split the air and the ball went back, back, back. Some people were on their feet, watching, stretching, hoping . . . but it came down just short of the back wall, landing soft and harmless in a glove. Groans all around, both teams still scoreless.

A trivia game popped up on the Jumbotron as the players jogged back to the dugout, and the crowd was shouting and laughing. Concession guys screamed about cotton candy, Miller Lite. In the chaos of it all, Sparrow and Tru were having their own little conversation, not private exactly, but certainly not including me.

"But have you talked to them much?" she asked.

"Yes, yes. You can get off my ass. I talked to Richard this morning. He wants us to start emailing each other in Latin, to see how I'm doing. You're laughing, but that's not a joke. As if he remembers any of that shit. He's so full of it."

"And . . . ?"

"And what?"

"Your mom?"

He shrugged. "We text. Basic stuff. Nothing heavy. I'm not you, okay? I don't chitchat with my mommy every day."

Sparrow pouted. "Don't insult my mommy. She loves you."

I was poking around in my Cracker Jack box with one finger, pretending not to listen, dying to hear more, when P.J. slid in beside me, smiling like crazy, hair gelled every which way, reeking of that horrible body spray the twins used to use.

"Lovely day for a ball game," he said, tipping an imaginary hat.

Sparrow gave a little wave, while Tru tented his fingers and stared deliberately at P.J.'s spiky head. Meanwhile I tried to sort out whether he was completely ridiculous or kind of adorable.

"I see you did your hair extraspecial for your date," Tru said. "Is it hard for you two boys to balance your relationship with your music?"

P.J. patted his head, unfazed. "It's hard, but it's worth it. He's such a handsome little bastard. But actually, it's not just us. Some of the groupies came, too. They're in the row behind us."

"The groupies?" Tru asked, incredulous.

Sparrow made a little noise of disgust. "That's what they call the girls they hang out with. *Their friends.* Their friends, I might add, who go to the arts school with them, and are just as talented as they are."

"Whoa, whoa," P.J. said, hands raised in the air. "I know, I know! It's a joke! We just like to mess with them. They're total rock stars. Hot chick rock stars. No doubt."

Hot chick rock stars. I felt completely crushed. I'd actually thought tonight was about me and Tru and Sparrow and the band. More than that, I'd dreamed that the whole summer could be, which I suddenly realized was ridiculous. As if they wouldn't have other friends. As if they wouldn't know other girls.

Still, P.J. was here. Next to me. Smiling that oversized smile and drumming his fingers on his thighs.

"So, ah. What have you been up to?" he asked. "Since our jaunt to the park?"

Tru mumbled, "Jaunt. Sweet Jesus," under his breath, and I ignored him, trying to think of something, anything to say, not wanting to talk about Prettyboy, not able to think of another thing, finally just giving a little shrug.

"Not much," I told him. Cardinal honesty.

"But you're coming to the battle of the bands next weekend? Because we officially signed up as Suck It, Sparrow, so you have to be there."

Now I laughed, and Sparrow leaned over to high-five P.J., while Tru acted like we were a bunch of idiots who were distracting him from the game.

"We'll be there," I told P.J. "I'll be there."

He started to say more, but his phone buzzed in his pocket, and he had to squirm to get it out.

"Shit, it's Devon. He's on his way. I just freaking got here, but whatever. Make sure you watch when he tries to come down. We're doing Black Guy, White Guy."

"I'm sorry, what?" Tru asked.

Sparrow sighed, very loudly and pointedly.

"What?" P.J. said. "*What?* What's the problem? Why do you have to ruin our fun?"

"It's not fun," she said. "It's depressing. It depresses me, and I don't know why you like doing it."

"It's an important sociological experiment to identify racist authority figures. And I didn't come up with it, Devon did!" P.J. spun around in his seat, scanned the stands behind us, pointing to the security guard who stood at the top of our stairs to the section. "Pudgy bald white dude. He didn't stop me when I came down. Keep an eye out!"

He patted my knee and then loped away, taking the steps two at a time, while Tru and I turned back to Sparrow.

"So I'm pretty sure I can figure it out, but explain, please?" Tru said.

She crossed her arms, huffed a bit. "Black Guy, White Guy is a game they play. They want to see if the guy who didn't stop P.J. stops Devon and asks for his ticket. They do this shit all the time. In stores, at restaurants, wherever. They think it's hilarious."

Tru was laughing. "And you don't?"

"No, I don't."

"I'm guessing that a lot of people fail Black Guy, White Guy?"

"Why, yes they do, Truman," she said. "How insightful of you."

"So then what happens?" Tru asked, already turning around and waiting for Devon to appear. "I hope they have a sticker or a button or something to pin on the person's chest. Just, like, a big red circle that says *RACIST*."

"No, Devon usually does this comically overly polite act to whoever the person is, and then the two of them laugh their asses off about it later."

Tru bit his lip, thought for a second. "I still like the idea of stickers. Maybe I'll make them stickers. Oh, shit, here he comes!"

Now we were all watching, joined in tense anticipation as Devon emerged from the tunnel doing a casual saunter and pulling his O's visor a little farther over his eyes. As he grabbed the railing and hit the first step, I exhaled, positive that everything was going to be fine. . . .

Then the guard leaned forward, tapped his shoulder, beckoned him back.

"Oh, what an asshole!" Tru said in delight, while Sparrow gave an angry little hiss. We all watched as Devon hopped back up to the landing and turned around, a bright, innocent smile on his face. The two of them spoke briefly to each other, and then Devon started scanning the crowd for us. We waved our arms, and he waved back. The guard gave an awkward minisalute, gesturing at him to go ahead.

A minute later, he was sliding into the seat beside me.

"Hey there," he said.

"Hey," I said back.

He leaned over, met eyes with Tru and Sparrow, who were elated and angry, respectively.

"What a world we live in, my brother," Tru said.

"Oh, did P.J. give you the heads-up?" Devon asked. "Just doing my part. Keeping tabs on the man. Don't look at me like that, Sparrow."

"I just don't understand why it's amusing to you. Do you watch the news? Do you know what happens to black kids because of the way people look at them? It seems like just this quiet, subtle thing to you, and a lot of times it is. But that's why it's so insidious."

"All right, all right," Devon said, tugging at his shorts, adjusting his visor again. "Don't break out the SAT words on me. I hear you. I feel you."

"I don't know if you do feel me," Sparrow said.

"Listen, I know. I get it. I live it. Excuse me if I need to laugh about it every once in a while, okay? You're a girl and everyone thinks you're perfect-looking, so trust me when I say the situation is not quite the same."

She wanted to say more, I could tell, but instead she gave him a dismissive little wave, mumbled something about having her own shit to deal with, and sat back in her seat. Tru rolled his eyes and leaned over my lap, asking Devon about his Blondie T-shirt, which got them going about a million bands I'd never even heard of. They kept talking about New Wave, which Tru said he thought of as poetic, intellectual punk, and Devon said, "Exactly, which makes no sense, which is why it's so perfect and great." At first I tried to mentally note everything they were saying, so I could steal the songs from Tru's collection later, but then I got distracted thinking about Black Guy, White Guy. I was cataloging my family members, my old friends, my old teachers, deciding who would pass. By the time I got to myself, I really didn't want to play anymore. I was reminded of searching for the racial breakdown of my new school and was newly ashamed. Then I remembered watching the band practice, how that somehow had made me think everything would be magically fine, and now suddenly that seemed naive and embarrassing, too. My mind was a jumble, and I tried to clear it by focusing instead on Devon's hands. His palms looked soft and were the rosy pink color of a seashell. He had calluses everywhere from the strings of his instruments, and I kept wanting to touch them with the tips of my fingers, to see how they would feel.

After half an inning, Devon got up to leave, annoyed with Sparrow and ready to go back to P.J. and the groupies. Before he left, he made sure Tru and I were coming to the battle of the bands. I felt myself blushing when I told him yes.

The whole time he was there, I'd been clutching the Cracker Jack box so tightly it was practically crushed to oblivion. Tru snatched it from me again, shook out the final crumbs. The prize landed in the middle of his hand, and he feigned excitement, telling me, "I win again. I always win, Frannie." He held the little treasure up to the evening light—a stupid fake tattoo. Still, he kept it aloft for a moment, bending it carefully between his thumb and index finger, seemingly deep in thought.

THIRTEEN

After the Thursday-night game, the weekend was a bust, Tru out
with the twins doing god knows what—he wasn't always in the
mood to report back. It was now the middle of July and miser-
ably hot, but Tru had started running in the mornings, and on
Tuesday I decided to go with him. For ten minutes or so we jogged
in relative quiet, but then he went flying, a block ahead of me in
half a minute, new shoes shining, not a word or glance back in
my direction. Sweaty and annoyed, I made my way home alone,
waited for everybody to leave, then hit the shower, thinking as I
did that there was no need to tag along again. I'd never really liked
running and wasn't particularly good at it. Tru seemed to have all
this fire spurring him on, so that was fine. I'd leave him to it. With
the shower on full blast, I sang loudly, thinking of P.J. and Devon.

Over at the Harts', Duncan had gotten a new haircut, shaved

shorter on the sides. Somehow it made him look infinitely more grown-up, but we still played the same games. Mazes. Trains. Twenty questions. I tried to stay patient, but my mom's words about my temperament still chafed me. When he brought up the chicken for the fifth time, I snapped at him, "I know!"

That night, Tru and I walked over to the busy street where Siren was. We went in a shop to look at records and comics but didn't buy anything. Sparrow was working and came out to say hi. Tru asked her when we could come back in, and she said we had to wait until there was a band worth seeing and one of the nicer bouncers was working.

The sidewalk was crowded with smokers, and I stood awkwardly close to Tru the whole time, keeping an eye out for the beer-bellied man, and wishing I weren't so freakishly tall and red-haired and conspicuous.

Wednesday night there was a blowout at The Mack's house, but when I asked Tru about it the next morning, he said the crowd had been pretty dull. I asked if Jeremy Bell was there, and he said, "What? I don't remember. No," and then quickly disappeared down to his room.

But that afternoon, he was home a little early from campus, waiting for me on the front steps.

"I was afraid you might call the authorities, turn me in for neglect and abandonment soon," he said. "So I called Sparrow. The good news is she wants to hang out tonight. The bad news is she wants to go the movies." He dropped his voice to a whisper. "One of *her* type of movies."

After dinner we met Sparrow at the indie theater, the one I'd been to a couple of times with Mom for Sunday matinees, when they showed old classics. But tonight we were coming to see an art-house film, a biography of sorts about a painter I'd never heard of. At the ticket booth, we had to pay with cash, and at the concession stand, we bought coffees instead of soda. They directed us to a small theater in the back that had a real purple curtain that covered the screen.

Two minutes into the movie, Tru announced that that this was some special version of hell. Twenty minutes in, he asked us, in a too-loud whisper, why nothing was happening except grass waving in the breeze and light glinting off windows. Sparrow finally shot him a look that shut him up for good, and he spent the rest of the movie messing around on his phone.

When it was over, we made our way back to the cars, both parked a couple of blocks away. The two of them walked in step behind me, Tru still complaining, Sparrow telling him all the reasons he was wrong. I didn't really get the movie either, but I did like the way everything looked. Like real life seen through some kind of hyper lens. I even liked the grass. Still, I didn't think that Sparrow would be able to disarm him. It just always seemed like Tru was right . . . or at least he had all the words to convince you that he was.

"You don't understand female directors," Sparrow said. "They work differently. They're more sensual."

"Sensual? There was a stunning lack of sex in that movie."

"I don't mean it in that way. I mean *sen*sual. Arousing the senses. Being one with the senses. The beauty of details. Don't tell me that wasn't a beautiful movie. Don't tell me it wasn't different from that crap we went to see with Devon. It's more than plot. It's *evocative*."

He laughed. "Okay, okay. Maybe I just like to give you a hard time. I get what you're saying. I appreciate *the evocative*. I like detail. I'm pretty sure F. Scott Fitzgerald is the master of the perfect detail."

Sparrow clucked her tongue and looked at him.

"Seriously? Still with the *Gatsby*?"

"What? I finally think I'm getting somewhere. I'm approaching genius levels of literary understanding."

"That book is depressing. If you keep reading it, I think it's going to warp your mind."

"It's not depressing. It's passionate."

"Passionate? Okay, now I think it's too late. You're officially warped."

"Gatsby's just Gatsby. You know? He's fucked-up but weirdly beautiful. It's possible to be both."

Sparrow responded with a skeptical look.

"Look, maybe we just have different tastes. I enjoy the finest in modern American literature. You like sexy grass or whatever."

She laughed at that, but I couldn't help dwelling on Tru's tone. For a moment there, he hadn't sounded like himself. He'd almost sounded unsure.

As if he could read my thoughts, he called ahead to me, interrupting them.

"C'mon, Frannie. We're waiting for your insightful commentary."

I'd actually just been dreaming that one day I'd be able to debate like they were doing. I didn't know people who talked about movies like that. They said they liked them or they didn't; the movies were cool or they weren't.

For a few moments, I fumbled with what to say. I almost told them that the movie felt like a poem to me—something beautiful that I liked without really knowing why. But then it seemed like a silly, girly thing to say.

And wasn't Tru right, after all? The movie was a little ridiculous. Nothing happened.

"I'm not sure," I finally answered. "I'm still thinking about it."

Behind me, Tru spoke to Sparrow in a faux whisper.

"That's code speak for something. Either *I didn't understand a thing* or *That movie was shit, but I don't want to be mean to Sparrow*."

She came up and put an arm around me.

"It's actually perfectly fine to take time and think, instead of running your mouth right away about everything," she said, speaking loudly for Tru's benefit. "And if you did hate my movie, that's okay. I happen to think everyone is entitled to their own opinion."

"And I," Tru chimed in behind us, "am entitled to tell them they're wrong."

On Friday night, Tru disappeared with the twins somewhere, and I was stuck home with Mom and Dad, watching a movie they picked. There was no sexy grass to be seen, no glimpses of light glinting off windows, just two people coming together, against all odds. It seemed kind of silly and obvious, like a million other movies I'd seen before. That was the first time I'd really thought about how alike they all were.

Though if I was being honest, I still liked it, despite all that. I still rooted for the odd couple, wanting them to make it.

Saturday finally rose, full of blazing, screaming sunshine. The battle of the bands was hours away. Endless hours. I was glad when Tru asked if I would come for a walk with him after lunch, because I needed something, anything to pass the time. He waited for me on the front steps, while I went to find Mom or Dad and let them know we were going out.

I saw Dad first, through the kitchen window. He was busy in the backyard—a place where he was managing to spend hours and hours this summer, even though it stretched all of fifteen feet by twenty feet. He mulched and planted. He patched the concrete walkway. Now he was building a trellis from some old scrap wood in the basement. I watched him for a moment from the back window. He was hunched over, sweating, his face hidden. He was usually a big whistler, but today he was quiet.

I decided to go tell Mom instead.

The vacuum roared upstairs, and I followed the noise to my room. I stepped through the door and almost ran right into her. The on/off switch was broken, so she had to pull the plug to hear me. I told her that Tru and I were going to go for a walk and that we might be gone awhile, but we'd back to have dinner and change before the battle of the bands. She smiled at me, but her face sort of scrunched when she did. She looked tired. Or maybe she looked sad. I could always tell when she was about to begin one of our rare serious talks, and I tried to rush out before this one began. Too late.

"You've been nice to your cousin. Thank you," she said. "Is he being nice to you, too?"

My cardinal honesty must have kicked in, because for a second I genuinely couldn't answer. But I thought about everything that had happened since he'd gotten here, how never in a million years would I give that up for the former peace of my sad, lonely summer. I was able to mumble something like *Yes, of course.* She stepped closer, looked me in the eyes, which meant she had to perch under me and peer up. I was five inches taller than her, at least.

"You met some kids from your new school, through his friend?" she asked.

I realized I'd hardly seen my mother at all in the past two weeks. She worked and worked and I babysat or went out with Tru or hid, brooding, in my room. I looked at her now and saw lines creasing her face like rumples on morning sheets. Again I mumbled some vague affirmative, but her eyes and her mouth didn't soften. Forcing a smile, I said the one thing I thought she'd want to hear.

"Yes. I met some nice kids. Really nice. One goes to my school. But he's just, like, a friend. Not whatever. He said I can eat lunch with him."

Before I left I wrapped my arms around her, hunching down to bury my face in her neck, the two of us clinging to each other. Then I bounded down the stairs and didn't look back.

Tru started walking, and I followed. We were headed in the direction of Siren, and he seemed to be moving with purpose, but when I asked where exactly we were going he only shrugged.

Tru was in good spirits, delightedly recounting the events of last night, another sloppy party at The Mack's house, where Jimmy had apparently gotten blasted, Tru had gotten mildly buzzed, and Kieran had stayed sober so he could drive. "They take turns doing that. Not a drop all night! A little Boy Scout streak they have. I find it kind of inspiring." He also told me that Jimmy currently had two decent-looking girls wrapped around his finger—an achievement made purely by acting like a jerk.

"He somehow has more game than Kieran. Can you believe that? High school girls, Frannie. Sometimes there's just no accounting for their taste."

I was surprised to hear him draw this distinction. I'd assumed the twins were one and the same to him, that he couldn't care less about them, but clearly that wasn't quite the case. I pondered that as we walked on, while Tru continued to spin tales about his night out. He told me he'd seen Jeremy Bell again. Apparently, Jeremy had come straight from his job at the pool and was wearing his swim trunks and lifeguard tank top.

"There was a point when we were right across from each other, on opposite couches, and I gave him *the look*."

"The look?" I asked. Beside me, Tru had a hop in his step. He was as happy as I'd ever seen him.

"If I'm trying to get a read on a guy, I use my eyes. It's the only real way to bridge such a delicate subject between teenage boys. You look at each other and linger a beat too long and that says it all."

"So did something happen?"

"No, no, no." He chuckled. "That's really, ah, not on my agenda right now. Trying to keep a low profile around your brothers and stay in your parents' good graces. Later, when he tried to give me the look back I stared back at him like he was insane."

"You didn't really do that."

Tru just laughed.

I wanted to tell him that was a terrible, mean thing to do, that I barely knew Jeremy, but he seemed sweet. Plenty of people were nice to him, but others made jokes behind his back or sometimes to his face. At St. Sebastian's, Jeremy was the only one. Or rather, the only one everybody knew about. The only one brave enough to be that open. I was searching for the words to explain all that, while also trying to summon the confidence to argue with Tru. But then I saw them.

Mary Beth, Dawn, and Marissa were heading right for us.

"Oh god," I said.

"Oh god, what?" Tru asked.

"My—my friends. Or my not-friends. The girls I never hang out with anymore. The Stix for Chix girls."

Tru peered ahead. "Those three?" He gave a snort. "Looks like we're going to have to talk to them. Put on your friendliest smile!"

They were now half a block away and coming toward us fast. They'd been at the coffee shop and all had those huge frozen mocha things with whipped cream. They must have gone there after practice, because they were wearing their field hockey gear and lugging their bags. The three of them spotted me, and I could see their surprise, their discomfort, and then their confusion when they saw Tru.

"Here we go," he whispered to me when they were still just out of earshot.

I looked at him and felt a ripple of fear. There was absolutely no way to control him.

And now the girls were here.

The three of them were sweaty messes. Hair a wreck, no makeup. I was kind of happy they looked so terrible, which I knew was petty, but I couldn't seem to help it. We greeted each other with a chorus of hellos that was the fakest-sounding thing I'd ever heard.

"We haven't seen you in forever!" Dawn said. "I mean, it *feels* like forever."

"Yeah, totally," I said, which sounded incredibly stupid and was not at all what I meant to say. "Uh, how was Stix for Chix?"

"Oh my god!" Mary Beth said. "You should have come. It was crazy. There were girls from some fancy prep school who wore bikinis—it was so ridiculous." She took her voice down to a whisper. "Everyone said they looked like sluts. And a bunch of guys who were seniors or something got kicked out for drinking. We won our first match, then lost, but it doesn't matter. You know?"

"Totally," I said and immediately wondered why I kept using that word.

There was a tense moment of silence while they all alternated between looking at me, looking at Tru, and looking at the ground. I realized I needed to hurry up and make an introduction, but too late. Tru was ready.

"Hi," he said, with his most charming smile, "I'm Truman."

He didn't tell them he was my cousin, and I could see in their faces that they had no idea. Since I never saw him, I never really talked about him. In a flash, he took out a cigarette, casually lit it, though I knew he almost never smoked unless he was in some sort of social setting with others who did. He repeated each of their names as they introduced themselves. Then he gave a little "Oh!" and pulled his cell out of his pocket. I hadn't heard it ring.

"Sorry, I know this is rude," he said, putting the phone to his ear. "Hey, Sparrow. What's up? Yeah, yeah, I'll be there. What time does the band go onstage? Got it. What's that? YES. Goddamn. Frannie's coming. Tell the boys to keep their pants on."

He hung up and looked at me, taking a very deliberate drag.

"Well," he said. "We better get going, huh?"

"Was that . . . was that really Sparrow?"

He dropped the cigarette on the sidewalk, half-smoked. He gave a playful shrug.

"Can you seriously tell those three apart?" he asked. "Yeesh. What a mousy bunch."

I looked the other way, embarrassed, mumbling something about how I wasn't even friends with them anymore. I glanced over to see if Tru had heard me, but he'd stopped walking and was now standing a few paces behind. Right in front of the tattoo parlor.

I'd passed this place a thousand times, had studied its bloodred awning, the shop's name in dripping black script: *Nice Ink*. There was an elaborate and beautiful mural painted on the front facade and door, devils and angels and dragons and butterflies, madly bright, all twisted together, climbing the building's brick walls.

Tru walked inside without waiting for me.

No. That was my first thought, singular and sure.

No.

No.

No.

No.

I will not go into the tattoo parlor. I will wait outside on the sidewalk, in the sunshine. I'll wait for as long as it takes.

Thirty seconds later I followed him in.

A man built like Jabba the Hutt was seated at a desk just inside the door. My throat constricted at the sight of him, but he was reading some magazine called *High Times* and never even looked at me. I tried not to stare at the army of—what were those, *trolls*? They began at his shoulder and marched all the way down to his wrist with their ugly faces and battle-axes.

The inside of Nice Ink was a different world from the outside. Sunlight didn't penetrate. The air was cold and smelled like candles and incense. Over top of the peeling floral wallpaper were framed photos of tattooed arms, backs, necks, ankles. The building was once a row house, just about the size and shape of ours. In the first room, our living room, there were the front desk and two display cases, one for piercing jewelry and another one for bongs and pipes. In the second room, our dining room, there were three tables full of thick binders. Tru was there, flipping through one.

Finally, the back, where our kitchen would be, was closed off by a curtain. Heavy metal played at a low volume, and above it came a persistent buzzing. I'd heard the noise before on TV, some reality show that Jimmy and Kieran used to watch because the girls were hot. I knew it was the sound of needle on flesh.

I was still exactly two steps inside the doorway. I hadn't moved. Now Tru whistled at me, waving me over, and I rushed to his side, trying to hide behind him.

"I don't think I'm allowed to be in here."

I said it so quietly that at first I was sure he hadn't heard me.

"It's not *a bar*, Frannie." I looked down at the binder, which was a catalog full of designs. Chinese symbols. Fairies. Skulls. He stopped on a page full of unicorns.

"What do you think?" he asked, in a voice reminiscent of Jimmy's mocking tone at the dinner table. "On my lower back?"

He put the binder down and picked up another. He flew through the pages, then stopped and smiled.

His arm blocked my view. I had no idea what he was looking at.

He walked over to Troll Man, who put down the magazine. Tru pointed to whatever he'd found, then glanced at the time on his phone.

"Any chance I can have this done in an hour or so?"

"That?" Troll Man asked. "Sure. That's easy. PAULA!"

There was a rustle in the back room and Paula appeared from behind the curtain. She was scrawny, pale, with hair the color of wheat. A ring hung from the center of her nose like a bull and her eyes were ringed in thick black, but her dress was delicate and lacy, like a doily. She had flowers inked everywhere. Daises circled her wrist like a bracelet; another strand looped her ankle. Ivy curled up her neck. Something pink and petaled peeked out from her neckline. She looked barely old enough to drink.

"Got half an hour or so?" Troll Man asked, inclining his head toward Tru and going back to his magazine.

"I got half an hour," she said, still holding on to the curtain. "You check this kid's ID?"

Troll Man didn't look up, just turned a page and sighed. "I don't know—did you? I'm sure one of us did."

She looked at Tru, her mouth screwed in a smile. Then she noticed me.

"Oh, honey. No way. I'm not doing you."

"Not her," Tru said, laughing. "Just me."

Paula paused and considered. "You're not getting her name, are you? I don't do names on young people. Will. Not. Do it."

Tru laughed harder. "Um, no." He turned to me. "Frannie, you're great and all, but, well . . . that's quite a commitment."

I tried to shrug with some measure of coolness, but it was more of an awkward squirm. Paula looked back and forth between us a few more times, and then she took a step back and opened the curtain farther. Without hesitating, Tru disappeared into the back room with the binder. She started to follow him, then looked back at me.

"You coming?" she asked.

Again, my first thought was strong and sure. *No. I should say no, and I should go back outside or go home or at least suffer through the coming minutes awkwardly with Troll Man.*

Instead, I scurried like a mouse through the curtain.

There were four black leather loungers that reclined like dentist chairs. Only one was occupied, in the far back corner. It was pushed down in a full horizontal position, and a man with a Mohawk was bent over a tiny woman whose face I couldn't see. Her back was becoming a landscape. I glimpsed a bit of it. A waterfall, a parrot in a tree. The bird was just an outline, and then I watched as the first touch of green came, bright and brilliant.

Tru was handing Paula the binder, pointing. She gave a quick nod, snapped it closed, and set it aside.

"Where do you want the damage?"

In a single fluid movement, Tru pulled off his shirt and tapped the top of his left pec, just above his heart.

He had no chest hair at all. He suddenly looked much younger.

"How big?" Paula asked.

He shrugged, and showed her with his fingers, holding them about four inches apart.

"It'll be seventy-five," she said. "Okay, sixty 'cause you're cute.

You have cash? I don't particularly want a paper trail on this one."

"I have cash."

Tru tossed me the shirt, which I fumbled and dropped, then grabbed from the floor. He got in the chair.

"I can load this into a machine that spits out a stencil," Paula said. "But I've got amazing hands. I can draw this out perfectly with a pen, a special one that doesn't smudge. Then I do the permanent ink on top of it."

"Let's go with option two," Tru said.

Paula's face lit up a bit, and she went to a small sink and methodically scrubbed her hands. She came back, opened a drawer, and began to arrange her instruments, her demeanor now a surgeon's. With everything prepped, she sat down on a rolling stool, dug in her heels, and, legs spread wide, she pulled herself as close as possible to his chair. She sprayed the area with soap and water, rinsed it, gave it a wipe of alcohol. She took out a disposable razor and went over the spot, laughing as she did, saying that it wasn't really necessary.

Tru watched the whole process with a detached curiosity. In the corner of the room I clutched his shirt like a lifeline, staring on feverishly as she pressed the pen into his skin and began to draw.

At first she leaned on him and I couldn't see, but then she pulled back and adjusted the overhead light. She leaned over again, but this time carefully, one hand in her lap, the other perfectly steady as it traced a soft, sensual curve that looped around and in on itself. A simple black shape came clear.

The sign for infinity.

When she picked up the needle, it buzzed like an angry insect against him, darkening the black shape and causing the flesh around to flush red. Troll Man was right—it didn't take long. At first Tru watched the whole process, calm and unflinching, but after a few minutes he turned away. He smiled briefly, then gazed at the ceiling, getting lost and dreamy.

When she was done, Paula bandaged him up and gave him explicit instructions for how to care for it—the cleaning, keeping it out of the sun, the signs of infection to watch for. She must have seen the carelessness, the utter disregard in his face, because she shifted her focus to me. In me, she must have seen something else. Something sturdy and reliable.

"You'll remember, right? You'll make sure he takes care of himself?"

I had nodded gravely and whispered, "*Yes,*" already repeating the instructions in my head, committing them to memory. But even as I did, I suspected it was futile.

I was sure that Tru would never listen to me.

FOURTEEN

I dressed for the battle of the bands in a tiny red sundress that my mom had given me last week. She'd found it in a box in the basement. Years ago, the dress was hers, and the cotton was soft and thin from lots of washings.

"Redheads are afraid of wearing red, but it can look great on them," she told me.

I put it on and she was right. I was sure she hadn't thought about how short it would be on me, and so I had rushed out the door behind Tru, a jean jacket wrapped around my waist. Now, seated in the passenger seat of our minivan, I kept pulling at the hem, stretching it down an extra inch over my thighs. Next to me, Tru was tapping his fingers on the wheel. He was in an extraordinary mood, even happier than this morning. He wore a white T-shirt, and in the right light, the outline of his bandage was visible. As we drove to the South City Rec Center, I kept glancing over at him, looking for blood.

Eventually I stopped tugging at my dress, deciding it looked just fine. I pulled down the sun visor for a second to check my makeup and was happy to see everything was still in place. At first I was kind of annoyed that Tru had the windows down, because the wind was tangling up my hair, but as I looked in the mirror and saw it flying, I thought that I actually looked pretty great.

Tru was blaring The Rolling Stones. As usual he drove fast and smooth.

The auditorium was roiling with high school students. They were black and white and Asian and Latino. Preppy and gothy and indie and sporty. They were lowerclassmen and upperclassmen, tall, short, skinny, fat. Some of them listened quietly in corners and some of them jumped and hollered by the front of the stage. Dozens were hiding behind the shields of cell phones, pretending to be occupied, popular, needed. I looked and looked but saw no one I knew.

Sparrow had told us where to find her—she had a spot staked out not too far from the front. Tru held my wrist and pushed shamelessly through the crowd while I watched my feet and tried to ignore the irritated looks and angry shouts. When we got close enough, we could see her hair peeking above the other heads, and we followed it until we reached her. She was wearing skinny black pants, shiny flats, and an oversized white button-down shirt that I was pretty sure was meant for a guy.

She looked amazing. When she saw me, she made a little *ooohh* sound, fingering the strap of my dress.

"Vintage?" she asked, having to shout a bit over the noise.

I thought about just saying yes, but then told her it was my mom's. She nodded in approval.

A hundred different conversations were reverberating off the high ceilings. Tru and Sparrow leaned in to talk. I heard her mention the "groupies," as she pointed somewhere back and to the right. Again, I felt a rush of disappointment that they were here, jealous and nervous without even seeing them yet. Meanwhile, Tru was bouncing up and down on his heels, laughing loudly, occasionally giving a fast, light touch to his bandage. When he took off for the bathroom, Sparrow turned to me with a questioning look.

"He seems . . . very amped up," she said.

First I froze. Then I couldn't hold it in.

"He got a tattoo."

For a full five seconds, she only blinked.

"He got *a tattoo*? When?"

For some reason I began to feel that this was my fault.

"This afternoon?" I swallowed hard.

"Oh good lord. Don't look scared, honey, I'm just—my god. That kid. Where in the world did he do this?"

"On his chest."

She threw back her head and gave a deep-throated laugh, uncoiling the knot of tension in my stomach.

"No, not where on his body. Like, where did he get it done?"

I told her all of it in a rush—the shop, Paula, how I'd watched the whole thing. Sparrow just listened, shaking her head.

"How does it look?" she asked me finally, her face skeptical.

I longed to roll my eyes, to laugh at him, to say it was ridiculous. But I couldn't help telling the truth.

"Actually," I said, "it looks pretty cool."

There were twelve bands playing two songs each, and Suck It, Sparrow went on third. They opened with "Heatwave," and I thought they sounded bigger and better than when we'd heard them in the basement, although Tru whispered down to me that they were nervous and playing a beat too fast.

He'd reappeared right before their set, drinking a can of Coke. Sparrow had said nothing, only given him a stern look. He'd turned to me in mock offense.

"Frannie!" he said. "You really didn't strike me as someone with a big mouth."

All through the first song, I could hear the pack of groupies behind us, though I couldn't see them when I looked back and scanned the crowd. They screamed for Devon and P.J. and every once in a while for Winston, with a kind of condescending sweetness the way you would cheer for a child. In that moment I hated them. Hated them completely.

There was a small break between songs, when Devon leaned into the mike and reminded everyone of their name. Sparrow began to jump up and down, fist-pumping, giving low, manly whoops.

"Very classy," Tru told her.

Winston clacked his drumsticks together four times, and then they launched into their second song. "Lola." Directly in my sight line was P.J., his hair gelled out in crazy directions, skinny arms gripping his low-slung bass, fingers moving surely over the strings. He started his mad tour of the stage, hopping, running, sliding on his knees to the very edge. For a moment I was mortified, sure people were going to make fun of him, but they didn't. Kids were screaming and clapping and laughing in a way that was amused, not mocking. I laughed, too, relieved.

P.J. leaped up and jogged over to the drum set to commune with Winston. I lost sight of him and began to maneuver around, trying to peek between the heads in front of me. That's when I realized if I leaned just the right way, I could see Devon.

There he was, Devon Jewell, planted at the very center of the stage, leaning up and into the microphone, teeth shining. His voice was deep and honeyed. He had that same ability that Tru did to wear a T-shirt better than everyone else. I shifted and stretched, struggling to see him, to see all of him, as he belted his way through the song.

Next to me, Tru made his hands into a megaphone and shouted a verse along with him.

> *"Girls will be boys and boys will be girls,*
> *It's a mixed-up, muddled-up shook-up world . . ."*

I giggled. Tru looked over at me and winked.

* * *

When Suck It, Sparrow was done, we made our way back through the crowd and waited by the door where the bands emerged from backstage. I was hot from standing in the middle of the mob and nervous that I was about to see the boys. To see P.J. I asked Tru for a sip of his Coke.

"Of course," he said, handing it over with a smile.

I raised it to my mouth, poured it down—and almost spit it out. I tried to swallow the medicinal burn of whatever it was without Sparrow noticing, but it was too late.

She looked at me. Then she looked at Tru.

"Excuse me? Aren't you driving tonight?"

Looking confused, Tru turned to me. "Aren't *you* driving?"

For a moment I thought he was serious. The words *I'm not old enough* were rising to my lips, but then I saw that, of course, he was joking.

"One drink, Sparrow. I swear," he said. "It was, like, one drink. And look, *I'm sharing it.*"

"Frannie," Sparrow said, "could you do me a big favor and throw that out?"

I looked at Tru, and he shrugged. I saw a trash can across the room and started walking. When I'd made it halfway, I took a quick glance behind me. Sparrow was on her phone, distracted. Tru, however, was watching my progress. He pointed at me and then raised his hand to his mouth, making a drinking motion with thumb and his pinky.

I arrived at the trash can and raised the can high, ready to drop it in.

But in that moment, I thought of the night ahead—of the band and groupies and who knew what else. Close quarters and talking and partying, maybe.

I brought the can back from the brink and swallowed what was left.

"Whoa, whoa, whoa. WHOA. Your brothers are *the Little twins?*"

We were in the back corner of the room, as far as possible from the crowd and the speakers, gathered in a clump: Tru, Sparrow, the band, and the six groupies. They were not a clan of beautiful, perfect snobs as I had, for some reason, suspected. They were just girls. White girls and black girls, my age or a year or two older, some of them pretty and some of them not, although all of them went to the performing arts school. That meant all were exquisite at singing or dancing or playing an instrument.

P.J. and I just had realized that we once went to rival K–8 Catholic schools, back when he went to Catholic school. Mine had been the oldest, most run-down of them all, while his was one of the most expensive, positioned right over the city line and into the suburbs. He only went there up until fifth grade, he explained, because he was "truly, madly, deeply ADHD, and the public schools will do way more shit to help with the spaz cases."

Since he was a year older than me, that made him a year behind the twins, and he remembered them from the Catholic schools' junior basketball league. He found a stray folding chair leaning against the wall and dragged it over, climbing on the seat and raising his arms to demonstrate how enormous they seemed to him when he was nine and they were ten. The groupies were giggling, yelling at him to get down, saying his name with sweetness and familiarity. It was clear that with P.J. there was an initial hump to get over, an overwhelming introductory period, after which he became rather lovable. Or lovable like a little brother at least. Lovable but exasperating.

"Were you there?" he asked, jumping down to the floor. "When the two of them scored, like, fifty points between them? Against my school? I was there riding the bench."

I was conscious of what Tru's can of Coke had done—creating a fuzz, a fizzle that spread through my head, making me think a beat slower. I spoke carefully, blushing as everyone's eyes turned in my direction.

"I was there," I said. "But I'm clueless about basketball. I was probably in the back row somewhere. Being a dork and doing my homework."

Some people laughed—Sparrow and Devon and P.J., I noticed—but most of the girls just kind of looked at me, and Tru was busy peering down his shirt and fiddling with his bandage. Someone asked P.J. if he'd been any good at basketball, and he was off on another story about dribbling and suicides and how he was pretty fast but always dropping the ball.

While he waved his hands and told his story, I was floating backward, thinking about Jimmy and Kieran all those years ago. I did bring books and homework to games, and it was a family joke, how bored I was by sports. Partly it was true, but not when the twins were playing—that's what no one really knew. I used to sit in the bleachers, looking down on them with a kind of reverence. I made up rhymes about making or missing baskets and would sing them to myself, trying to bring them luck. I remembered the day that P.J. was talking about, how at first it was just a good game, and then it became something extraordinary, and the whole room buzzed. My parents were so happy. I was so happy.

A little whistle sounded to my right, and I jumped. It was Devon.

"You still with us?" he asked with that smile, his unreal teeth. There were still some beads of sweat on his forehead, the aftermath of the stage with its glowing lights.

Smiling back at him, I felt my gentle buzz receding like a tide. There really hadn't been much left in the can when Tru had given it to me. The initial flash of bravery it brought was almost gone. I clung to that last crest of courage, angry and awed at how fleeting the power of a drink was. I rode the end of the wave while I still could.

"So," I asked Devon, "what are we doing next?"

The battle of the bands was not actually a battle at all, no judging or winner or prizes, so we stayed for half the groups, then headed to the park by Devon's house. Sparrow had caught a ride with Devon and now she wanted to drive the van, but Tru convinced her he was fine, so he took the wheel, with just Sparrow and me as passengers. He drove particularly slowly and was overly cautious to stop at yellow lights, while pointing out to Sparrow how responsible he was. She gave him the finger, told him he was an ass. We parked on a different street from everybody else, so we didn't see them until we got to the playground. Tru was leading us by a flashlight he'd dug out of an old emergency kit in the back of the van. Other people had little lights on their key chains or were guided only by the glow of their cell phones. The groupies had come, too, so we were an even dozen, a crew of shadows overtaking the swings and slides.

I sat down on the dolphin with the broken handle, and Devon and P.J. followed me. Devon took the whale. P.J. hopped on the sea horse and started rocking.

The boys had come to the show polished and pristine, but they'd been hauling their equipment around all evening and taking cigarettes on the sly. Now they smelled like soap and sweat and smoke. The richness of it made my skin tingle. I felt too nervous to even look at them, staring down at my lap and pulling on the hem of my dress while they talked to one another. One of the girls had brought a plastic bag that strained with beer cans. Tru took charge of passing them out, bringing the first three cans to Devon, P.J., and me. He moved away from us then, toward a couple of girls who were chatting nearby, and started talking to them immediately about music. But he was standing in a spot where he could see me and the boys, and I could tell he had an eye on us, like he was waiting for something to happen. I tried to ignore him, popping my beer and taking a sip.

Two drinks. I'd now had two drinks in my whole life—some of Tru's mystery Coke cocktail and now a Miller Lite, lukewarm and bitter. It tasted like something gone bad, but I didn't care.

P.J. asked what I'd thought of the show. Clearing my throat, I told them they were amazing, in another league from everyone else. I meant every word.

"Thanks. It's awesome that you came," P.J. said. "Especially since you're our namesake. Or no, that's not right. You're, like, our name giver. Or something. You know what I mean."

"It's a good name," Devon said, and put up his hand to high-five me.

Our palms touched, lightly, just for an instant.

Devon and P.J. started recapping and critiquing the other bands. P.J. jumped in with wild, nuanced imitations of each one, Devon and me dissolving into laughter as he screeched out awful notes and strummed an air guitar. I told myself to drink the beer slowly, but before I knew it I had gulped it down. A new buzz tickled around edges of my head. I felt a little airy, a little floaty. Like my head was stretched.

As P.J. crooned out a nasal ballad and pretended to bang on a tambourine, one of the girls came over to us. I remembered that her name was Tara—Tara with the big golden eyes and dark skin that matched Devon's. She stood in front of him and flipped her hair. It was long and shiny, pin-straight.

"It's new," she told him. "What do you think?"

"*I* think it looks nice," Devon said. "But do you know what my mother will say?'

"Oh, she's already seen it. Just this afternoon." Tara put her hands on her hips and adopted a serious voice. "'I liked it short and kinky. Why do you need a weave? Would you like me to out-line the many political ramifications of your hair?'"

"Damn," he said. "That was pretty good. Watch out or you're going to turn into her."

"Ha! Not likely."

Her eyes shifted to me, then back to Devon. She smiled at him, and I felt embarrassed, though I wasn't sure exactly why. Maybe just because I always felt embarrassed.

Devon coughed, rocked a bit on his whale. "So what did you think of my singing?" he asked.

"Good," Tara said with a shrug. "Not as good as mine."

P.J. let out a long, low whistle. "That is cold, Tara. Ice-cold."

So that was her talent. Singing. I could easily imagine her onstage, all confidence, pitch-perfect. She would be strut-ting around, flipping that gleaming sheet of hair that Devon's mother didn't like. Even clueless me knew what she was talk-ing about, at least a little. I knew that there were endless com-plexities to being a black girl and keeping your hair natural, or not, and that it meant different things to different people. That changing it could be expensive or painful. I suddenly flashed back to my homeroom last year at St. Sebastian's. There had been an Indian girl named Anya, and two of the black girls, Danielle and Monet, liked to sit behind her and joke that they were going to bring scissors and steal her perfect shining locks. Indian hair cost the most, they said—she had a thousand-dollar head and didn't even know it. Anya always laughed. I laughed, too. Even the teacher did. But I wondered what would happen next year, if I was sitting at the lunch table while a bunch of girls had a conversation like this. If I should laugh, and when, and how much. I couldn't decide if I was overthinking this, or if the real problem was that I'd spent most of my life never bothering to think about these kinds of things at all.

Tara and Devon were still bickering, and then she came over and started poking him in the stomach, telling him to pull the notes from his diaphragm. The two of them joked and slapped at each other, easy and familiar, until she said something about him showing off tonight, and he gave her an annoyed look.

"Fine," she said. "Whatever."

As she walked away, Devon glanced at me.

"Tara's my cousin. I just . . . didn't know if you knew."

"Oh!" I said. "So she's Sparrow's cousin, too?"

"No, no," he said. "Other side. My dad's side. I actually see her more than I see him. My parents are divorced, and he's a professional musician. He travels a lot."

"Wow. That's cool. I mean, it's cool that he plays music for a living."

I had no idea what else to say, too afraid of asking music questions that would make me sound like a moron. I was saved when someone called Devon's name and he hopped up, jogging off into the dark. I looked over at Tru to see if he still seemed to be watching us, but now he was deep in conversation with the girls, gesturing wildly, telling a story that was making them laugh.

Sparrow appeared then and took Devon's place, gracefully straddling the whale.

"So," she said, "what's this about us all going to jump in some creepy reservoir? In the middle of the night?"

P.J. launched into an elaborate explanation of how Tru was planning a getaway to Prettyboy, at the end of the summer when the moon was full. "You're not allowed to swim there, but we can totally sneak in and do it. There's this perfect spot to jump," P.J. said. "It's going to be badass."

Sparrow was shaking her head and grinning.

"My god. Truman. Always with the schemes and the danger. Last year, after prom, you won't believe what he had us all do...."

"Tru went to *prom*?" I asked.

Sparrow laughed. "I know, can you believe it? Talk about someone I thought was too cool for that. But this guy Andy was desperate for Tru to come with him. And Andy, well, he's a sweetheart. He and I had done this big art project together, so he enlisted me to convince Tru, and somehow I managed. It wasn't a real date, more just a group thing, but Andy could at least have the illusion he was actually at prom with a guy! And if he was cute, all the better."

I tried to imagine this, struggling to picture the Tru I knew taking part in a night of punch bowls, posed photos, and terrible music. The whole idea sent a twist to my heart, made me think that he was a little more human than I thought. I wanted to ask Sparrow a million more questions—about Andy and Tru in a tux and whatever wild thing he'd planned for after the dance . . .

But then a question needled me. This was last year. Before Aunt Debbie and Uncle Richard knew. So had Truman told people at school before he told his parents? Or did Andy just know because he was friends with Sparrow? I was pretty sure Tru would kill me if I asked her stuff like that—he never talked about school or home when I was around. I looked to see where he was and found him at the edge of the trees, smoking with Devon and talking quietly. I decided I should ask Sparrow more while I had the chance.

"So I guess he just went without telling his parents about the Andy part? And they didn't notice, since it was a group thing?"

Sparrow looked a little confused, but just as she opened her mouth to say more, there was a light. No, two lights. A pair of beams coming from somewhere down the path. With them came a crunch of shoes on gravel. And then a loud voice.

"Park's closed, guys. Who's there?"

I dropped my now-empty can.

"Cops!" someone hissed. *"Cops, cops, cops!"*

We were all running before I knew what was happening, trying to get back to the main path and tripping over tree roots and playground equipment and one another. I heard a terse "Where the fuck is Frannie?" and I called out, "Here," in a terrified squeak. Seconds later Tru was next to me, and I looked to him, wide-eyed and frightened.

He was laughing.

"Hey there," he said. "You ready?"

He grabbed my arm and pulled me in a different direction, whispering that it was safer to split off. Our legs were pumping like crazy, our strides matching each other. He had the flashlight on, but it barely did any good, fast as were moving and weak as it was. We kicked our way through a patch of thick brush, barely able to see in front of us. He was a pace or two ahead of me when we came up against a short, white fence.

Tru ran right into it with a grunt, falling backward on his ass. I scaled it in two swift moves—a step to the center bar, a hop over.

"Holy shit," he said from the ground. "You're a goddamn gazelle."

A moment later he was over it, too, and we were flying together through the trees, changing course to head back in the direction of the car.

My short dress whipped around my legs. My lungs heaved. My toes gripped my flip-flops like they were clinging for life. Tru was right beside me, step for step. From deep inside my chest welled something like happiness, but madder, wilder.

I never wanted to stop.

I wanted to run forever.

Creeping out from the woods, we hustled into the car, and Tru said he would circle the park a couple of times to look for anybody who might still need a ride. The van swung in a slow loop, once, twice around the perimeter. We didn't see anyone, and then he got a call from Sparrow, who was with Devon, Winston, P.J., and Tara back at the house. Tara had heard from the other girls, who were in their car and headed for the safety of home. Everyone had gotten away.

Tru hung up and tapped the dashboard clock. "Guess we have to go home, too."

It was eleven forty-five. The battle of the bands was scheduled to go until midnight, and Mom had ordered us to be home by twelve fifteen.

"We have a little extra time," he said. "Want to cruise?"

I nodded, sinking down into my seat, still afraid of seeing flashing lights and hearing sirens. Tru flipped through the CDs, picking Bruce again, and we left the green, happy sprawl of almost suburbia behind, coasting back south. My forehead was pressed against the glass as we rolled past streetlamps and neon signs, their harsh light made beautiful purely by the motion of speeding by. The night was one big blur or fluorescence, a seemingly endless ripple of warmly glowing announcements for fast food, discount mattresses, oil changes. Neither of us spoke.

The clock had crept past midnight when we drove by Loyola, the college where he took Latin. Looking up at the high-rise dorms, I saw only a few windows glowing—lonely summer boarders.

"Your dad went here?" I asked. "Where did he meet Aunt Deb, exactly?"

For a few seconds Tru said nothing. Then he sighed.

"Let's skip the romantic tales. I'm not really in the mood."

This was definitely one of those times when Tru wanted me to just shut up, but right at that moment we were passing a strip mall anchored by a familiar restaurant. I couldn't help pointing out the little brick pub as we drove by.

"See that? O'Malley's? It's where Grandpa John was a cook and a bartender. I mean, that's a different name than it used to have. . . ."

Tru stopped abruptly, and I jerked forward against my seat belt. He did a three-point turn in the empty street and drove back to the restaurant, pulling the car into a space right in front.

"I knew it was around here, but I didn't know that was it," he said.

He seemed to be talking more to himself than to me as he peered at the skinny windows, the shut front door of the restaurant. It was impossible to see inside.

"Do you remember them?" I asked. "Our grandparents?"

They'd married when they were much older, had their two girls very late. Miracle babies, they used to say. Then they'd both died young. In their sixties. I was named for my grandmother, Frances, but I didn't have one memory of her. Grandpa John either. I thought Tru might, but he didn't seem to be listening. He tapped his fingers on the wheel, kept staring at O'Malley's, the door closed up tight as a coffin. No one coming or going.

"I know I just requested no romantic tales, but since you asked, *that* is where my parents met."

I felt a shift in the atmosphere. Something wasn't right.

"Every Thursday, when John worked the bar, our moms used to go have a burger. When they were in high school. They'd sit and eat and talk to their dad. And guess who used to go in there to have a beer?"

I waited a second, not sure if he actually wanted me to answer.

"Your dad?" I said finally.

"Bingo."

I looked out, considering the restaurant anew. This place was a part of his history. We'd made an accidental pilgrimage to his very beginning, and I could tell he wasn't happy about it. Tru's tone was starting to feel a little dangerous, but I didn't want him to stop talking. My family was so buttoned-up. Tru was my only chance to know anything.

"So Debbie met Richard there? And they started going out?"

"Well, sort of." He snorted and looked at me. "At first it wasn't my mom and my dad. It was *your mom* and my dad. Did you know that?"

The silence seemed to crackle between us, as I took a second to absorb and understand what he was saying.

No, I hadn't known my mom had dated Richard first. I hadn't known at all, but he was well aware of that. It was clear from that satisfied look on his face. He was enjoying this opportunity to unnerve me. I tried to will myself not to care, not to be affected by what he was telling me, but it was too late.

I was already getting upset.

For weeks now I'd been trying not to feel so silly and childish and clueless around him, and now here he was again—knowing things that I didn't. Things about *my own mother.*

Tru was tapping his fingers on the wheel, still seeming to enjoy gauging my reaction.

"News to you?" he asked.

I didn't want to give him the big reaction he was obviously looking for, so I shrugged. Tried to speak casually.

"How long did they date? My mom and Richard?"

"Well, I don't have all the exact details. Not a particularly long time. But they were certainly, you know, *a thing* of sorts, before it all ended."

He stopped talking, and silence descended between us, leaving me to wonder what else there might be to the story. I could tell he was waiting for me to ask more, but I didn't want to play this stupid game with him. I told myself to just sit and wait.

I couldn't do it, though. There was one thing I really wanted to know.

"How did they break up? Richard and my mom?"

His fingers stopped tapping, and he pulled out a cigarette but didn't light it. Just flicked it around with that elliptical motion of his fingers.

"I believe they hadn't officially broken it off before Debbie slipped in, although it's a bit of a gray area, the way she tells it."

In that moment, I was very sick of Tru. I didn't want to be in the car with him anymore. But even as a lump had formed in my throat, I pushed it back, kept talking.

"Is that why our moms aren't close?"

He laughed at that, his fingers still twirling.

"Oh god, no. That would be awfully petty, at this point, don't you think? I mean, it was superdramatic at the time, when he and Debbie took up with each other instead. She's recounted it for me, with lots of hand flourishes. But it's nothing anyone cares about anymore. My mom married a college guy from a rich family. Your mom married a nice boy from the neighborhood. That's that. Just a family history lesson for you. Didn't want you to be in the dark."

I was crying a little. I didn't want him to see, but of course he did. He put the cigarette away, cocked his head to the side to see me better.

"Seriously? It happened a million years ago. You can't be that upset."

I wiped my eyes with my hands, then crossed my arms.

"You were telling that story to upset me," I said. "Or shock me or whatever. You know you were. So mission accomplished. Now we're late, and I want to go home."

He paused for a moment more and then slipped the van away from the curb, back toward the house.

When we'd gone a couple of blocks, he glanced over at me. My tears were dry by then, but I kept my eyes focused on the road.

"I know it's a little unsettling," he said, "to find out that your mom would ever associate with him. But think how I feel. Half my DNA is his."

He was waiting for a laugh, but I didn't give him one. Two minutes later we were parking the van. As he turned off the lights, he spoke again, much more softly than before.

"I'm not sure why they don't talk, to tell you the truth," Tru said. "I don't know if *they* know why they don't talk. My guess is they're just different people who wanted different things."

The whole neighborhood seemed asleep, and the two of us shut our doors quietly. We went to the front porch without another word, and I opened the door as quietly as I could, hoping that no one was waiting for us. By now we were twenty minutes late.

The lights were off in the living room, but Mom and Dad were still on the couch, the TV on low. She was leaning against him, asleep, his arm draped around her. He looked at us and glanced pointedly at his watch. But then he smiled. Put his finger to lips in a *shhhh* motion.

Tru and I parted then, him slipping downstairs while I tiptoed up.

I crawled into bed without washing my face, without changing into my pajamas. I tried to focus on the band, the show, the park, but instead I kept thinking about my mom and Richard.

Why couldn't I be like Tru? Why did I have to care?

Maybe I didn't like to think about my mom as a teenager, dating people. Maybe I didn't like that she'd been dumb enough to date someone who was apparently awful. Or maybe I didn't like how random that made everything seem, like Mom could have ended up with someone else . . . and then I might never have existed.

For a few minutes I pondered that. At first it made me feel small and alone, but then I sort of collapsed into the abyss of it— and that made me feel free. I was just a speck of matter in the middle of creation. Nothing mattered. Like Tru said in front of the reservoir: look head-on into infinity and it doesn't fill you up, it empties you out.

I came out from under my pillow, thinking that I was okay, that I had calmed down enough to close my eyes and sleep.

Except I wasn't quite there. Something still nagged me.

In those dark minutes when we'd sat outside O'Malley's, the moment I'd felt the absolute worst was when Tru had confirmed that Debbie stole Richard away from my mom. But it wasn't even the betrayal that bothered me so much—it was the fact that it made my mother seem like the second choice. Which then made my dad seem like the second choice. Which then implied that my family was second-tier. I was second-tier.

That thought burned in my chest, a bitter little ember, and I realized that I'd been nursing this feeling for a long time. And why exactly? Because Tru's family was rich and he went to a fancy school? Because he'd been brilliant enough to be on TV? Because he made friends so swiftly and easily here in this city that was my home, not his? Yes, yes, yes. All of that.

I realized that it was a terrible thing to think about my family. A pathetic thing to think about myself. Still, in a strange way it was a relief to admit it. To put it into words.

So maybe I wasn't a brave little speck in the universe anymore, but at least now I understood my own feelings, even if some of them were ugly. I really did believe that gave them less power.

And besides, I might not want to face infinity and be emptied out. Maybe I was the kind of person who wanted to be filled.

FIFTEEN

I hid out most of the next morning in my room, until Mom came to retrieve me and drag me to the grocery store with her. She wanted to know everything about the battle of the bands and these "young musicians" I was spending time with. At first I pulled Tru's old trick of rolling my eyes and answering in annoyed monosyllables, so that I wouldn't risk revealing anything about our late-night trip to the park, our run from the cops, everything I'd learned about her and Richard. But I could tell right away I was hurting her feelings, so I finally opened up a little. I told her how the guys played crazy covers of "Heatwave" and "Lola," and she laughed and said she loved those songs and that she wished she could have heard them.

That afternoon, she and Dad dragged us all to the beach again. Tru sat shotgun and played Bruce, while I sat in the wayback. I was glad for the distance, because I was still mad at him. Not because of what he'd told me, but because of the way he'd treated me.

We emptied out of the van and surveyed the park before us. Everything was different from the first time we'd come. Summer had reached its full rage, the sun merciless, the quarry water thick with bodies, lifeguard whistles screeching overhead.

Jimmy and Kieran went off to play volleyball. My mother and Tru settled at an empty picnic table, her with a mystery novel, him with his phone. I joined them but kept my head down, methodically making my way through my chemistry workbook, the one I'd shoved under my bed and tried to forget about after Tru had arrived.

Dad had gone back to the car for the cooler, and when he got back, he plopped it on the grass. Then he took a spot across from me, awkwardly folding his giant's body to fit the gap between bench and table. He snatched the workbook from my hands and held it before his face, upside down.

"This? This is easy. I could do this in my sleep." He lowered the book just enough so that his eyes peeked over the top. They were big and warm and moist. He winked and looked back down at the page.

"Oh, right!" He flipped it right-side up, pretending to fumble as he did so.

He handed it back to me, face crimson in the heat. "At least one of us understands this stuff."

He gave me a smile that creased the lines around his eyes. I smiled back and felt my mouth waver, as I suddenly wanted to cry. Bending over my book, I hid my eyes, pretending to shield them from the sun.

Dad announced he was going for a dip, then lumbered down to the quarry, swimming out until the found an empty spot and flipping over. He was an incredible floater. Even here, in freshwater, he could suspend himself for hours. I watched him for a minute, then felt overwhelmed by the need to get away. I said nothing, just took off for the pavilion to get a soda.

I'd fed my dollar in, but hadn't pushed a button yet, when I heard someone whistling. It was a Stones song, "Sympathy for the Devil," and there was Tru, leaning against the machine. He had a roll of SweeTARTS and was doing that trick again, weaving it through his fingers. He paused and offered them to me, but I shook my head.

"So, after I'd given up chess, but before I'd taken up spelling, I had another hobby."

I looked at him briefly, then hit the Dr Pepper button. The machine spit out my can with a rattle and thunk.

"Magic," he said. "I wanted to be a magician. I had a cape and a top hat."

I tried to arch an eyebrow but failed.

"I begged my parents for a rabbit," he added.

This was a form of apology. I stood there and weighed it in my mind.

"I don't believe you," I said. "I can ask Sparrow. She'll tell me."

The edges of his mouth lifted just a bit.

"Please don't. This is one thing about me she actually doesn't know, and I'd never hear the end of it. Seriously."

Popping the tab slowly, I let the mouth give a loud, cold hiss. I took a long drink before I spoke again.

"Did you have a name?"

His smile grew. It reached his eyes.

"That's the best part. For some reason—and don't ask me where I got this—I called myself 'Truman the Destroyer.'"

I laughed. Then Tru laughed. Another moment passed and the two of us were laughing together. At first we did laugh for Truman the Destroyer in his top hat, but then we kept laughing. The laughter was its own spark and its own accelerant. Once lit, it burned and burned.

Tru caught his breath and wheezed out a confession. "Last night? In the park? Those weren't cops. I caught a quick look, and I think they were some dads from the neighborhood. Huge dorks. They looked even more scared than us. I would have told you, but I was having too much fun running through the woods, smashing into fences. I probably have internal bleeding. I'm going to need one of your kidneys."

I wasn't even mad; I didn't care that he'd lied, because we were laughing harder than ever and it felt so good. I laughed until my insides were sore. I laughed until it hurt to breathe.

Then I decided to take a chance.

"Are we really friends?" I asked.

For once, I'd caught Tru off guard. He gaped at me, looked almost embarrassed.

"Frannie! Oh my god. Don't do that."

I could have let it go, like I'd let so many things go with him before, but I didn't want to be deflected. Not anymore. I wanted to talk.

"It's just . . . if we're friends, you should tell me things. Nobody tells me things!"

"I told you things last night," he countered, with a bit of his old wicked smile returning.

I scowled at him, even though I was starting to feel better. Like I was going to be okay. Like Tru and I were going to be okay.

"That's not what I mean," I told him. "I don't know anything about what you're thinking. About how you feel about important stuff. About your parents. I don't want you to go back there to them. Not unless they change."

I hadn't planned on saying any of that, and now my eyes filled with tears. Tru took my elbow, gently.

"Let's walk," he said.

We trudged in silence up the steep hill that led to the hiking trails, but before we got to the trees, Tru veered off, sat us in the grass where we could look down on the quarry, the water shining in the sun like a coin.

"Do you remember my parents much?" he asked

I thought about it first, answered carefully but truthfully. I even said the stuff that made me feel guilty.

"Just a little. I haven't seen them in years. Your mom talks exactly like my mom, and looks a lot like her, too. But, you know. Thin. Nicer hair. Your dad is short with glasses and a big chest and shoulders. That first morning when we drove out here, you were joking about the Hamptons. You did an impression of him."

I'd surprised him again, I could tell. He chuckled a little. "Maybe I did."

For a couple of minutes we just sat there quietly, looking down, listening to distant laugher, splashing. Happy little-kid screams. Everyone looked small and insignificant from up here. I felt calmer.

"Can I tell you a story?" Tru asked.

"Yes," I said. "Of course."

He looked at me, then away. "When I was thirteen, I got in a shit-ton of trouble with these four other kids, kids I'd known forever. Cameron. Brandon. Brody. And, ah, Skip. Skip was there. We were just so pent-up all the time, burning to do bad shit, but we were still too young and dumb to do anything real, you know? But we were desperate for it, so we did all the terrible boy things you can think of. Setting fires in the woods. Stealing stuff from convenience stores. One afternoon, we just went on a tear. Knocked down a bunch of mailboxes. Popped people's car tires. Set firecrackers off. We left this perfectly obvious path of destruction, a perfect little bread-crumb trail of our transgressions. And at the end of it was this enormous house that everybody in town knew, because it belonged to some guy who won the lottery and then had a string of terrible luck. His family died or something. So cliché, right? Supposedly he had a bunch of people that waited on him, and he never left the house. Or that was the exaggerated version kids told. The place is insane, looks like a castle, a turret at the top with a little stained glass window. So we top off our campaign with a giant rock launched right through that perfect, beautiful window. It was a serious triumph. Three stories up, small target. I can still hear the sound of it shattering.

"So we get picked up right there in front of the house and dragged to the police station. Our parents are all there, and the cops are giving us some stupid talk they reserve for white, upper-middle-class idiots like us, who aren't really going to get in any trouble. But they're still definitely screwing with us, saying, 'Wow, whoever did that window must have some arm; that was a hell of a throw.' None of us will say who it was, so there's this awkward silence. And then Richard starts yelling that it was me, that he knows it was me, that it had to be me, so whatever was coming, they should just dish it out. My mom is mortified, and everybody is giving him this *whoa, whoa, settle down* look, even the police officers. The other parents just think he's being a dick, because, I mean, these people know him, and he is a huge dick, but I just have a feeling that's not really it. There's this weird insistence to what he's saying, and eventually I figure it out."

Tru looks at me now. He seems to be gauging my reaction so far, but I've tried to quiet my expression. To keep my entire body still and just listen.

"He wants me to have thrown it. Because it was this crazy, impressive, manly feat of strength. He doesn't give a shit about anything else at that point, not about me getting in trouble, none of that. He just wants me to have launched that rock. And I'm not . . . I'm not talking about my being gay right now; I'm not saying he suspected or anything. That doesn't factor in here. Not yet. All his weird Napoleonic insecurities predate that, trust me. But anyway, as I realize what's going on in his head, I meet eyes with my mom, and I know she knows, too, and she's horrified."

He was running his fingers through the grass, watching the blades get pushed down and ripple back into place.

"In that moment, I had this pure realization that he was never going to *get it*, you know? Whenever something great or something terrible happens, he's going to cloak whatever it is in his fucked-up issues and priorities. And I know Mom feels the same way, which in a way makes it better, but in a way makes it much, much worse. What is she doing with her life? How does she stand it?

"Anyway, Skip's dad, who's at least as big a dick as mine, is this rich-ass defense attorney. Eventually he gets us out of there with just a bunch of warnings. The next day, Richard has me up at the crack of dawn, running laps at the track and doing push-ups in the rain until I puke."

Tru stretched his legs out in front of him, looking at his Nikes, now scuffed a bit from their first weeks of wear.

"The other day, I said I was good at running until I puke, and you asked me why. That's why. I'm pretty sure some people think he hits me. He gives off that vibe, to be honest. But he never does. He just does stuff like that. But that morning, for the first time, I really didn't care, because I felt like I knew what his specific brand of bullshit was, and that I was never going to be like that."

The grass was sharp and itchy against my skin, but I didn't dare move. I felt a million things all at once. I felt like a useless know-nothing, a little girl with an easy life who had zero to offer or say. At the same time, I felt drawn close to Tru in a way I hadn't all summer, knitted up with him.

"Can I ask a stupid question?"

"My favorite kind," he said.

"I know it's not the point of the story. But I really want to know who threw the rock."

He laughed, one of his real laughs. "Of course you do. That's the best part of the story, that I don't tell you. Look, let me be totally honest, that's not the first time I've told that story or anything. I don't know if you do this yet, but when you get older, you'll have your own set of favorite stories that you've perfected. You'll take them out after a night of drinking, or when you've been dating somebody and you're starting to get serious, because they help explain who you are. So that's one of my stories. And most stories are, you know, at least half bullshit. But that one's the truth," he said, and looked right in my eyes.

"Of course," I said. "I believe you."

He bit his lip a little, glanced away, and shook his head. "You're not just honest, Frannie. You're trusting, too."

I looked back down at the water, searching for my family and finding them slowly. First Dad in the water, then Mom at the picnic table. Finally, the twins, standing at the edge of the sand.

"I'm trying to think," I said, "if I have a story like that I could tell. Maybe something from this summer."

Tru cocked his head and thought.

"Well, it's got to be something with danger. All good stories have a little danger."

First I thought of last night, the battle of the bands and our run from the fake cops. But that didn't seem like enough. I thought of that first night in Siren, but the danger there was the man, and that wasn't something I wanted to think about, let alone talk about.

Except sitting there with Tru, after everything he'd said, I thought that maybe I should. I angled myself toward him, but kept my eyes on my shoes.

"Um, that night at Siren. The man you yelled at?"

He didn't say anything, just looked at me and waited for me to go on.

"I don't know if this is really anything? I don't want to, ah, be dramatic. But he kind of really freaked me out. Not just because he touched my hair. He said something about how I looked really young, but he wouldn't tell on me. And then he asked where I lived and said he thought he'd seen me. Walking in the park."

I'd actually been hoping he might laugh, but his brow was furrowed and he looked mad. *Really* mad.

"The dog park? He said he's seen you there?"

I wanted to downplay everything right away. I wanted to take back everything I'd said, because seeing Tru worried was making the whole thing seem creepier, which was bringing back everything I'd felt that night. Revulsion. Fear. Guilt.

"He didn't say what park. There are tons of parks. I think he was full of shit."

Tru's jaw was clenched, and he ran his hands through his hair, then pointed at me when he spoke.

"If you see that asshole anywhere, you tell me, okay? At the park, on the street, in a fucking church—I don't care where he is, you tell me. He's a creep."

He found my eyes with his, to make sure I understood.

"Okay," I said. "Okay, okay. I got it."

"He's worthless, you have to know that, and you can't let him get to you. He's a piece of shit, and you're golden. He doesn't deserve to speak another word to you."

I didn't answer. I couldn't. I was too busy turning my head the other way, pretending to look at something off in the trees.

For the second time in two days, Tru had made me cry.

SIXTEEN

And the summer blazed on.

I began a campaign to have Duncan spend a little time outside every day. At first, I had to coax and convince, but soon he accepted it as part of our routine. I would take him around the block or down to the park, pointing out the different kinds of flowers and trees, describing to him how they worked, the quiet ways they grew and thrived. He smiled sweetly and sometimes held my hand. I was never sure how much he liked these little excursions, and sometimes his arms flared with bug bites or his face flushed pink from the heat. Still, I didn't stop.

Our house, meanwhile, seemed to be shrinking, or maybe we were all growing within it. Always there was something to grumble or yell about. Jimmy obsessively shaved his head and left the aftermath in the bathroom sink, a defiant pile of short, sharp hairs. Kieran went crazy from being cooped up with Jimmy and took up residence on the couch most nights, smashing the cushions out of shape and sweating all over the fake leather. Dad got a temporary gig at a car repair shop down the street and he never could seem to get the grease and oil off his hands, leaving fingerprints everywhere. The hot water heater began an ominous dripping, a sure signal of coming death, and twice I caught my mother down in the basement just staring at it.

The days got hotter and hotter, and still we didn't turn on the air-conditioning. Tru, meanwhile, was still running in the mornings, going for longer and longer stretches as the weeks passed. Nothing stopped him. Not rising heat. Not humidity. Not rain.

After the thunderstorms and all the delays, fireworks finally came that year, the third week in July. Mom still insisted that we watch them as a family, so we went to visit her friend Maria from work, the one who had a house with a roof deck looking over the water. It was the kind of place that made me think if only I could be a grown-up with a roof deck, then everything else in my life would be fine. Maria lived alone, so it was just the six of us and her. We sat there together on high, in a collection of sagging beach chairs. Mine was in front, and I had a clear view of the night sky exploding in neon wonder. I felt the reverberations in my chest, and imagined that each glowing asterisk sent out a shock wave that traveled in a direct line toward me, fizzling and finishing somewhere near my heart. But of course that wasn't really how it was. Everyone else must feel them just the same.

I turned briefly around right as the finale was reaching its peak, fireworks on top of fireworks, color raging, the air acrid with smoke. Jimmy and Kieran were staring up, but Dad had his arm around my mom. He was whispering in her ear, and she was laughing. I noticed that Tru was watching them, too. The darkness hid his face.

There were nights when Tru went out with Jimmy and Kieran and there were nights when he went out with me, Sparrow, and the band. We would listen to them practice or go to the movies or eat pancakes at the diner in Towson, Tru always finding some way to pay for the two of us without actually asking me and without anyone noticing. Every time we hung out with them, I got nervous about P.J. At home, when I was alone, I'd been picturing what it would be like to be his girlfriend, to finally kiss someone. I thought maybe I wanted that, because he was pretty nice, and even more so, just because I wanted to finally have the experience of it all. But then when then he was actually there, I'd change my mind. I'd hide or slip away, avoiding him. Avoiding whatever might come if we got too close.

Of course there were nights when the boys were busy with their own jobs and music lessons and other friends. And then, Devon and P.J. disappeared at the beginning of August to spend ten days at a music camp in the woods of Virginia. So a few times, it was just Sparrow, Tru, and me, which was both disappointing and a relief. Once, Sparrow took us to a party with some friends she'd made at MICA. There were four of them living in an enormous open loft on the top floor of a crappy building in a crappy neighborhood. They'd painted a beautiful mural on the wall, a bunch of famous paintings all mingled together. I kind of recognized them, but Sparrow could name them for me. DaVinci's *Mona Lisa* in Van Gogh's café. Michelangelo's god reaching toward Adam on a background of Jackson Pollock paint splatters. Sparrow's friends drank wine and played music that sounded like nothing but noise, and the whole time Tru shot me looks. He mocked things with nothing but a single glance in my direction, and I was proud to realize that we shared that much understanding between us.

When you know someone, you can say so much without saying a word.

Marissa actually invited me to her birthday party the second week of August, or maybe her mom made her—just as my mom made me say yes. We slept over at her house in the basement, eight of us, all St. Sebastian's girls except for me. We were a bit too old for that, and I think we all knew it. I could see more clearly than ever before just how far my group had been lagging behind. Those girls still weren't friends with boys. They didn't do cool things. I asked them about SSR and they talked madly for minutes and minutes on end, seeming to have loved it even though I was pretty sure they hadn't done anything bad in the woods. I was a little surprised to find that I wasn't even jealous of the retreat anymore. Maybe just the softest twinge. When they asked about me, I was vague, said a little about meeting someone from my new school, about the battle of the bands, but mostly I kept quiet. In the morning, I neatly rolled up my sleeping bag and went home.

The heat hit a fever pitch. On a particularly miserable night, when the whole house turned into an oven, Mom and I escaped to the library. While she stocked up on new mysteries and romances, I wandered by a table of "suggested summer reading," saw some of the books we'd done in English last year—*Romeo and Juliet*, *Lord of the Flies*. There were also books we hadn't read, but that I wanted to. All the Jane Austen ones, because everybody said they were romantic. *Atonement*, because one of the AP classes at St. Sebastian's had been assigned it, and some parents got mad about the sex. Ever since, I'd been meaning to pick it up.

And then there was *Gatsby*.

The cover had the same shadowy blue face as Tru's copy. I took it tentatively, skipping over the strange poem and reading the first couple of paragraphs again, then on through the first couple of pages, embarrassed by how long it took me. Every line seemed cloaked in so much meaning, and I had to go slowly, consider each word. Then I hit a part that stopped me dead.

> If personality is an unbroken series of successful gestures, then there was something gorgeous about him . . .

I pictured Tru cocking an eyebrow, lighting a cigarette, driving our van with just the lightest of touches to the wheel. I remembered clever jokes and cutting insults, told with equal charm. I thought of every time he'd said the right thing, just when I'd needed him to.

My insides prickled, though I couldn't say exactly why. What was wrong with being gorgeous? I read a little further, feeling almost guilty. Like I'd found Tru's diary or something. I knew I could take the book with me, but I hesitated. I imagined some cold winter day a few months from now. Snow would be falling. Tru would be long gone. But I could sit in my room or in a coffee shop or in the library at my new school and make my way through these pages. Look for secrets. Maybe feel like he wasn't really gone.

I put the book back and went to go find my mother.

The next day Tru was home from Loyola earlier than usual, and we took a blanket over to the park. I'd finished with chemistry and moved on to some algebra prep work that arrived last week, and he of course was reading *Gatsby*.

"Do you understand it any better now?" I asked him. "Better than you did at the beginning of the summer?"

He put the book down, rubbed his face with his hands.

"Yes, Frannie. I think so. And let me tell you, I'm really starting to think that Daisy and Gatsby are just a couple of assholes."

Still, he picked the book back up and kept reading, murmuring to himself every once in a while. His Latin books sat next to him, unopened.

I looked toward the bridge and knew that beyond it was the safe, the vodka inside. I still liked thinking of it, hiding there, waiting for me to surprise Tru. Like a secret weapon of sorts, tucked away like a promise. As long as I didn't use it yet, didn't drink it yet, then I felt like good things were still waiting, like some epic night lay ahead.

A packet arrived that day in the mail, full of information about my new school. I kept opening it up to look at the same photo— a fancy science classroom, kids in goggles doing serious-looking experiments. I was instantly over my old fantasy of my basketball boyfriend and his sister. A new one emerged of me in a white coat with a girl like Tara as my lab partner, someone smart and outgoing and funny. Someone who would want me as a sidekick. I'd sit with her and Winston at lunch. They'd introduce me to all my new friends. My mind kept inserting Devon into the picture, although I knew he wouldn't be there. After a while I didn't fight it. I just let him hover there. I thought about how soon I'd be in school.

Summer was suddenly nine weeks gone.

Tru came into my room that Sunday to tell me he had set a date for the jump-off: his very last Saturday. I couldn't believe how quickly the summer was going—how quickly it was almost gone.

"Before the big jump, we need to get away, Frannie. This weekend. Me, you, Sparrow, and the boys. We need to go camping. I heard there's some island that has wild horses. Do you know what I'm talking about?

"Assateague? You want to go to Assateague? We camped there when I was little."

He looked at me incredulously.

"*Assateague*? ASS-ateague? What genius came up with that?"

He picked a dirty T-shirt off the floor, balled it up, and tossed it, hitting me square in the face. I threw the shirt back at him, but he leaned easily out of its path. I rolled my eyes at him, then answered in my best imitation of the way he talked. Slow delivery. Bored tone. Punctuated by sighs. "I'm pretty sure it was the Native Americans. You know, the ones who lived there before we killed them all or kicked them out."

It was a pretty half-assed impression, but it still got him. He laughed for real.

"How do you even hear about these things?" I asked him. "How do you know about everything around here?"

He gave me the eyebrow. "I talk to people, Frannie. I'm a very sociable person."

I rolled my eyes. "Well, Mom and Dad will never let us go. The two of us with the car, and a bunch of people they don't know? Dream on."

"What if your brother comes? Jimmy's picking up a couple of extra shifts this weekend, but Kieran is free, and I've planted the idea. Your mother is easy to persuade when she thinks we're all happy and having fun together."

I'd never thought of that before, but as soon as he said it, I knew it was true.

"Kieran won't be into it," I said. "He'll feel like he's babysitting me."

Tru shrugged, almost gracefully. His nonchalance was an art form.

"Maybe something will change his mind," he said.

He turned around and left abruptly. Just as I was digging my algebra work and calculator out of my nightstand, he called to me from the top of the stairs.

"Did I mention that Sparrow is coming for dinner? Tonight?"

SEVENTEEN

Because the weather that day was blistering and mysterious company was coming, we finally, finally, finally turned on the air-conditioning. It rumbled to life very slowly.

I was setting the dining room table while Mom, Jimmy, and Kieran fumbled around one another in the still-sweltering kitchen. Mom was in her heels and apron, rustling through the pantry. Jimmy was inhaling pretzels, on his usual rant of "Who eats *this* in the dead of summer," this time about a massive pot of chili. Kieran was filling the water glasses while the two of them traded insults in one of their fevered and furious wars that none of us could penetrate. In the middle of it all, we had missed the light knock and Dad opening the door.

Sparrow had just stepped inside.

"Oh!" he said, with an uptick of surprise. "Well, hello."

I swear the boys heard something in his voice and composed themselves. Jimmy walked into the dining room first, rubbing his head, and Kieran followed him, gripping four glasses, water sloshing out the sides, his fingers rudely touching the rims. I trailed after them, and all three of us could now see Sparrow, standing just inside the front door in a patch of waning evening light. She had the black-and-white dress on again, the one she wore the first time I met her. She told my dad that she heard we were having chili, so she made jalapeño corn bread. She held up a pretty little basket, covered with a bright yellow dish towel. He took the basket from her and whistled appreciatively.

"Jalapeño corn bread? I didn't know Martha Stewart was coming."

Sparrow laughed, genuine and sweet, while I stood there gripping the silverware, absolutely certain that I would not survive even an hour of this. I would die first, painfully, of complete and absolute humiliation.

The twins, meanwhile, were frozen beside me. Jimmy's mouth was hanging open, literally hanging open, while Kieran had this distant, awed look on his face like he'd just stumbled, completely unprepared, upon the pyramids.

Sparrow came over and introduced herself to them in a breezy way, all smiles, then threw her arms around me as she always did, warm and welcoming. Jimmy and Kieran looked on in disbelief until she released me and disappeared into the kitchen to help my mother.

In her wake, something passed between my brothers and me.

For years the twins and I had shared not only a house, but the same school hallways, the same bus, the same playground, always aware of where the others stood, who they were at home and outside. But here was Sparrow, a spectacular friend I had that they knew nothing about. That meant we had secrets from each other now.

From here on out, we always would.

I hurried to finish setting the table, and heard a rustle then from below—the sound of Tru coming up the stairs. He opened the basement door with a slow creak, revealing a face that was eager, delighted. He came to see his act in motion.

Truman the magician.

Mom and Dad had put the leaf into the dining room table to give us more room. Why they hadn't done this before, so that we didn't bump elbows after Tru came, I had no idea. But now everything opened up. We could move. We could breathe. We asked nicely for things to be passed, handing spoons and bowls carefully, no one spilling.

Under Sparrow's gaze, we seemed to have remembered ourselves as polite and thoughtful people. The family became a bunch of chatterboxes, everyone talking at once, having loud, overlapping conversations. Tru was telling my mom about Sparrow's aunt, how she was a professor, and how excited she was that I was going to the science and engineering school. Meanwhile, my father was asking Sparrow if she rooted for the Patriots. Her eyes got all wide and excited.

"I do! In fact, this is so crazy: my mom was a cheerleader for them, just for a year. In between when she stopped doing ballet and when I was born. She has a photo of herself in uniform that she keeps in our dining room. Our dining room! It's mortifying! I'm always trying to make her put it away. So yes, I like the Patriots, but I'm more of a basketball girl."

When she said this, Jimmy and Kieran resumed their idiot looks, Jimmy all slack-jawed, Kieran silently worshipping some wonder of the world. Sparrow looked up at them.

"Frannie told you about P.J., right? My cousin's friend?" she said. "How he remembered you two from basketball games?"

But I hadn't told them. I'd been so wrapped up in myself that it hadn't occurred to me. Now Sparrow explained the whole story, complete with the part about P.J. standing on the chair, and my whole family was laughing.

After that the conversation lulled for a moment as we all turned to our bowls, and I was afraid that we might descend back into the same kind of grumpy, halting dinner we'd been having all summer. But then Kieran jumped in and with stories about camp, and we all listened and looked happy and reminded him to tell the funniest ones.

"Frannie, have you told Sparrow about Duncan?" Kieran asked.

"Ugh," Jimmy said. "No more Duncan stories. It's the same thing every day."

"Well, I haven't heard it," Sparrow said. "Tell me about Duncan. Is he the kid you babysit?"

So I started to talk all about him, how sweet he was, but how hard it was sometimes, too, and my parents listened quietly, smiling. Looking proud. Meanwhile Kieran was just openly staring at Sparrow, who was looking at me and pretending not to notice all the attention. And as I talked about the mazes and the blocks and the chicken, I looked over to see Tru, who'd been so quiet for the last few minutes, you could almost forget he was there. He was tipping his chair back, twiddling his thumbs, and looking completely satisfied.

What a trick he had pulled, right before our eyes.

Sparrow washed the dishes and I dried while my mother for once just stood by, letting others do the work. She thanked Sparrow for introducing me to new friends, someone from my school, and Sparrow was gracious and humble, saying that it was no problem at all.

Halfway through the pile of bowls and spoons, Sparrow broached the camping trip, emphasizing that it was one night only and that she would be in charge, that she was terribly serious about watching over Devon. She added that Tru had talked to Kieran about coming and keeping an eye on everyone, too. She somehow made the trip sound like a playdate, a bunch of kids goofing around. She explained that we wouldn't be off in the woods alone, that the camping areas were packed, that we'd be on top of a million other people on an island that was patrolled day and night by park rangers. My mom listened carefully, nodded tightly a couple of times, saying that we'd been there years before and she remembered what it was like. A nice place.

I couldn't believe it—she was charmed into saying yes.

* * *

The next day I was a wreck. I was anxious about what would happen, with beer and boys and who knows what, and I was just as afraid that my mother would come to her senses and say we couldn't go. I couldn't focus on anything in my workbooks. I gave up forever on my summer reading. I lost my patience with Duncan, and had to stop and breathe, regain my composure. Setting the table, I broke a glass.

That week The Mack's parents had disappeared to god knows where, and Tru was over there Monday and Tuesday with the twins. Wednesday we met Sparrow, P.J., and Devon at the diner, where we talked about who had tents and coolers and sleeping bags, making all the final plans. After that, the boys relayed what had happened at music camp, Sparrow talked about her final art project, and Tru told the best stories from all the St. Sebastian's parties he'd been to with my brothers.

I'd been mostly quiet, fiddling around with my pancakes. Tru started smiling at me, and I knew I was in trouble.

"Frannie, you've barely said a thing. Maybe you can walk us through some of the chemistry equations you've been working so hard on this summer."

I narrowed my eyes at him, pouring more syrup on my plate.

"What?" he said, with that wicked smile of his. "Winston's not here. That makes you our designated dork, right?"

I righted the jug, clicked the top closed, and set it down on the table.

"This from the spelling bee king of Connecticut?"

Sparrow did one of her head-back, deep-throated laughs, while P.J. and Devon went wide-eyed, turning from me to Tru.

"I'm sorry," Devon said. "What was that?"

I picked up my fork and knife, resumed eating like it was no big deal.

"Tru was in the National Spelling Bee. The one on ESPN."

P.J. absolutely lost it, shaking his head wildly, rubbing his eyes and looking at Tru like he was seeing him for the first time.

"You were not one of those kids," he said to Tru. "Those kids are mental. They are not right in the head. You were not one of those kids."

Meanwhile Devon was looking at me like I'd just done something surprising. Impressive.

"I can't believe you've been hiding that from us," he said, and I noticed that he seemed to be talking just to me, not to anyone else.

Then he smiled his killer smile, and I ducked my head, not sure what to say.

When P.J. had finally calmed down, Sparrow confirmed what I said, and that's when I glanced at Tru, looking to see if I'd thrown him off even a little. He was staring down at his plate, then looked sideways at me, gave me a little smile. He appreciated that I'd tried to get him, I could tell that he did. But this wasn't a real secret. I should have remembered from earlier this summer, at the dinner table. This was a piece of the past that he already owned.

He'd challenged me, and I'd deflected. I challenged him, and he was ready to revel in it. Looking up, he pushed his omelet out of the way and folded his hands together, gazing at the boys.

"Indeed, I was one of those freak-show kids. Let me spin you a tale of spelling and woe."

Thursday was cooler than it had been in weeks, and that night after dinner, the twins went to play basketball. Tru wanted to go for another run, even though he'd been that morning as usual, and asked if I wanted to come. I said sure, and we both got our shoes and headed out the front door, started jogging down the sidewalk without bothering to stretch.

"Should we race?" he asked.

"Race? I don't think it's racing if we know who's going to win."

"Well, sure. With that attitude you're never going to beat me."

I thought for sure he was going to tear off down the block, but instead he kept moving at a leisurely jog. We passed an old couple walking a pair of poodles, a young couple pushing a pouty toddler, a tired guy in a suit, laptop bag slumped heavy on his shoulder. Tru didn't seem to notice any of them. He had his head craned up at the cloudless blue, a white moon stamped unexpectedly on the not-yet-dark sky.

"Are you ready for our big camping trip?" he asked. "There's going to be stars and a fire and everything. Very romantic, you know."

I knew, of course, that he was about to mess with me. I tried to veer the conversation away.

"Porta-potties and bug spray and sleeping on the ground," I said. "Totally romantic."

He fought a smile then, as I knew he would. He always liked when I was sarcastic.

"I just want to make sure you've thought about, you know, everyone who's going to be there. Maybe there's a certain someone you're excited to see."

I refused to look at him. I kept my eyes straight ahead, took a second to tighten my ponytail.

"Well, I do have a crush on Sparrow," I said. "But who doesn't?"

Just at that moment we were rounding the corner, the basketball courts coming distantly into view.

"Who doesn't indeed?" he said, with a jerk of his head in the twins' direction.

I laughed a little, and for a moment we were quiet. I thought he was actually going to drop it. Then he sighed.

"So you're not going to tell me anything? About how you might be feeling? All these weeks we've spent together, I just thought I could help prepare you for a big night."

"I'm quite prepared," I told him. "I've already packed my toothbrush and everything."

He smiled again, and then kept quiet the whole jog home. A couple of times I thought he was going to say something more, but he always stopped himself, as if thinking better of it.

We both knew what I was doing, after all. That I was practicing the kind of game he had taught me to play—the shield of clever answers, or rude ones, when you didn't want to talk. In this case, of course, it wasn't really working, because I wasn't fooling him at all.

Still, he seemed amused enough that he decided to let me be. At least for now.

EIGHTEEN

Tara and the groupies all had tickets to a concert that weekend, so that left the seven of us—the band, me, Tru, Sparrow, and Kieran. Just enough to fit in our old monster of a van.

Kieran and I had taken Friday off, and Tru was ditching class. Sparrow drove over with the boys that morning. We spent half an hour shoving all the gear into the trunk until it was a solid block of tents and bags and coolers. Then, to my horror, Mom appeared. She had come home early from work, and she made us unpack the whole thing so that she could check it for beer while we sweated on the sidewalk. She found nothing.

I wondered where in the world it could possibly be hiding.

After she gave the okay for us to reload it all, I thought we were finally free. Not yet. While I stood there red-faced and mortified, she lined up Devon, P.J., and Winston and stood before them with arms crossed, her face an angry mask, full of that look she always got before the twins went out: peremptory disapproval.

"I've already talked to my kids and Truman, and I know Sparrow is an adult who knows how to be good, but let me tell you boys—*you are going to behave.* There are rangers *all over* that island. If you do anything, they will be on you, and you will be sorry."

Winston just stood there in shock. P.J. drummed his fingers worse than ever and was driven into an uncharacteristic silence. Devon looked simply solemn, nodding along to every word. When she was done he was the only who managed to speak.

"I think you would like my mother, Mrs. Little. I got almost that exact same speech this morning."

I saw a flicker at the corner of her mouth that could have been the start of a smile.

The whole time, Tru had been standing down at the end of our block, talking on the phone to one of his parents, his body stiff and turned away from us. He came back just as we were climbing into the van. He ran his hands through his hair a few times, seemed to be composing himself.

Kieran drove, with Sparrow next to him, Tru and I in the middle, the three boys stuck in the back. As soon as Kieran left our street, we realized that no one had CDs, only phones and iPods, which our van had no way to play. So we were stuck with what we were always stuck with: U2, Bruce, and the Stones. P.J. and Devon had no problem with that, yelling out requests for "Gimme Shelter." Kieran warned everyone to roll down their windows, because the air-conditioning barely worked. He then turned the music to a very specific, and strategic, volume: just loud enough that he could talk to Sparrow but no one else could hear them. That meant the only person I could really talk to was Tru, but he had his earbuds in.

As we made our way south toward the highway, P.J. tapped my shoulder, and I turned around. He tried to tell me something, but it took several times for me to catch it over the wind and the music.

"Your brother is taller than ever. And your mom is scary but also kind of awesome."

We both settled back into our seats, and behind me, the boys became wrapped up in their own conversation. I gave silent thanks for this little blessing: a three-hour car ride that I would be able to spend with my thoughts, searching out the window and readying myself for whatever might come.

We joined a long line of cars chugging over the bridge and onto the island, water sparkling and sloshing below. At the guard booth, Kieran handed them our pass, which Tru had mysteriously provided, and the attendant told us how to get to our designated square of campground. He warned us the wind was supposed to be bad tonight. In fact, it had been getting steadily worse the whole way down. Now it was actually rocking the car.

"Tru, how'd you get a spot so last-minute?" Kieran asked as we pulled into the parking lot. "Usually they fill up a few weeks in advance."

"Weren't you there? It was at The Mack's party last week. Some kids from your school—drama kids, I think. They'd gotten two, but then some people bailed, and they said we could have one. So I guess I should apologize. We're probably going to be stuck next to a bunch of insufferable, attention-starved star wannabes."

"Um, did you forget where Devon and I go to school?" P.J. asked.

"We don't know anyone *but* insufferable, attention-starved star wannabes," Devon said.

"Well, they brought our beer, so we should all be thanking them anyway," Tru said.

I whipped my head toward him. "So that's how you did it."

He gave a little shrug, looking proud of himself.

Kieran asked which drama kids, and Tru said Kylie Bennett and Rachel Bobbins. Kylie was the fresh-faced, perky girl who was always the lead, and Rachel was her cute, chubby friend who usually got stuck playing some old lady. Kieran said they were nice girls, and Sparrow teased him, asking whether they were special friends of his. He whispered something back that made her laugh.

After Kieran eased the van into a parking spot, we all tumbled out, stretching and marveling at the madness of the weather. Sunlight glinted dimly through gray clouds, while the air whipped us violently, blowing as if it wanted to rip our clothes from our bodies, our feet from the earth.

We divided up most of the gear, deciding that we'd come back later for the rest. Burdened with our loads, we made our way slowly down the path toward our designated campsite. The island was spotted with tents, many bending in the wind like sails, some already tipped or collapsed. Barbecues were smoldering. Portable speakers sent out thin music. Kids were running around and screaming like savages.

"Where the hell are the horses?" Tru asked.

"We'll probably only see a few," Kieran said. "Maybe closer to the beach."

The wind blew and blew. My hair whirled around my head, snaking tendrils covering my eyes. Half-blind, I did the best I could to keep up.

Our designated spot was a little patch of land about the size of our dining room at home—lot number 367. We were much more isolated than Sparrow had implied to my mother. We could hear the din of other people, but were mostly shielded from them by patches of thin, young trees. The only campsite we could actually see was the one right next door. Kylie and Rachel's. A big red tent bowed in the breeze, and there were three beach chairs held down by rocks placed on the seats. No people around. Tru kept looking over there, arms folded, annoyed.

Dropping our things, we got our bearings. A concrete bunker of bathrooms and showers was a two-minute walk to the east. The beach was just south of us. We had one small tent for Sparrow and me, one giant tent for the boys. Everybody was jumpy and jittery, staring reluctantly at our hopeless jumble of equipment.

Kieran looked at our impatient faces and laughed.

"Jesus, I thought this was a vacation. Apparently I'm a permanent camp counselor. Get out of here. I'll set up."

Sparrow offered to stay and help. The boys took off and I

started after them, then looked back for Tru. He was coming slowly, glancing back at the other campsite.

"Is that Kylie and Rachel's?" I asked. "Is it just the two of them?"

"Hmmmm?" He gave me a look like he had no idea what I meant, then breezed by me, following the boys.

The five of us walked single-file down the skinny path that ran through the woods, thick greenery blocking out the sky. There were roots and rocks to dodge, and we had to walk carefully. *Like a tightrope walker,* I told myself, thinking back to the beginning of the summer.

I could not believe how much had changed. I could not believe I was here.

The leaves shushed together overhead, and we hurried along, rushing toward the break in the trees. One by one, the boys slipped from the woods. Last in line, lagging several steps behind, I finally reached the path's end, hovering there to take in the view of the beach, the way it opened before me like a picture book, an expanse of perfect sand with the ocean brewing like an angry cauldron behind it. There was no one here but us. Tru was just a few steps away, hands in front of his face, like maybe he was trying to block the sun. Winston, Devon, and P.J. were farther off down the beach, and they were laughing like mad. I couldn't figure out why it was so empty, why they were cackling like that, until I actually stepped out of the protection of the trees and stood next to Tru.

The wind had taken over. Sand flew everywhere, stinging our

skin. I put my arms up instinctively, but that did nothing. We were battered from all sides. I yelled to Tru, asking if we should go back. He looked toward the trees, swatting at the air as if the sand were a swarm of gnats he could shoo away. Then he shrugged.

"Too late to stay clean and pretty, I think."

He was right. I already felt hopelessly grainy. My hair was blown to hell. The two of us stumbled down toward the boys, who waved us over and shouted about the weather—"Look at this; oh my god, can you believe it?" Winston got out his phone and took a picture of all of us, hair and shirts flying, shielding our eyes as the water churned behind. He started to put it away, but then P.J. said, "Wait, get this!" and tried to launch himself into a handstand. Halfway up, he failed, crumpling into a ball, while we all shrieked and laughed. Devon tried next, managing to hold on for a moment, though his knees were bent.

Before he fell his shirt slipped down and showed his chest, lean and smooth.

They told Tru to go, but he declined with a dismissive wave of his hand, heading toward the water. Then they turned to me. I tried to wave them off, too, but they started chanting my name and clapping their encouragement. I gave in, tucking my shirt into my shorts and putting my palms into the soft, shifting sand. One foot at a time, I pushed myself into a perfect line and counted slowly to five, holding on against the wind. I came down lightly. When I was back on my feet, rubbing my palms against my hips to dust them off, I saw that the boys were all staring at me, impressed—or maybe something more.

I wasn't embarrassed. It felt good.

"Are you, like, a gymnast?" P.J. asked.

"I was," I said. "When I was younger. Then I got too tall."

At first they just kept staring. Then Devon smiled.

"That's okay. Tall is good," he said. "I'd kill to get too tall for things."

A new gust came, stronger than before. I felt as though sand had infiltrated every part of me, working its way under my clothes, through every strand of hair, between my toes, behind my ears. P.J. put his arms out straight and collapsed backward to the ground.

"BURY ME!" he said.

For a moment, we all looked at each other, unsure. Then Devon shrugged, dropped down, and started to push a pile of sand toward P.J. I looked at Winston and he smiled. We dropped down and dug in our hands. As I was giggling, covering P.J.'s knobby knees and feet, I remembered Tru. I looked up and found him at the water's edge. He stood in the soft, puckering sand, not flinching when the surf reached his feet, not moving as it swirled around his ankles, up almost to his knees.

He looked small to me then—small but sure, standing strong against the rage and power and endlessness of the ocean.

Devon, P.J., and Winston went off to smoke their cigarettes, in search of some sheltered spot where they could possibly get some peace and strike a match. Tru and I had settled on a giant rock that rested where the trees met the sand. We were watching

Kieran and Sparrow, who had finished with the tents and joined us on the beach.

The two of them were down by the water, trying hopelessly to throw a Frisbee. Every time they released the red disc, it flew wildly, captured by the wind and whipped off course. They kept racing to retrieve it and couldn't stop laughing.

After a while they flopped down, looking exhausted. They, too, gave themselves over to sandiness, lying side by side, staring up and talking.

"Is Kieran cute?" I asked Tru.

The eyebrow cocked.

"Is he cute? I didn't realize that Maryland was the South. I'm not really into my cousins."

"Shut up," I said, kicking sand in his direction. "I'm just wondering. I'm his sister. It's hard to tell."

Tru tented his fingers, leaned his head to the side, and thought.

"He's not handsome exactly, but he's nice-looking. He really needs to cut his hair. He's got that tall, broad-shouldered thing, though. That goes a long way."

Sparrow jumped up and tried a cartwheel. She completed one perfectly, arms and legs straight as a windmill, then got knocked down by a roaring gust. Kieran clapped as she rolled back to his side.

"But he has no chance," I said. "Right?"

Tru gave a playful shrug. "Actually . . . I think he might."

I looked back at the two of them in wonder. "You said Jimmy had all the game."

"With high school girls. Sparrow's in college. Or almost. Things change."

Kieran's hair was flying everywhere. He tried to hold it flat with both his hands. He shouted something, Sparrow laughed, and in that moment I saw him so differently. As someone more grown-up than I realized. Someone with his own kind of charm. Someone who maybe had a lot to offer.

Tru turned and looked at me. "That's one good thing about life, Frannie. High school rules don't last forever."

Back at the campsite we realized that lunchtime had long since passed. All of us were famished, and we dug into the coolers, making sandwiches and passing a bag of chips, a box of cookies. The wind hadn't stopped, and napkins and plastic bags were wrenched from our grips, tossed away and lost forever. Still we saw no horses.

On the walk back from the beach, I'd noticed that some families were packing up and heading for home, giving up in the face of the gale. We just walked around the tents and gave the stakes an extra push. Sparrow suggested that she and I set up our sleeping bags, doing so in a loud-ish way that reminded everyone the two of us would be together. No funny business, as my mother would have said. The guys followed suit, arranging their things in the other tent.

As I was crawling back out of the flap and rezipping it, I heard the crackle and warble of a speaker. The noise had come from down the path, and we all went and stood at the edge, just as a pickup truck drove slowly by, blaring a message from the bullhorn on its roof.

"There is a tornado warning in effect. I repeat, there is a tornado warning in effect."

As it passed us, I caught a glimpse of a bored-looking ranger in the front seat. He repeated the message, then disappeared from view.

P.J. tilted his head sideways, knocking his hand against his ear. "Um, I'm not crazy, right? Did you guys hear that?"

"Were there instructions attached?" Devon asked. "Or was that just a heads-up that we're probably going to die?"

Kieran and Sparrow took a step away and began having a quiet conversation about whether we needed to leave, and Tru slipped over, began talking in his most soothing voice about how that wasn't necessary. Meanwhile P.J. started running around in circles and waving his arms, pretending to lose his mind. I giggled, and that set everyone off, all of us laughing, shirts flapping in the breeze.

"This is fucked-up," Winston mumbled, one of the only things he'd said all day. We all laughed harder.

"Whatever," Devon said. "What will be will be. If that thing sucks us up, I guess we just go to Neverland."

"Yeah," P.J. said. "Neverland's not so bad. You never grow up and there's, like, pirates."

"Except the tornado doesn't take you to Neverland," I said. "It takes you to Oz."

"I guess that's right," Devon said. "Good thing we brought the smart girl."

"Oz," P.J. added. "That's midgets and flying monkeys. Not as cool."

Kieran and Sparrow were still a few steps away, having their quiet conversation, but I noticed that Tru had wandered off, back toward the empty campsite. While everybody else continued to debate the merits of Neverland and Oz, I went to stand beside him.

"You keep looking over there. Do you want beer that bad?"

He looked at me in a way that he hadn't for weeks and weeks—the annoyed stare that made me feel like a child.

"You're right, Frannie, I should be entertained solely by your stimulating conversation about Peter Pan and Dorothy."

I was nursing the sting of that when I saw them coming up the path from the other end of the island, the north side, where we hadn't yet been. It was the drama girls, Kylie and Rachel, and somebody else behind them.

Not just somebody else. Jeremy Bell.

I should have known, should have guessed, but I just hadn't made the connection. Because when Tru had said "drama kids," I'd never thought of Jeremy, who was not a drama kid exactly. He was just friends with some of the girls and helped them build sets for the plays.

Now I turned to Tru, hands on my hips.

"THAT?" I whispered, low enough that the others wouldn't hear. "That is why you wanted to come? That's what this whole trip was about?"

"Oh, gosh, no, Frannie. I came so you and I could tame a pair of ponies and join the circus!"

He could see my feelings were hurt, and he put an arm around me.

"I'm sorry, I'm sorry. Look, I want to have fun. I want you to have fun. I want your brother to have fun. I just want us all to have fun and live a little. Okay?"

I said okay, but didn't know if he even heard me. He had already taken off, sauntering over to meet the three of them. The girls looked thrilled to see him, jumping up and down and calling his name. Behind them, Jeremy raised his hand in a shy, tentative wave.

I hadn't seen him in months, and I realized he was even better-looking than I'd thought. Details came flashing back to me. His dad was Irish Catholic like my family, his mom from the Philippines. I took in his olive skin, his romantic eyes, the scattering of unexpected freckles on his cheeks, and that's when I remembered the nickname given to him by some of the girls at school.

Jeremy What-a-waste.

In the flurry of hellos, Kieran introduced the St. Sebastian's kids, first to Sparrow, and then to the band. I was mortified by how jealous I felt then, not wanting the boys to meet these other people from my old school, as if it would suddenly reveal that I was in no way cool or special. I hung back, trying to ignore the whole exchange, pretending to be busy with something in my bag, but then Kieran pulled me over.

"You know my sister. She's two years behind us."

The girls politely pretended that they did, though I could tell they had no clue. Blushing, I tried to move away, but as I did

Jeremy gave me a wink, a wave, and a quick "Hi, Frannie." He said it warmly, a little aside just between the two of us. He actually remembered me. I managed to mumble a hello, touched to have been recognized, to know that when I disappeared from the halls of St. Sebastian's, there was a chance someone might actually notice. In that moment I adored Jeremy, totally and completely. I wanted him and Tru to get together and be happy forever.

Moments later, we all broke apart, busy getting cleaned up and organized. A few went to shower, though most of us didn't bother. Some went searching for cell phone reception, so they could check in with their parents. Others went down to see the beach one more time, to put their feet in the ocean before the wind got any worse.

With everyone hustling around and getting ready to leave, Tru produced from his pocket the world's smallest, most perfectly rolled joint. He held it out between his finger and thumb like some glittering gem, saying he could share if anyone was interested. Jeremy raised his hand like he was in class. Sparrow, supremely annoyed, ordered them into a little grove just outside of our site, which offered some cover. She threatened that they'd better be quick.

She took off then, too, leaving Kieran and me alone. There was one Coke left, and we decided to split it, trading it back and forth as we rested side by side on a log. From that position, we couldn't help but look directly at Tru and Jeremy. They were just visible through the thin branches of the trees. I could see they were talking, but they were too far away for us to hear. Their chairs were angled slightly toward each other, and Jeremy was resting his foot on the leg of Tru's chair. They sat very close.

The silence between Kieran and me grew heavy. I searched for something to say.

"So . . . I guess they kind of know each other. From the parties this summer."

He sighed. "You know, I'd never have gotten into some fancy magnet school, but I'm not as dumb as you think I am."

I turned and looked at his profile. After a moment he turned, too, and met my eyes. We had one of those silent exchanges that I seemed to be having more and more of lately.

"You and Jimmy know?" I asked.

He let out a singular laugh, a sharp, humorless exhale.

"Well, I figured it out. Not Jimmy. Jimmy actually *is* as dumb as you think."

A small weight was lifted from my chest, the burden of secrecy, and I wanted to tell Kieran everything. Absolutely everything that had happened all summer. Siren and the tattoo and Mom dating Uncle Richard. But I wasn't quite ready. Instead, I turned back toward Tru and Jeremy. I grabbed a stick and made scratches in the dirt.

"Do you know that's why he's here?" I asked finally. "It's because his parents found out and couldn't deal."

Kieran straightened up and let out a low whistle. "I didn't know that. Jesus. That's messed up. His dad . . . I don't know if you remember him. He's not a nice guy."

I wanted to ask more about that, but then Kieran looked at

me, and I saw that his mind was somewhere else. His face was flushed and sad. More than that. Ashamed.

"I'm sorry, Frannie. About next year. About St. Sebastian's. I'm an ass. I should have gone to public school. I can't believe I just sat back and let them do that to you."

Then his head was in his hands. His ears burned red, and the fire of his emotions passed to me. I knew how hard it would be to admit what he just said, to be vulnerable like this. Most boys his age, I didn't think they'd ever dream of it. But what he was doing right now he was doing for me, and that meant everything.

I felt loved in that moment, deeply loved.

I started to say his name but choked on it. I wanted to reach out and touch him but couldn't figure out how to.

"That wouldn't make sense," I said finally. "One year of your tuition wouldn't make up for three more years of mine." My voice was breaking.

"Yeah, but in another year Dad'll find steady work again. At least, I think he will. Everything would have been fine. You could have stayed with your friends."

Not until he said it did I realize that I no longer wanted to go to St. Sebastian's. Not at all. I looked at Kieran, but his face was still hidden.

"My friends sucked," I said.

"Frannie!" He laughed and finally looked up.

"Well . . . they kinda did."

He shrugged. "They were okay. You're cooler than them, for sure. I mean, look at the new friends you made."

Just then we saw Sparrow, coming back from the showers, now wearing a pair of tiny gym shorts and a tank top, her hair under a bandanna.

Kieran coughed. "A serious improvement."

When everyone was back, the beer appeared. Kieran managed to get me alone for a moment and ask for a favor. He wanted me to only have one. He told me it was okay with him if I wanted to pretend to have more—he would help me do that, even—but for him, please, I had to be good. I was only fifteen. I was the youngest person here.

"How many are you having?" I asked.

He paused. Smiled. "Four? What if I say four? Frannie, I'm huge. Four is nothing. I'm going to space them out all night."

"Then how about I get one and a half?"

He shook my hand and divided one between us on the spot. I said that he could have four and a half if he wanted, and he put me in a headlock, which was his way of saying thanks.

Devon and P.J. had brought their acoustic guitars, and they got everyone around the fire pit, which we had not lit because of the wind, instead relying on a pair of electric lanterns. They played Motown and then The Beatles and then terrible pop songs that everyone secretly loved and knew all the words to. Kylie and Rachel jumped in to sing along with their big, beautiful sopranos, and I could see that Devon and P.J. were impressed, which made me proud of where I'd come from. Our little Catholic school had good singers, too.

I kept waiting for Tru to join in with that supposed angel voice of his, but he didn't. He just sat on the ground, in front and to the left of Jeremy's chair, leaning back on his palms. I tried not to look at them too closely, but my eyes kept creeping back in their direction, as I wondered what, if anything, was going to happen. And then I saw Tru shift.

Such a small motion, just a rearranging of weight. Except it wasn't. It was more. His right arm was now touching Jeremy's leg, ever so slightly. Jeremy didn't move.

Goose bumps broke out on my arms. I knew what that touch meant—it was the lightest bit of friction, but it said everything, because they were both letting it happen. I thought about that: how life might come at you and sometimes you could say yes without doing anything at all. All you had to do was not pull away.

I knew I shouldn't watch them, so I turned, only to see that Kieran and Sparrow were now sharing the log, her leg resting against his leg, skin to skin. I felt like there was electricity jumping in little bolts all around us, jolting us, connecting us, and the wind was still screaming, screaming, screaming.

P.J. was sitting across from me, staring.

He and Devon started strumming something new, and Rachel jumped right in, belting the words. Everyone was cheering and clapping and then a bunch of people were shouting along and laughing, but I didn't know what this song was and I wondered how that could be—how everyone could know something except for me.

And Kieran was whispering in Sparrow's ear. And Jeremy's leg was jiggling nervously against Tru's arm. And P.J. was still looking in my direction.

I closed my eyes and chugged my beer, almost gagging on it. I felt sick. I didn't want any of this. The pairing off, the separation. I could feel everyone's desire to get away, to be alone, to fall on one another and do . . . whatever they would do. I resented how obvious it all seemed. Just put people in the vicinity of one another and they attracted like magnets, no magic at all, no meaning. I hated it, and I hated that we couldn't just sit here and sing and be together. I hated the taste of beer, and I hated the fuzziness taking over my head as I drank it. I felt off-kilter. Everything was in motion and would never, ever stop.

Just then there were giggles from out in the darkness. A girl and a guy, teenagers, stumbled from the path into our campsite, holding hands. He flipped his baseball cap backward, and the girl slipped behind him shyly.

"Oops," he said. "Not the way to the beach."

Kieran told him no problem, pointed out the direction they should go. Right as they started to scamper away, the guy pulled back.

"Just a heads-up. They've got patrols coming through. They're definitely poking around if they see a bunch of kids together. You might want to break it up for a little bit. That's why we're on the move." With a wink, he pulled a flask from his pocket, then slipped it back in. Then the two of them were gone, back into the trees, while all of us went wide-eyed, clutching our beers.

"Oh, shit," Kieran said. We paused for only a couple of seconds and then everyone was grabbing flashlights and lanterns and cans, trying to figure out who should go where and for how long. I noticed that there was more excitement than nervousness in people's voices, and I realized that this was it. This was the excuse people needed to pair off and disappear.

I grabbed my flashlight and beer, told Kieran that I was going to the bathroom, escaping during the height of the chaos before anyone could object or try to join me. I hurried down the path into the concrete bunker, rushing to lock myself in the stall at the far end. I huddled there, not caring that the toilet seat was dirty, just sitting and drinking, reading graffiti over and over, saying nothing when I heard Kylie and Rachel come and go. There was writing all over the walls, and I tried to distract myself by taking in all of the love and anger and silliness that were inked there. Who loved who and who was a terrible person and jokes that were fading and not making sense. More than anything, there were just initials—signs that people had been here and wanted to leave some trace of themselves behind. At first I pretended that I'd never have to leave, never have to face whatever was about to come. But as I drank in that grimy stall I grew restless.

Ever since that first band practice in the basement, a tension had been building. I'd been flattered by P.J.'s staring, and then I'd spent all this time avoiding him, to the point that I was sitting here. Alone. In a bathroom.

I just wanted something to happen. I wanted to kiss somebody.

More than that, I wanted—for once—to feel bold and unafraid.

* * *

Back at the campsite, I found Tru sitting on a log, alone. I was filled with Bud Light and resolve.

"Where is everybody?" I asked.

He came to stand next to me and started ticking people off on his fingers. "Kylie, Rachel, and Jeremy went to look for a Windbreaker that Kylie left at the beach on the other side of the island—good luck with that. Pretty sure it's blown to Timbuktu. I think Winston is sleeping in the tent. Not a big drinker, that one. Couple of beers knocked him out. Kieran and Sparrow walked off that way somewhere to dispose of the empty cans, or so they said. Scandalous!"

He paused then, crossing his arms and cocking his head. "So let's see. Who am I missing?"

I stood there and would not answer.

"Oh, right," he said. "Devon and P.J. Well, P.J. went back that way, to the car. His bag and some other stuff were still in the trunk," Tru said, pointing west. "Devon went down the beach." He pointed south.

Right then, all I wanted was for it to be over. I wanted to kiss P.J. and have it be done. I cleared my throat, but still sounded shrill and squeaky. "I should probably go to the car. I had a couple of things in there, too."

I started to move in that direction. Tru's arm shot out and blocked me.

"*P.J.?* P.J., Frannie? I mean, c'mon."

I stood there, behind his arm, unmoving. I said nothing.

"If I were you," he said, "I'd go for Devon."

I hoped the darkness hid my face. "Devon doesn't like me like that."

But even as I said it, I knew that it wasn't true.

Maybe P.J. had been more obvious about it, especially in the beginning, but Devon had been flirting with me, too. I knew he had. And Devon . . . Devon was the one I liked.

So what the hell was wrong with me?

Why was I talking myself into running after someone I didn't even want? At the beginning of the summer, when I was at my lowest, I'd spent nights dreaming of my perfect imaginary boyfriend on the basketball team, but when real, live Devon arrived in my life, and *actually showed interest in me,* I was—what? Too scared to see it?

No, that wasn't quite it. Not scared but intimidated. Intimidated for so many different reasons. Because he was shorter than me, because he was cooler than me, because he was black. All of that caused some great mass of confusion that had been blocking out everything else—that he loved my band name, that he could command an entire stage, that every time I saw him I could barely keep myself from staring at his perfect face.

With P.J., it would have been easy. I knew how he felt and that he felt more than I did. There would have been so little at stake. If I backed out at the last minute, if I was a terrible kisser, it would have been embarrassing, but I would live.

With Devon, I knew it wouldn't be that easy. With Devon, I was putting myself on the line.

I covered my face with my hands and tried desperately to think. I was standing in the middle of an island, in the middle a windstorm, my arrogant ass of a cousin standing there and blocking my way, making things so much harder.

Because now there was only one person I could imagine running after.

Tru sighed loudly.

"Listen, it's up to you."

He moved his arm and took a step back, hands raised in a posture of surrender.

I was angry, not at him exactly, but still, I glared at him because it gave me something to glare at. I kicked the dirt at my feet.

"You were really rude to me when I first told you about Jeremy. And now look at you two!"

I stomped off like an angry child. I stomped to the south. To the beach. To Devon.

The more quickly I moved, the easier it was not to think.

I jogged down the path, my flashlight glowing dimly. On both sides, I caught glimpses of people taking cover in struggling tents. Leaves conspired overhead with an eerie rustling. My old fear of the dark returned, and I hurried faster now, almost running, the beach coming into view, awash in moonlight.

I burst from the greenery onto the sand and ran right into Devon.

Bouncing off each other, the two of us laughed and made confused, overlapping apologies. He had dropped his flashlight, and

I stepped back, flaring mine around until we found it. He picked it up but didn't turn it on. I kept mine trained on the ground. Standing there in the shadow of the trees, it was too dark to see his face. Sand still blew hard against our skin, and it crept around my feet, too, as the ocean hissed in the distance, an inky blackness stretching on forever. We stood there together on the edge of the world.

I swallowed hard.

"I guess . . . Were you going back?"

Those were my words, but the tone in my voice said something else. It said *Don't go back, stay here, stay with me*, and I knew in that moment that I had laid the truth before him.

He said nothing, just shifted his body toward me, closing the gap, three inches, two inches, one . . . The wind whipped around like it was wrapping us up, and now we were as close as two people could be without touching, so close that I went dizzy with closeness, my mouth so near to his I might have been breathing in the air he was breathing out. My mind flew back to biology class, thinking how this would make me a plant, a flower in the ground, just waiting for someone to come along and exhale. To feed my core. To give me life.

Breathe, little plant, breathe.

That was the very best moment, when his lips had not touched mine but I knew they would and all I could think was, *Oh!*

Oh!

Oh!

NINETEEN

First there was just the softness of his mouth crushing my breath, cutting me off from everything but this, everything but him. Then he dropped his flashlight, I dropped mine, and his tongue was moving in. It was like some desperate creature had invaded my body. I didn't like the feeling, it was so much wetter than I'd thought it would be, and weirder. I tried to move my own tongue but couldn't will it far enough to make it past his lips. Instead, I stayed locked in place, his tongue seeking, both our lips tussling. Fighting almost.

Movies and books and love songs had taught me that this would be different. I expected to be utterly lost in the moment, but it wasn't that way at all. I couldn't stop thinking about what he was thinking about. I had never been more conscious of my body, of myself. I wondered if he thought I was flat and scrawny, and I wondered if he could tell I'd never done this. I wondered how many other girls he'd kissed, and I wondered if he'd ever kissed another white girl, and then I wondered if that was a terrible thing to think about.

I could feel myself tensing against the strangeness of it all, but then he moved one arm gently on my neck, and one arm around my waist, and he was pulling me closer, and this I liked. This felt romantic. I realized my arms were hanging limply at my sides, and so I moved them to mirror his, one on his neck and one around to his back. As I touched him, I fell in love with his cotton T-shirt, how incredibly thin it seemed. Just below that was his skin, and just below that were his ribs, caging and protecting his heart, his lungs.

Through it all, the wind did not relent.

His lips parted from mine, the two of us taking a moment to breathe. He touched my hair and seemed relaxed. That made me more nervous than ever. His arms loosened, releasing our embrace, and I felt some small relief, that there was air between us and I could remember myself, secure my footing.

Next to me, Devon sighed.

"P.J. is going to kill me."

The words buzzed in the air around us, and right then, all I could think of was Tru. I wanted to find him and tell him that both these boys liked me, to say how amazing that seemed. He would have laughed in my face, I was sure, but still—even as Devon delicately took my hand, what I wanted was my cousin, my friend. I wanted him to hear the story of this kiss. I wanted to relive this moment with him, this moment that wasn't even over.

Our flashlights were still at our feet, as we hid away in the darkness, but next to me, I could tell that Devon was shuffling his feet. Now he seemed nervous, too.

"I, uh . . . Pretend I didn't say that. I shouldn't have said that because I don't even know. I mean, we haven't actually talked about it, about you . . . I just kind of got a vibe that, you know . . . Yeah. I'm going to stop talking now."

I laughed, pulling my hand from his to cover my face. He started to move toward me again, but then we heard Sparrow's voice, calling Devon's name through the trees.

"Ignore her," he whispered, pulling me closer, and in that moment I forgot about everyone else except for him. Something started pulsing inside me—a second heart that was pounding, pounding, pounding, and part of me wanted us to fall down together in the sand. The other part of me was so terrified about what came next that I needed to be anywhere but here. I searched for my voice and felt my lips chapped and burning, abused.

"Maybe," I whispered, "maybe we should go back? She's probably worried?"

I felt Devon pulling away from me, and for a second I thought he was mad or annoyed, but then he took another step back, toward a patch of moonlight. I could see that his mouth was open as he stared at something off in the distance.

He took my elbow softly and turned me around. "Frannie," he said, "look."

I turned toward the night-dark water, and there in front of the ocean were horses. A herd of beautiful horses. Finally, we'd found them, and they didn't look real. They looked like mythic creatures, powerful but graceful, too, pawing at the ground, snapping their necks. They huffed against the wind, backs to the sea, hot coats pressed together. I tried to count them, but they blended together, legs meshing with legs to make a swarm.

"Wait here," Devon said. "I have to get everybody. Wait here."

I was so distracted by the kiss, the storm, the horses, that I said nothing, didn't even nod. But just as he was turning to leave, he paused, reached out, and placed his fingers on my arm. He said my name, and I turned toward him, hair flying in the breeze, still speechless.

"Do you want to come with me?" he asked.

His voice and his touch were gentle, and part of me wanted to say yes, but the other part of me just needed a little space. Time to recover.

"I'll stay here," I told him.

Then he was gone and it was just me there on the beach, watching the horses with a fast heart. I looked up for the first time all night to see the sky, unobstructed by the endless grid of lights that mapped out the city. The stars were thick here, thicker than I could ever remember. I stood there, spun mad by the wind and almost wishing that no one would come, that I could just be alone.

I moved in slow steps toward the herd, and as I got closer, their figures became clear. They lost that edge of magic, looking earthy and strong. I counted seven of them.

When I was about twenty yards away, I sank down to sit and

watch. Two of them turned their heads toward me. I looked back, but nothing seemed to pass between us. I didn't even know if they saw me.

Time moved strangely, quietly. After some undetermined minutes, I heard a soft noise. Sparrow and Kieran were settling into the sand at my right, and in the moonlight I could see that their fingers were lightly entwined. Behind them, Kylie and Rachel were kneeling down to watch, too, and next to them, Devon and P.J. Together we whispered and pointed, shielding our eyes from the flying sand with hands and hoodies, talking about how beautiful the horses were. For a while we just sat there in silence.

Eventually Tru and Jeremy appeared, walking over very slowly from somewhere down the beach. When they reached us, they didn't sit. They were inches from each other but didn't touch, didn't hold hands, even though all of us knew, even though none of us cared.

Seeing them together, a pair of shadows, the tension between them palpable, I understood, just a little more deeply, how lonely it would be to live like that.

Next to me, Devon was sitting cross-legged like a child in class. I looked at him and smiled. Just when I was starting to feel perfect and relaxed and wonderful, we heard the sound of the bullhorn, the rangers coming through. We jumped up, some of us still clinging to beers and cigarettes, and we agreed to go back separate ways.

I felt a hand on my shoulder and was surprised to see that it was Tru.

"I've got Frannie."

And so it was just the two of us. Together again. He led us away from everyone, away from the horses, away from the path back to camp, just taking me down the beach into darkness. Into nowhere.

"So," he said, "what happened?"

Embarrassed, I remembered storming away from him.

"I . . . I kissed Devon."

"*You* kissed *him*?"

He sounded proud, and I almost didn't correct him.

"Okay," I said after a few beats. "He kissed me."

He chuckled at that as we kept walking.

"Why does he like me?" I asked.

"You're having a confidence crisis now? You just made out with him!"

"I know, but . . . I don't understand why he likes me."

We kept walking, Tru looking out toward the water.

"Look, this isn't meant to be harsh, just honest. But, yeah, on the surface he might seem a little out of your league. I mean, I attribute that to his age and confidence, so don't get all bent out of shape about it. But so what? He likes you. You're tall and thin and have lots of shiny red hair. I'm sure you know on some level how appealing that is. Plus none of these kids really know you. Quiet equals mysterious. Or something."

I tried to digest all that, but it was too much. I didn't want to think about any of it right now. Besides, I wanted to know about Tru.

"So," I said, "are you going to tell me what happened with you?"

He stopped dead in his tracks.

"I just realized something, Frannie. It's not the red hair. It's the science thing. He's one of these weird guys who wants to date his mother."

He tried not to laugh, failed completely, and I started punching him hard in the shoulder with both fists. I pounded and pounded, squealing angrily at him until he danced away, crying out that he was joking.

"Now you *have* to tell me what happened with you," I demanded. "You owe me."

He ambled along, staring straight up at the stars, hands in his pockets, making me wait a bit before he answered.

"I kissed him." He said it nonchalantly, never breaking stride.

We walked for a while in silence, but then the wind kicked up a fierce howl, forcing us to stop. Tru leaned into the gale, shirt, shorts, and hair whipping behind him. I wrapped my arms around my shoulders and waited for it to subside, to tame back down to the standard madness of the day. When it did, we kept going.

"So now what?" I asked.

"Well, Frannie, I don't know. I don't think that we can hope for much else tonight. This is not exactly a night for romance. More like the scene of a disaster movie."

Then he stopped and looked at me. "Do you feel like running? I feel like running."

On one side, the ocean crashed. On the other, the wind in the trees made a papery music. Before us, the beach was a long, lustrous stretch of black.

"Yes." I said. "Devil take the hindmost."

And so we ran, fast and hard, sand kicking everywhere. We ran until my lungs burned and my legs ached. We ran from nothing. We ran for our lives.

TWENTY

Tru was right. We got back to the campsite and the wind had gotten worse. There was nothing to do but take cover in the tents. As Sparrow and I hunkered down into our sleeping bags, Kieran came over and lifted the flap. "Good night, ladies," he said. Sparrow responded with a firm good night that I knew meant *Go to bed; don't even think about coming back*. Kieran flashed a big grin, and she giggled.

We whispered to each other for a bit about nothing at all, both of our minds elsewhere. Then we drifted off. Again and again, I woke in the night to the wind howling overhead, bending the tent down low, the shiny polyester rippling just over our heads.

By the next morning, the weather had calmed only a little, and we agreed to pack up early and leave. We said good-bye to Kylie,

Rachel, and Jeremy. He blushed and looked at the ground when he waved at Tru. Tru's smile was easy as ever.

We piled into the car, and this time I ended up in the wayback, between Devon and Winston. Soon we were over the bridge, back on the highway, music blaring.

Devon reached out to take my hand, and Winston looked politely out the window, pretending not to notice. Devon's thumb twitched against my thigh. There in the backseat, I felt fluttery and nervous, but happy. Really happy.

At least for now.

What would happen when we left the van? Was last night a one-time nothing that he'd forget about, or was this going to turn into something? And if it turned into something . . . then what? What would that something be?

My palm was growing warm against Devon's, and I found myself watching the back of Tru's head as he stared out the window. As long as he was here, I could ask him these things when I needed to, and yes, he'd laugh, but at least I'd be talking to someone, not just leaving all of it buried.

Soon, though, Tru would be gone. I'd have to learn how to navigate without him. I'd have to open up to other people, too.

Dad had taken a temporary construction gig on the eastern shore, so he was gone that last week of summer, staying with a family friend in a little town on the Chesapeake Bay.

The rest of us carried on. Monday dinner was unusually quiet. Mom asked Tru if Sparrow would like to come again, and he said,

"I don't know, ask Kieran maybe?" He managed to say it with an innocent face, while Mom turned to my brother with a look of surprise. Later, she asked for Kieran's help drying dishes, and I could hear them talking. "Well, do you even know how to talk to an older girl, how to treat her? No offense to your past prom dates, but I'm not sure they were quite that classy." Embarrassed, I hurried away before they could catch me spying.

I'd given Devon the landline number, and he called me later that night. I managed to snag the receiver before anyone else got it. Then I ran to my room and curled up in a ball on my bed, stuffing my head under my pillow as we talked. I was terrified of having nothing to say, because I knew, I was absolutely sure, that Devon was right on the verge of realizing I was dull and plain and not worth his time. But nothing like that happened. First we talked about our days, about the school year to come, then a little about music. I asked about his family, and he told me more about his dad's work as a musician, his tour schedule, how he wanted to grow up and be like him, but at the same time he was mad that he was always away. He asked about my family, too, and I talked about my mom and dad, about what had happened with his work, how we were struggling. It was easier than I thought it would be, and Devon was a good listener, asked lots of questions. He wanted to know everything about underwater welding, at which point I realized just how little I knew—I'd never really bothered to ask.

I was waiting for Devon to say something about hanging out this week, but apparently he was totally booked the next few days. The new school year was only two weeks away, and there was something intense going on with auditions, something about competing for placements in different groups and ensembles next year. He and P.J. were both swept up in that, and we wouldn't see them again until the weekend. He said he'd call me again later in the week, and I was starting to feel really good, until he ended by saying, "Good night, see you Saturday." Then my heart went like a drum because Saturday was the jump-off, and I knew that I still wasn't ready. I was certain I'd be left there on the edge of the rocks like a scared little kid, while everyone else leaped down, sure and fearless.

Just after I'd hung up, Tru poked his head in my room to tell me that Friday we were going back to Siren with Sparrow. Nobody else, just the three of us. It was an eighteen-and-up night, and even Sparrow could only work so much magic.

"Who's playing?" I asked.

"That's a surprise," he said. "You'll see when we get there."

Normally Tru loved lording surprises over me, but right now he seemed too distracted. His phone was beeping with incoming texts and he was flipping through them quickly, annoyed and frowning.

I asked who it was and thought at first that he was going to ignore me.

"The ever-charming Richard!" he finally said, shoving his phone in his back pocket and running his hands through his hair. Just as I started to ask more, he cut me off.

"Since we're so close to our big trip to the jump-off, I'd really like another recon mission. Maybe Wednesday? We'll say we're going to the mall, give it one last look."

"I guess we should make sure the rope's still up?"

He crossed him arms and leaned against the door frame. "Actually, that's a really good point. We should do that. Mostly I was just in the mood to stare down at the water. You know, indulge in our forever feeling, Frannie. Taking on the infinite void."

And with that he turned around and was gone.

TWENTY-ONE

Mom was standing in the doorway to my room, and I was looking at her like she'd lost her mind.

"You're taking us to *what*?" I asked. "With *who*?"

It was Tuesday, one night before the Prettyboy recon mission. Three nights before Siren. Four nights before the jump-off. We'd just finished an early dinner, and I'd been planning to spend at least one evening holed up peacefully in my room, getting ready for it all. I'd said I was going to do my summer reading, but really, I was going to blast a New Wave mix Tru had made for me at my request, while I tried on clothes. I had to figure out what I should wear to Siren to not look like a child, and what I should wear to swim in a forbidden reservoir and still look okay for a boy who was "on the surface" a little out of my league. If I actually worked all that out, then maybe I could decide what the hell to wear to a special new-student orientation that was looming on Monday.

But here was Mom was standing in my doorway, having just announced that she was taking Tru and me to some theater thing with her friend. I asked when, and she said right now. I was still looking at her like she was insane, and she was looking at me like I was the most annoying, ungrateful child who'd ever walked the planet.

"It's a storytelling show, all right? They pick a theme, and people tell stories based on that theme. It's supposed to be a lot of fun. My friend from work has four tickets. We're going."

"Your friend Maria? With the roof deck?"

I hadn't meant to, but I still sounded skeptical. She was completely fed up.

"No, not Maria with the roof deck! Nancy, okay? I have more than one friend at work, you'll be shocked to know. Go put on your shoes!"

It wasn't that the plan sounded all that awful, I just wasn't used to my mom having mysterious friends who invited us on cultural outings. But she was telling, not asking, and ten minutes later she'd loaded Tru and me into the van. We flew down the highway, pulled into a parking garage, and jogged up the block, hoping not to be late.

I hadn't been here since a field trip in eighth grade, but the lobby looked the same as I remembered. Soaring ceilings, rich carpet. A little concession stand with T-shirts and candy and wine served in plastic cups. We got there with five minutes to spare. Just enough time to meet Nancy, who was perched on a bench, excitedly waving at us.

She was younger than my mom, maybe thirty-five or so. Pretty and petite with a pixie haircut, and even though I felt bad about jumping to conclusions, I saw her and I just knew. Even before I spotted the little rainbow pin on her canvas bag, I knew. And it was immediately, painfully obvious what Mom was doing. I wanted to drag her aside and tell her she was an idiot, that she didn't know Tru at all, that this was exactly the kind of gesture he would hate.

Except as we were all getting introduced, he had his mouth scrunched in this kind of half smile, clearly not pissed. Certainly not excited or grateful, but at the very least amused.

And with Truman, *amused* was sometimes the best you were going to get.

"Well, hello, Nancy," he said as he shook her hand, and a minute later, the four of us were heading inside the theater, grabbing the last of the programs from the usher, and taking our seats as the lights dimmed. I squinted in the dark at the cover, looking for the title of the show. When I found it, I almost groaned out loud, ran for the exit, hid under my seat.

The theme for the night was "Coming Out."

I thought the storytellers were going to be actors, but they weren't. There was a lawyer and an AIDS research scientist and a guy who ran a homeless shelter. Just regular people, telling regular stories, which somehow seemed to make them sadder or funnier than they would have been otherwise. Some of the stories were devastating and some of them were hilarious and then there were kind-of-devastating stories that were told as if they were hilarious stories, and those might have been the best. Like the librarian, who described the time she made out with her college roommate, the first love of her life. "Which was really unfortunate," she explained, "because she was most definitely straight, just really horny and in the immediate vicinity of me, who looked conveniently like a dude as long as my pants were on."

Nancy was laughing a lot. Tru was laughing a little. My mom and I were too busy leaning away from each other, pretending we hadn't both heard the word *horny*.

The last storyteller of the night was a big, handsome guy with a shaved head. He talked about growing up in Cleveland and being a loud, obnoxious kid always grating against his superconservative family. To save money, he went to college at the Catholic school down the road from his childhood home, worked part-time all the way through. He majored in business, and probably would have stayed there his whole life if he hadn't gotten an unexpected job offer in Baltimore. Before he left, he sat down with his dad, because there was something they needed to talk about, something he couldn't leave without saying, something that he hoped his dad would understand. Sometimes, he said, you have to find your own way. Sometimes the path is unexpected. Sometimes you go against the way you were raised.

"And my dad is sitting there under this creepy picture of Jesus, so it's like they're both staring at me, I shit you not. Dad's got his bifocals on to read the recap of last night's Browns game, and he slowly puts down the paper. He takes off his glasses. Something crosses over his face, and he says to me, 'Brandon, you are my son. There is nothing more important to me than your happiness. I want you to find someone to love the way I love your mother, whether it's a woman or a man.'"

The place had grown absolutely hushed. I didn't dare look at Tru, who I knew must be thinking of Richard. Instead, I just hung there in the silence with everybody else, waiting.

"And that's a beautiful thing. A really beautiful thing. It touched me to the bottom of my heart, to know that he felt that way. The only problem is, I'm totally straight. I was trying to tell my dad that once I moved to Baltimore, I'd have to root for the Ravens."

The entire room lost it.

Mom was laughing harder than anyone. She put a hand on my shoulder and a hand on her chest, little tears in the corner of her eyes. I was laughing, too, feeling like I'd let go of something I'd been holding in all summer, though I couldn't say exactly what had been released or why. I just knew it felt good to be here together, listening to people open up.

My mother turned to me and mouthed the words, *I love you.*

By the time the show ended, it was pretty late, so we talked to Nancy only briefly. We all said that the show was great and thanked her for the tickets, and she asked Tru and me about when we were heading back to school. She told me I had great hair. Nothing groundbreaking. No indication of why we were all there. After that we headed back to the car.

For the first few minutes we drove in silence—not awkward silence, just thinking silence. My mind was on my mother, the fact that she brought us here, that she'd done so with such deliberation and confidence and meaning. I wondered if something had changed in her these last long months, because she'd had to shoulder so much for our family. Or maybe what I was seeing tonight had always been there, I just hadn't been looking for it.

While Mom still hadn't spoke, there was a tension in the air, and I knew she was going to say something. I started to think this whole night had been an excuse to break the quiet.

Tru, though, was the one who spoke first.

"Aunt Barb," he said, with that naughty little sparkle in his voice, "you never told me you had such hip friends."

"Ha-ha," she said. "There are all kinds of things you don't know about me."

Tru loved that, I could tell, and we drove on for a few more minutes without talking, though I could sense my mom wanted to say something. Eventually she did.

"That last story actually reminded me of your mom," she said, glancing over at Tru. He stiffened a bit, but she kept going.

"When she was eighteen, she could vote for the first time, and my god, she'd never cared or thought about politics ever. But all of a sudden, it was all she wanted to talk about. Our parents were devoted Republicans. Old-school, or whatever you kids call it now. This was when Bill Clinton ran against George Bush, the first George Bush. So Debbie makes this big, grand announcement about it, just like the guy did with the Ravens, only hers was serious, and our parents were mad. After that, there's Debbie, wearing this 'I'm with Bill' button every day, yammering about who knows what, I can't even remember. It doesn't matter, to be honest, because she didn't have a clue what she was talking about. She just wanted to have her opinion and say it loudly. And she did. Over and over."

"Sounds like it made for lovely family dinners," Tru said.

"Well, it was a tricky time in our lives," she said. "Our parents wanted us to find nice boys and settle down, the sooner the better. They'd done it so late in life, and they wanted us to have all that right away—they thought it was the most important thing. Don't get me wrong. I think so, too, but I would never push my kids the way they pushed us. Anyway, her yelling about politics was just her yelling at Dad to back off. She was my little sister, but I admired her. I never could have done it. I always stayed quiet, did what I was told."

"But so did she, in the end," Tru said. "She got married really young. And to someone conservative. Popped out a kid pretty fast."

"I suppose. But maybe that's just what she wanted to do. I've never seen her as happy as when you were born. I was six months pregnant with the twins, and I came to Connecticut to see her, to meet you. I stayed for a week. Everything seemed so magical. We just stared at you endlessly."

"How entertaining," he said.

"It was," she answered. "Anyway, my point is that she acted out, with all the political talk, and a lot of it was silly, some of it was mean, but it was important, too. We were growing up; we were going to be leaving. Our parents were so overbearing, especially our father. He needed to be pushed away a bit. To start the break. It's hard to explain, but I think you know what I mean. She was such a pain, but what she did was right in some way, or maybe just needed. We were kids. It was all she knew how to do."

"So there's a right way to be an asshole sometimes?" Tru asked. "Or is it only okay when you're young?"

A gentle rain was starting, and my mom sighed. Put on the wipers.

"You don't have to talk like that, you know. You're better than that."

"Well," Tru said. "It's nice that somebody thinks so."

"I do," Mom said. "I hope you know I do."

Tru started shuffling through the CDs in the glove compartment, picked Bruce, as he so often did. At least two times out of three. He put it in and pressed play.

"Does Debbie still love Springsteen?" Mom asked.

There was a pause while the music started to rise.

"Of course," Tru finally answered.

"Is Richard still the only kid from Jersey to ever hate him?"

This time Tru said nothing, but he leaned his head against the window, and I could see his face reflected in the glass, wearing the trace of a complicated smile.

TWENTY-TWO

Devon called again on Wednesday just after dinner, right before Tru and I were leaving for our recon mission to Prettyboy. I took the phone upstairs and talked to him curled up in bed, heard all about his audition that day. It had gone well, he thought, but he'd have to wait until next week to hear the official outcome. He asked if I was nervous about starting at my new school. I told him that I was, but that Winston had told me I could sit with him at lunch, and that it had meant a lot to me. He said that Winston was the best. He told me it was worth it to be patient and really get to know him, that he was worth the wait.

"You, too, Frannie," he said. "You're kind of like that, too."

After I hung up, there was a knock at the door, and Mom poked her head in, asked me if she could grab the receiver. I handed it to her, and she moved back to the door, but lingered there.

"Who was that, if you don't mind me asking? Was it one of the boys who went camping?"

I pretended to be very occupied with smoothing out my blankets and sheets.

"Yes," I finally said. "It was Devon."

"Sparrow's cousin?"

"Yes."

She looked at the phone, studying it at least as hard as I was studying the bed.

"Is he . . . Are you dating?"

I could have lied or dodged this at the very least. But I didn't want to. Not anymore.

"I don't know," I said. "Maybe almost? But not exactly. Not yet."

It was oddly relieving, to say all that out loud. Mom laughed a little.

"I guess that's how things are now. He seems very nice. He must be talented and hardworking, with music. He's cute."

I gave her a look that said *Stop while you're ahead*, and she laughed again.

"Okay, okay. If you do start officially dating, will you tell me? Please? Moms like to know."

I thought for a second, then shrugged.

"Okay. I'll tell you."

She turned to leave, then stopped again. She stood there with the door ajar, hand nervously twisting the knob. She looked uncomfortable, and I knew that whatever she was about to say was hard for her. But I could tell that she was bracing herself to say it anyway.

"Maybe you'll think this is ridiculous, old-fashioned, but there are still people in this world who won't like seeing the two of you together. I like to think it's not a lot of people, but . . . I know that they're out there. I'm sorry to say that Devon probably already knows that. But you . . . I'm not sure that you do. Not really, at least. It's something to be aware of. You can hate it, but you still have to be aware of it. You have to know that it's there."

I stared at my hands, face burning, not sure yet what to say or think.

"Do you think I'm being ridiculous?" she asked.

I looked up at her, then, saw how she was still wedged uncomfortably, half-in and half-out of the doorway, looking intently at my face.

"No," I said. "You're not being ridiculous. I just . . . I feel bad. I feel bad that there are things like that I never used to think about."

She gave me a sad sort of half smile.

"Well," she said, "that's probably the right way to feel."

Then she slipped out the door and was gone.

Because Tru and I would be out until after dark, we told my parents we were going to the mall again, and then took off for Prettyboy. We parked in the same spot as before, the one close to the jump-off. The last shafts of sunlight were streaking through the woods as we walked, illuminating all the million dust motes floating slowly to the ground. Tru was holding *Gatsby* in his hand. I listened as dry leaves crinkled beneath our feet, turning to confetti on the forest floor. Just like last time, we heard the rush of water first, then saw the rocky ledge.

The rope was still there.

We settled down on the rocks again, but this time the evening was mild, felt almost like fall, and they were cool to the touch. We both lay down on our backs. I stared at the sky. Tru stared at his book, flipping pages mindlessly.

"How's Devon?" he asked, but seemed distracted.

"Good, I guess. I think we're good."

"But are you *a thing*?"

"Maybe? I mean, he calls me."

"Well, in that case, I'll reserve the chapel, you pick out the cake."

I covered my face with my hands, thought about Assateague. Devon's shirt slipping down during his handstand, showing that flash of skin. Then later, lips. Tongues. My hand on the back of his neck. His hand slung low on my waist. I rolled over, trying to clear my mind, searching for the right way to ask Tru about Jeremy and get a real response, not a sarcastic deflection.

Before I could, he let out a long, terse sigh.

"I was wrong, Frannie. Last time we were here. Looking at the water. I was very wrong."

"About what?"

"About *Gatsby*. The romance isn't real. It's just sad, pathetic adults inventing meaning where there isn't any. Screwing each other to escape their pointless existence. Which means the tragedy is just that. Tragedy. Ruined lives and destruction. No beauty or meaning behind it. What a load of shit."

I didn't know what to say, so I turned and stared at the rope, studied the knot that tied it to the tree branch, wondering how strong it was. How safe.

"You know, last summer I did this same thing with *The Catcher in the Rye*," Tru said. "And the more I read it, the sadder and more pathetic it got. But that was okay, because it was about being a kid, and being a kid . . . well, it ends. You're just surviving to make it to something better."

Tru stood suddenly, wound the book back like he was a pitcher on the mound. I sat up quickly and actually gasped a little. Maybe it was silly, but I didn't want the book to fall that long way down. To disappear.

But Tru didn't throw it after all. He dropped it at his feet.

"And that whole 'cardinal honesty' thing? The line you read? I'd been missing the point there, too. Nick's a goddamn liar. Everyone's a goddamn liar. We're all just telling stories about ourselves, and we're all full of it."

He nudged the book with his foot, moved it an inch or two. Not quite far enough to fall.

"Maybe not you, Frannie. I've gotta say, you might be my last great hope."

Tru turned and headed for the woods. We'd barely been there five minutes.

Before I followed him, I walked to the edge and looked down one more time into the glittering water. I was thrown off-kilter as I did, tilting forward for one terrifying second before I got my footing. I backed up slowly and carefully. Then I grabbed the little paperback copy of *Gatsby*, with its tattered pages and broken spine. I had to jog to catch up with Tru. When we were back in the car, I placed it between us on the console, not sure if he noticed or cared. We rode home with only the sound of Bruce, not speaking at all until he was pulling the van up in front of our house.

"Can I take you somewhere tomorrow?" I asked him. "It's just a short walk. Please? It's something special. I promise."

A little of his old self returned. He raised his eyebrow just a bit.

"Now *you're* taking *me* on a secret errand? How the tables have turned. I'll go, but if you're not getting a tattoo, I'll be very disappointed."

In fact, I was worried that my secret errand was going to be a disaster. I'd been planning it for week—going back and forth on whether Tru would love it or just think it was silly—and now I wasn't sure at all. Assateague had been everything I'd wanted, it seemed like it had been everything Tru had wanted, but now he was clearly so upset, unsettled. Soon he would be gone, and I didn't yet know what that meant for me here in Baltimore or what it would mean for him back in Connecticut, with his parents.

Still, I decided not to give up on what had once seemed like a grand idea, hoping the magic I'd planned might still come off okay.

I whispered a quick thanks, and Tru just nodded. Then he shut off the ignition, flipped off the lights, and grabbed the book, heading inside without another word.

* * *

We left after dinner Thursday night, walking past the lacrosse field, moving toward the big brick buildings of the Johns Hopkins campus. It had that eerie ghost-town emptiness of a school in summer. I got lost, crossed the street too far down, had to circle back. Tru was beginning to lose patience, and I thought that maybe I had the wrong block or maybe the thing was gone or maybe I'd totally imagined it. I wasn't even sure if he'd want to see it, not anymore, but I just had to try. . . .

And then there it was. I stopped short, and he bumped into me. "That's it!" I said.

"A gross college dorm? Stunning!"

Ignoring him, I approached the building, and placed a hand on what I'd come to show him: the plaque. He came to it skeptically, with his arms crossed. But as soon as he started reading, his posture changed. He loosened up and leaned in. I stood close by his side and read the words along with him, feeling that same little thrill as when I'd first found them a couple of weeks ago on a walk with Duncan.

THE AUTHOR F. SCOTT FITZGERALD LIVED
IN AN APARTMENT ON THE TOP FLOOR OF
THIS BUILDING FROM THE FALL OF 1935
THROUGH THE LATE SPRING OF 1936 WHEN
HIS WIFE, ZELDA, WAS A PATIENT AT THE
SHEPPARD PRATT HOSPITAL. DURING HIS
STAY IN THIS BUILDING, THEN KNOWN AS

THE CAMBRIDGE ARMS APARTMENTS, HE
WROTE HIS FAMOUS MEMOIR ESSAY "AFTER-
NOON OF AN AUTHOR," PUBLISHED IN 1936.

Side by side, we stared at the dull bronzy sign. He reached out and put a hand on my shoulder, but didn't look at me. He didn't say anything, didn't need to.

"Sheppard Pratt—is that the local loony bin?" he finally asked.

"Yeah," I said. "How did you know?"

"Because. Zelda was *fucking insane*."

After a minute of quiet, I moved to leave, but Tru didn't follow me.

"So," he said, hands on his hips. "How are we going to get inside?"

The lie he spun to the security guard was truly a thing of beauty— an elaborate tale about how this had been his freshman dorm, and his little sister here had never seen it. Now he'd had to leave school because his parents couldn't afford the tuition anymore, his father a marine welder who was running out of contracts, and he just wanted to show her where he'd lived that first year.

"Sorry," he said, as we slipped inside the stairwell and shut the door. "Didn't mean to borrow your dad, but it's always the true details that really sell."

I said nothing, not even sure how I felt about it.

"Should we try to find a kegger?" he asked.

"It's not that kind of school," I told him. "They're *nerds*. And they're not even here. It's the summer!"

He shrugged, and then he was off, sprinting up the stairs while I followed, the fluorescent lights flickering and buzzing. He climbed all the way to the top floor and we exited the stairs into a large common room. The door banged loudly behind us, breaking the stillness. A soda machine hummed. Nothing else seemed to move. We were surrounded by empty bulletin boards and shut doors. Without hesitating, Tru stepped forward and tried a handle. It swung open, no resistance.

We walked into the room and saw two stripped beds, two empty desks, two shut wardrobes. Tru sat on the floor and pulled out a joint. I sat next to him, and we both faced the window and stared out, even though we couldn't see much from that angle, just a patch of sky.

"So," he said with a flick of his lighter. "You've had a drink now. Are you interested in some of this?"

I thought for a moment and went with my gut.

"I don't think I'm ready."

He gave me a smile that looked almost proud. Then he took a deep drag.

"Are you worried about going back?" I asked.

He shrugged, exhaling a smoke ring. "Sort of. Did you see that perfect circle? I've really been working on this. You should take stock and appreciate my skills."

"How have your parents sounded lately? Are they acting any different?"

Tru stood up, walked over to the window, and looked down at the earth below.

"Thanks for rescuing my book," he said.

I thought about pressing him, decided this wasn't the time. We had a whole weekend ahead of us when we could talk.

"No problem," I said. "It just didn't seem right to leave it there. I mean, even if you really hate it now."

He inhaled slowly, exhaled another ring. "I don't hate it. I think I love it."

I watched the ring dissolve, read his face to see if he was serious. "You do? You love it?"

"I do. Because it's true. About people. About life. All the harshest, grimiest, dirtiest parts. But there's beauty in the way it's told. I don't know. For some reason, that makes it better."

He drummed the fingers of his free hand on the glass, while I watched from the floor, feeling distant from him, wishing there were some way to pull him back to me.

"So you can still use *Gatsby* to sleep with people?" I asked him. "At cocktail parties?"

He didn't move, just shifted his eyes in my direction. "I've taught you well this summer. And yes, of course. I've got my favorite line all ready."

He ground the mostly unfinished joint into the windowsill, still gripping it as he spoke.

"'They were careless people, Tom and Daisy—they smashed up things and creatures and then retreated back into their money or their vast carelessness, or whatever it was that kept them together and let other people clean up the mess they had made.'"

He directed the words out the window, not to me in the least, and I said nothing more. A minute later we left. We walked back through an inky twilight. When we got home, he went inside while I stayed on the porch, staring off into the park, remembering the safe for the first time in days.

I realized that, of course, I should bring the vodka to Prettyboy. After all, it was supposed to set off a perfect night, be the key to something special. Part of me still didn't want to drink it yet—as long as it was there, then I felt like something great was waiting ahead. But the summer was so close to over, and I had always meant to share it with Tru. It seemed almost like a bad omen if we didn't drink it together.

The time had come.

I thought about digging it up now, but I wasn't sure where I'd hide it, and decided I should wait until right before the big night at the jump-off. For a few more moments, I looked down into the park, then turned around to go inside. But with one hand on the screen door handle, I paused.

Tru was standing in the dining room with my mother. They were partially blocked from my view, but I could see that she was hugging him and saying something in his ear. She pulled away, keeping her hands on his shoulders, looking him in the eyes, saying something more firmly. Secret words that didn't reach me.

I waited for them to separate, then came inside and went straight to my room.

TWENTY-THREE

Friday evening Mom was going out to a wine bar and then to a late movie with Nancy and some of her friends. Jimmy had cackled like a hyena when she told us what she was doing, and he didn't even know who Nancy was—if he did, he probably would have laughed until he died. To be honest, I'd almost laughed, too, because Mom never did things like that, and for a moment I'd thought she was joking.

Then I thought of my father gone. I thought of how hard this summer had been on her. I thought of her taking Tru and me to that show. Suddenly, I felt like an ungrateful little monster.

She got ready to leave and came downstairs in a black wrap dress and her big gold jewelry. Watching her stand by the door, adjusting her hair in the mirror that hung there, I saw that she was young, younger than I'd ever stopped to realize or think about. Barely past forty. When her ride honked out front, I ran over and hugged her before she left. I told her she looked nice.

"Nice for an old fat lady," she said, and patted my head. "You look so pretty lately I can hardly stand it."

She smiled and told me that I should be good. Then she was gone.

I started to go upstairs but paused on the first step when I heard whispers in the dining room. I shifted to the left and saw Tru, conspiring with Kieran in the corner. I paused, hoping they wouldn't turn around and see me.

I overheard Tru telling Kieran that he didn't want to stay at Siren all night for whatever this mystery concert was. He wanted to go for a bit, but then he and Sparrow would drive over to The Mack's last party of the year. Kieran and Tru started debating who would stay sober to drive the minivan home.

"You realize I'll also be bringing . . . ?" Tru said this in a loud voice and pointed in my direction, looking dead at me, knowing all along that I had been there.

Kieran turned and saw me at the bottom of the stairs. He looked worried, but said that it was fine.

We walked to Siren, just Tru and me. He kept looking around, seeming to take everything in, first the houses in our neighborhood and then the busy street with all the shops. Kids on skateboards passed us by, then couples on dates, just like that first night. As I watched Tru watching everything, I realized that we wouldn't make this walk again. Tomorrow was the jump-off. Sunday he was going home.

I almost cried.

"Déjà vu," Tru said as we approached Siren, only this time Sparrow was outside waiting for us, leaning on a lamppost, smoking a cigarette in tight black ankle pants, black flats, and teeny little black tank top with a sweetheart neckline. She looked like some newer, better Audrey Hepburn.

"Nice outfit," Tru said when we reached her. "But if you're dressing up for Kieran, he seems like more of a jean-shorts-and-tube-top kind of guy. Or maybe your mom's old cheerleading uniform?"

She ignored him, snuffed out her cigarette, and took me by the elbow. Tru followed us inside, past the same sad, loser bouncer, who looked no happier than last time to see the two of us. I forgot to hide behind my hair, and he seemed particularly upset by my obscenely young face.

But it didn't matter. We were in.

This time there was no water music, no girl in a purple bob. Just a bunch of guys in T-shirts and jeans playing a Madonna song, while a girl who looked extremely drunk clung to the mike and sang passably along. A big red banner hung over the stage, screaming, *KARAOKE . . . LIVE!* in glittery letters.

"You wanted to come to *this?*"

I hadn't meant to be rude, but the question burst out before I could think. Sparrow leaned on her knees she was laughing so hard, only standing up to point at Truman—who, surprise, didn't seem to care what we thought.

"Actually," Sparrow said, "I saw them last month. The band's pretty amazing. They play weddings, too, so they know everything. There's just no machine to follow, so you have to know the words."

Madonna girl stumbled back into the crowd to a series of loud cheers, and she was replaced by a bearded man in flannel who sang Johnny Cash while half the crowd shouted along. Sparrow began dragging the two of us from the entryway toward a place in the back, because, "Frannie, darling, you are lovely, but in the middle of this crowd you look about twelve."

We were halfway to our hiding spot, dead across from the stage, when Tru stopped in his tracks. Sparrow tugged on his arm in annoyance, but he was looking at the guitarist with a wily grin and would not be budged.

"His T-shirt—that says Rutgers, right?"

Sparrow didn't answer him, just finished ushering us toward our dark corner. We were there all of ten seconds when a guy next to her started chatting her up. As soon as she turned her head, Tru was gone, moving up through the crowd and next to the stage, waiting for the song to be over. I gently poked Sparrow's arm, and when she saw, she just sighed. "I knew he was going to do this. At least I've worked my last shift."

The last notes of the Johnny Cash song faded away and the two of us watched as Tru signaled to the guitarist, then whispered in his ear. The guy smiled like crazy and nodded.

"What's Rutgers?" I asked Sparrow.

She shrugged. "A college. In New Jersey."

Of course. Tru was going to sing Springsteen. I couldn't believe I was finally going to hear his voice.

He didn't have the biggest voice. He didn't have much range. But what he had was liquid and honey, the tone pure and clear. He did the song very understated, never pushing it, hardly moving. His eyes were open. I could feel the people next to us going still. I felt shivery, a sadness soaring inside me, high up in my chest—that certain sadness you only get with perfect pop music, when whatever magic there is in the melody and notes makes you feel alive and mournful all at once. He pronounced the lyrics with precision, and I took in each word.

"It's like someone took a knife, baby, edgy and dull,
and cut a six-inch valley through the middle of my soul."

This was a song about being sad and screwed up, but it was also a song about sex, about sex that helps you forget yourself and the world and everything, everything. In that moment, I stopped thinking of Tru and started thinking of Devon, and I let myself get lost in a big rush of happiness and fear and desire and confusion, the music making all of it seem beautiful.

As the song moved past the final verse, I didn't want it to end.

Tru finished with a repetition of the chorus, *"I'm on fire,"* and the guitarist was winding down and then people were whooping and hollering and raising glasses in the air, and beside me Sparrow was just clapping and smiling and shaking her head. For a few seconds, Tru stood there, absorbing the love, but he didn't look as happy as I would have expected. He looked distracted, distant. He turned to leave the stage, and the guitarist

As a pint-sized girl with a burst of curls ran up onstage, Tru wove back to us through the crowd, looking very happy with himself. The girl warbled out the first notes of a song that I thought was The Beatles.

"You seem to have forgotten that I asked you to lie low and not sing, but of course I never really expected you to listen," Sparrow said. "You up soon?"

"Well," he said, "there was a line, but I seem to have worked around that. I'm next."

He was popping up and down on his heels, fiddling his fingers, absentmindedly whistling. Lacking in his typical cool resolve. Happier than he'd been in days. Seeing him like that made me smile.

When the girl finally stuttered through the last chorus of the Beatles song to a round of polite applause, Tru made his way to the stage, cool and calm as could be. At the same time, the band members started leaving, heading over to the bar for a drink. Only the kid in the Rutgers shirt stayed, and Tru hopped up next to him and arranged himself before the microphone. He gripped both hands around it as the first chords came in, and I recognized a song that I'd been hearing for years in my parents' van, a song that had come on again and again this summer. It always made me think of driving late at night, of going somewhere and doing something bad. And then Tru was singing.

At first, there was too much noise to hear well; people were shuffling around, distracted by the band leaving, not sure what was happening. But after Tru got through the first verse it grew quiet. They turned their attention to the stage.

reached out to shake his hand. As he did, Tru pulled him over for a moment, whispering. The guy whispered back and wrote something on the sheet of paper next to him.

I wondered if Tru was going to have another turn, and I hoped he would. I wanted to stay there all night. I wanted him to sing a million songs. But as he came down the short set of stairs, I thought again of the spelling bee, and just like all those years ago, I was watching his face and trying to understand what he was feeling. This time there was no smirk. Just a smile that was forced and hollow.

I was sure that in his mind, he was already halfway back to Connecticut. Back to his father. Back to whatever fresh miseries waited him there.

After that, people kept coming up to Tru to say nice job or to try and talk to him, but he was aloof, brushing everyone away. He had burned off his jitters from earlier, but they seemed to have been replaced by something new. A sadness, but a fierceness, too. I was watching him nervously, but then he caught me and wiped the expression clean.

The band returned from the bar, drinks in hand, and the guitarist was at the microphone, announcing that the break was over, digging out the page of singers to come. Tru further recovered his cool. He straightened up, looked expectantly toward the stage. The wicked grin returned. He was completely animated. As if he'd boomeranged back from low to high. Sparrow was talking to the two of us and he shushed her, put a hand to his ear, signaling that he was trying to hear.

"All right, everybody! We've got three more singers coming at you. Up next is Jake. Then Sarah. Then Frannie."

My name hit me like ice water. I said nothing, just looked at him. Sparrow was looking at him, too, arms crossed, jaw set. He turned on an innocent expression.

"What? She can sing! You can sing! Not great, but better than these jokers."

I felt a childish urge to push him. "You are so full of shit. You have never heard me sing."

Sparrow put a hand on my shoulder.

"I'll go fix this," she said, then gave Tru a withering look before inching her way over to the band.

As soon as she was gone, I turned an angry gaze on Tru, while he stood there grinning back.

"You're a dick," I told him.

"What else is new, right?"

And now I was sure, there was something off about him tonight. An extra edge, but without the usual sparkle. A moment later, he left me, taking off without another word in the direction of the bar.

I was alone for all of two minutes when I felt a hand. On my ass.

"Little girl is back."

I whirled around and for a moment could only stare, shocked and disbelieving. And then I realized it was him. The creep with the potbelly, the neck tattoo. The two of us locked eyes, and I wanted to scream or kick him in the shins, but I was frozen, able only to look at his smug face, my hands quivering. I watched him part his lips.

Already, the words *little girl—little girl*, of all things—were crawling all over my skin, and now he was going to say something else horrible. I couldn't stand it. I didn't want to hear whatever it was, because I knew the words would stick there in my mind. . . .

"Get away from me."

I hadn't said it as loud as I'd wanted to, but I'd said it loud enough that the people around us were staring. He started to put on an act, looking around in confusion like he didn't know what was happening. More people were turning toward us, but I was still trapped so close to him, packed in with too many people, no clear way to get out.

Then, just to my right, the crowd was parting. People were being jostled, falling aside.

Tru was shoving his way through.

Before I could think or talk he was beside me, his fist swinging up in a beautiful arc. I watched the path it cut through the air and could see that he'd done this before, he'd thrown a punch, and he knew how to do it with gravity and assurance.

His knuckles smashed nose, and then there was color. Red. Electric, sticky red, like a burst juice box.

The man staggered back, hands on his face, eyes shut, almost tripping as people shrank away and space opened all around him.

I couldn't believe the violence of it, of that single hit, because in the movies people get punched again and again and keep going. Now I knew what bullshit that was, because this guy was laid low with only one, though Tru was still there beside me, not backing away, his thin frame locked and loaded. He bounced on his toes and shook out his fist, angry and righteous.

The background noise came back to me slowly—first the shouts and then the scraping of bar stools and the screeching of microphones with no one singing into them. Firm hands gripped my arms from behind and I gasped, tried to pull away, but then I saw it was only Sparrow. With one hand still on me, she grabbed Tru and yanked him hard, one time, two times, three, until he finally relented and started to follow behind her. I chanced a final look back at the man as we began our retreat and the blood was ghastly, curving around his mouth and dripping down into the wispy hairs of his chin. The whole way to the back door Tru was pointing at him and yelling—yelling crazy things like "You fucking pig, I will kill you!"

And then we were outside. I was hanging there like a rag doll; Tru was still tensed and sputtering, and Sparrow had to push us down the alley in the direction of her car. We stumbled ahead of her, and I couldn't stop looking down at Tru's hand, where a trace of red lingered on his knuckles.

"No. No. No. You are out of your mind. There is no way in hell we are going to the party."

We had scrambled into the car and driven several blocks away, now parked on a quiet side street, engine and lights turned off. Sparrow glowered in the driver's seat, while next to her, Tru defended himself, insisting that no one would try to track them down, and even if they did, the best thing we could possibly do was to go somewhere else, where we wouldn't be found, or where we could establish some kind of alibi. I cowered in the back, wishing I was home in my room.

"An alibi?" Sparrow said. "*An alibi?* 'Cause if they actually find you and try *to charge you with assault*, you think that would work? I repeat: you are out of your mind."

"Charge *me* with assault? They should charge that asshole with assault!"

Sparrow turned around and looked at me very seriously.

"What did he do to you?"

I wished she hadn't asked. Just like before, when Tru and I had talked at the beach, I didn't want to say it aloud. It seemed like that made it more real, and I didn't want it to be real. But she kept looking at me, brow furrowed.

"He just . . . called me 'little girl.' Grabbed my ass."

I looked out the window instead of at her face, but I could feel the anger coming off her.

"What a fucker," she whispered. Then she looked at Tru. "You *saw* that?"

"I saw enough."

Sparrow sighed loudly.

"All right, okay. But still. I could have had that asshole kicked out. We could have had somebody threaten him, scare the shit out of him. Johnny from behind the bar or someone. You had to go all Rambo on him instead? Jesus Christ."

Again, I saw the fist. The blood. Tru in a rage. Sparrow was right—it was not the way to handle it.

But I was still glad that he'd done it.

More than that, though, I just wanted to forget the whole thing happened. Not that I thought it would be that easy. The exchange with him had lasted less than a minute; counting the punch it was still less than two. But that didn't matter. I could already feel it taking up space in my mind, preparing to lurk in some dark corner.

But that was something to think about and deal with later. For now I just wanted to drop it. I squirmed in the backseat, ready to get the hell out of there.

"So what are we doing?" I asked.

"Going to the party," Tru said.

"I have so had enough of your shit tonight," Sparrow said. "We are *not* going to that party."

He blew out a hard singular breath and put one hand on the dashboard in front of him, seeming to steady himself.

"Look," he said. "We're supposed to meet Jimmy and Kieran there. I told Kieran I'd drive the minivan home. Which means he's already been there for two hours, drinking. And if I don't show up, I don't know what they're going to do."

Sparrow angrily rolled down the window and lit a cigarette, puffed on it for half a minute. Finally, she spoke.

"We will go there. We will get Kieran and Jimmy. You will drive them home immediately."

Sparrow turned the key without waiting for an answer, and her sporty little car roared to life. Before she pulled out, she looked back at me.

"Frannie, honey. I'm sorry."

We sped off into the night, Sparrow clicking through a couple of songs, unable to settle on anything, no music right for this moment. She turned the sound off, and we sat there in silence. I was left with the echo of Tru singing at the bar, those dangerous words.

A little question wormed its way back into my mind, something I'd started to wonder before, but had forgotten in the midst of everything.

"Why did you say I could sing?" I asked Tru. "You have *never* heard me sing."

For a moment he said nothing. Then he spoke, in a kind of faux-serious tone, thick with sarcasm.

"Well, I've heard someone singing. In the morning. In the shower. That's why I signed you up for the song by that ex-Disney girl. That seems to be your favorite. Or I know you do some of your own versions of the Suck It, Sparrow catalogue. Something Motown maybe, or The Beatles? Or how about "Lola"? You're pretty good at that one."

I was having one of those moments when I felt like a moron, slow and dumb as could be. *How?* I kept thinking. *How? How? How?* Then the pieces fell in place, but with agonizing slowness.

If Tru had heard me in the shower, then he'd been home in the morning.

If he was home in the morning, he'd skipped class.

If he knew I sang all those songs, he'd skipped class more than once or twice or even three times. He'd skipped it a lot.

I started to wonder if he'd ever been at all.

The very idea unraveled me, loosened my insides. I couldn't imagine skipping even one class, and Tru might have blown off an entire course, doing it without a care, doing whatever the hell he pleased all the time. He turned so he was sideways in his seat, looking back at me in the dark.

"You know that little window in the basement, the one in the bedroom? You should really have it fixed. Very dangerous. You wouldn't believe how easy it is to slip right back inside."

Sparrow told him to please just be quiet, he was giving her a headache, but he kept holding onto the headrest, staring at me as if he wanted me to cry or freak out. And I *was* freaked out. He was riled like I'd never seen him before.

I started to wonder who he'd really thrown that punch for—me or him.

The Mack's family lived in a neighborhood within the city limits but set apart, an enclave of winding roads and great big stand-alone homes. His was grand and white with columns out front. The street was already thick with cars, and we parked a couple of blocks away. Tru wanted to go in alone, but Sparrow didn't trust him, and wasn't willing to leave me abandoned in the van either. That meant we were all going in.

We crept through the backyard, Tru leading the way to a pair of sliding glass doors that opened into the basement. He knocked three times and the curtain was brushed aside by Preston Ames, a soccer player I knew vaguely as a happy stoner.

He let us inside with a goofy smile.

"Greetings! You're, like, fashionably late."

I was so wrecked by everything that had just happened, I'd had no chance to prepare myself. I wasn't ready to be here, in a room full of my former classmates who were older and cooler than me. I went in last, tripping over the doorjamb.

The basement was a huge open room with a pool table, a bar, a keg in the corner, and eyes—so many eyes, sweeping in our direction. I saw dozens of people that I hadn't thought of once in all these weeks of summer: beautiful girls, bitchy girls, JV basketball players I'd had moronic crushes on freshman year. Way in the back, The Mack was pouring shots behind the bar. Jimmy sat on top of it, next to a little blonde I didn't recognize. "Sweet Jesus!" he yelled. "Who let my freaking sister in?" I knew my face was red, red, red, but I also knew that no one was looking at me, because everyone was looking at Sparrow. Not looking, staring. And they were staring because nobody knew who she was and because she was beautiful and because she was dressed too nicely for this party. But I knew they were also staring because she was the only black girl there. There was cattiness and envy coming off the other girls in waves, while boys everywhere were taking her in, and I hated everyone, hated all of it.

Kieran appeared at our side, Sparrow and me both relaxing at the sight of him. He put a hand on my shoulder, his other hand holding a red plastic cup.

"How's it going?" he asked, his face bright and happy.

Sparrow bit her lip, and I stood there, without a single word at my disposal. Kieran wrinkled his brow.

"Don't worry," he said. "I know I'm driving. This is just Coke, I swear."

"Wait, you're driving?" Sparrow asked. "Tru told us *he* was driving."

And that's when I turned and realized he was gone, across the room.

Standing with Jeremy Bell.

I could see in an instant that things were bad.

He was standing close to Jeremy, too close, inclining his head in Jeremy's direction, telegraphing what was between them. Jeremy was totally freaked. He wasn't ready for this, wasn't ready for people to see him here with a boy. He actually started edging away until his back was against the wall with nowhere to go. I wondered how the hell Tru could be so oblivious, how he could possibly miss how upset Jeremy was.

But then I realized that he hadn't missed it at all. He never missed anything. He was just on some mad war against the world, burning everything down in his path.

I touched Sparrow's elbow and whispered her name. She turned to look where I was looking.

"We've gotta get him out of here," I said.

For a moment she just stared, and then she was speaking into Kieran's ear. I wanted to scream at her to hurry because all I could think of right then was the sweet way that Jeremy had said hello to me at the campground. All I cared about was saving him. I wanted to run over there, grab Tru's arm, pull him away, but the chaos of the room was making me dizzy. The staccato voice of a rapper drummed from the giant speaker, and all over this enormous space with its oversized furniture, boys and girls were moving and churning. Kids were pressed together, laughing, dancing. They were lounging over chairs and pumping hard on the keg.

Sparrow and Kieran were still talking too low for me to hear. Then fury took over his face, and he grabbed my arm.

"Are you okay?"

Again I heard that nasal voice, calling me a little girl. I felt the hand on my ass. I watched his nose get destroyed. I never wanted to think about it again, and I never wanted my brother, *my brother*, to know anything about it.

"I'm fine," I said. "Fine. Fine. Fine. I just think we should leave."

"We're leaving," Kieran said. "Let me just get Jimmy."

He hurried back to the bar, where Jimmy was in close talks with the mystery blonde. Sparrow and I turned and headed toward the corner, rushing to retrieve Tru, to free Jeremy from him. We were almost there. Another five seconds and we could stop this.

But just as we reached them, Tru leaned in and kissed Jeremy. Swift but sure on the mouth.

Jeremy jerked away, his face going blotchy and red. He glanced at us for half a second, then looked back at Tru, taking a step away from him.

"Dude," he said quietly. "C'mon. What the fuck are you doing?"

"What the fuck are *you* doing?" Tru asked. He spoke like they were joking around, but he said it loudly. There were a couple of knots of people close to us and they were already watching, listening, whispers starting among them. Sparrow maneuvered her body around, trying to block everyone's view, mumbling Tru's name, soft but angry.

"Did I miss something?" Tru asked Jeremy, now practically yelling. The whole room could hear. More people were looking. I turned back toward the bar, and saw everyone staring. Jimmy. The blonde girl. The Mack.

And I remembered then what he said whenever Jeremy came in the door. *"No date tonight? Good."* A sinking started in my chest, went down to my stomach, as I turned back to Jeremy and Tru, watched Sparrow try to casually step between them while smiling as if nothing were going on. I was almost certain Jeremy was going to cry, and now Kylie and Rachel were hurrying over from the other side of the room.

"Truman Teller," Sparrow said, the false smile still plastered on her face. "It's time you took your worthless ass outside."

He looked down at his watch, like all of this was no big deal.

"Okay," he said. "I'll wait by the door. It's getting kind of hot in here anyway."

He inched his way through the crowd, ignoring the gawks and murmurs. He stepped through the sliding doors and stood there in the grass, hands in his pockets.

By then Kylie and Rachel had arrived at Jeremy's side. Sparrow started to mumble something, but then sensed it was better to leave them alone. I felt so bad, I couldn't even look at them. Sparrow grabbed my hand and pulled me back toward the bar, where Jimmy was telling Kieran to get lost, that he'd find another ride.

Kieran, Sparrow, and I went out the back, and I could sense more chatter gathering all around us. Enough people had seen that the room was buzzing about it. We exited into the night air, but Tru was no longer standing there. I felt a little twinge of nervousness, but Sparrow said he was probably just waiting around the corner, by her car. The three of us started to hurry, jogging across the shadowy green of the backyard, emerging beneath the glow of a streetlamp, making our way down the block to where we'd parked.

Tru wasn't there.

"The van's close by," Kieran said. "Maybe he found it."

He started off in the other direction, and we followed. Our feet pattered down the asphalt, past hulking houses, and I could feel the worry grow between us. We tripped a motion-sensor light, and I jumped. A cat darted from beneath a car, and I jumped again.

"Right down here," Kieran said, and we turned the corner, edging around a mansion with a menacing, spiked fence, onto a shady street ending in a cul-de-sac.

Kieran stopped walking. Sparrow and I stopped, too.

"What is it?" she asked.

Kieran looked around him in disbelief. He backed up and checked the street sign. He stared at it as though it might change.

"Oh, fuck," he said.

"Oh, fuck, *what*?" Sparrow asked.

"The van. The van was right here."

For the first couple of minutes, it was as though Kieran and I could bring the van back through logic, arguing that he didn't have keys, he couldn't. Sparrow was very quiet beside us, then spoke in a low voice.

"He got a copy," she said. "Sometimes . . . sometimes he crawled out the window late at night and drove."

"Drove *where*?" Kieran suddenly looked very tall and very angry.

"I don't know," Sparrow said, her voice still quiet. "A couple of times he met me at parties or whatever. But sometimes I think he just . . . drove."

The three of us stood there, lost. The streets here were wide, the yards big, and empty space echoed all around us. Bugs made soulless music. I felt as though I were falling, even as I stood there on the ground. I didn't know where Tru was because I didn't even know *who* he was.

He was a ghost.

A liar.

Truman the Destroyer.

Apparently a fucking car thief, too.

Sparrow and Kieran must have called Tru ten times between the two of them. No answer. We got into Sparrow's car and sat there for a few minutes, radio turned low, waiting for him to reappear.

Kieran jogged back to the house and went inside, checking to see if Tru had returned and parked somewhere we couldn't see. He came back alone, climbed into the passenger seat, and slammed the door. Said nothing.

Nausea rose in my throat. Scenarios kept running through my head: Us going home without the van. Having to tell my mother. Her calling my father.

In the front seat, Sparrow and Kieran were debating. He was a mess and thought we should call Mom now. She was sure Tru would come home before there was trouble, swore he was a master of sneaking around and not getting caught.

From the backseat, I cleared my throat. "He was different tonight."

They turned around to look at me.

"What was that?" Kieran asked.

"He was different tonight. He was . . . I don't know. All keyed up. Jumpy. Sad and then happy and then sad again. He's not acting as cool as he usually does."

"So you don't think he's going to show up at the house?" Sparrow asked. "Before your mom?"

I paused, unsure.

"I don't know. I think . . . I think he just doesn't want to go back to his parents'."

It was eleven thirty. We had an hour before Mom would be back. We decided to check Siren first. We didn't really know where else to try, and when I suggested it, the other two reluctantly agreed that he might be crazy enough to go back there—to try and drink, to heckle singers, to look for the guy he had punched. Who knew.

Sparrow was driving nervously and carefully, so it took some time to creep out from where we were parked, in a back corner of the neighborhood. My fantasies were running wild: every time we rounded a corner, I imagined him there in the van, remorseful.

Truman, remorseful? I knew it was ridiculous even as I kept picturing it, over and over again.

As we pulled out of the neighborhood, back onto the main road, Sparrow and Kieran were fuming, cursing, boiling mad. Totally disgusted with him. The heat of their anger wilted my own. I was still mad, but I was worried, too.

"I know this is bad," I said, leaning forward and cutting off their back-and-forth. "But he's afraid of his parents. He doesn't want to go home to them."

"Yeah, well, he pissed them off pretty good," Sparrow said.

I leaned back, shocked that she would say that. Now I was angry.

"That's not right!" I said. "It's not like it's his fault or something."

"How is it not his fault?" she asked, sounding annoyed with me for the first time ever. "His mother . . . She obviously screwed up on a whole different level, but that doesn't excuse what he did. The whole damn school knows. The whole town."

I looked at her. Kieran looked at her. I felt like I was swimming in a pool that was slowly draining, sucking me down, down,

down. There must be some mistake. We just weren't understanding each other.

"Tru is here because . . . because he's gay," I said. "Because his parents found out and sent him away."

Sparrow's eyes looked up sharply, meeting mine in the rearview mirror.

And then I knew. I had the story very, very wrong.

TWENTY-FOUR

At first I just curled up as small as I could and said nothing. Then I asked how long his parents had known.

"He told them a year ago. No, more than a year ago. They weren't . . . Don't get me wrong, it wasn't easy. They weren't happy. Especially his dad. But he wasn't nearly as awful as I thought he would be. I mean, he didn't try to send him to an insane psychiatrist to fix him or anything. It's more like he put up a wall instead, just doesn't want to think or talk about it. I actually think his mom is okay with it now."

I waited for Sparrow to go on. She stayed quiet. I was afraid to ask any more, but Kieran was not.

"So I don't understand. What do you mean that he screwed up? And Aunt Debbie screwed up? *Why is he here?*"

For a moment she stalled and hedged, stammered, sounding almost as confused as we were.

"I thought . . . goddammit. He told me you knew. He told me you all knew what happened and why he was here. He asked me not to talk about it with you, and I . . . I didn't question it. I thought it made sense, because, well, shit. Because it's a subject better left alone."

"Okay, okay," Kieran said. "I'm sorry—I'm not pissed at you, of course. I believe you. But whatever it is, you should tell us now. You need to tell us."

For a moment there was only silence, Sparrow shifting in her seat.

"I don't know if it's my place," she said. "It's about your family."

Kieran looked at her, while she kept her eyes on the road.

"Exactly," Kieran said. "It's our family. Whatever it is, I think it's time we fucking knew."

Her shoulders slumped, and I could tell she was fed up, exhausted. She gave in.

"His mother," Sparrow said. "She had an affair."

The word bristled in the air, seemed unreal. Something from soap operas or romance novels, not real life. At first, she said nothing more, but then Kieran whispered her name. She said the rest in a fevered rush.

"The man . . . He was someone Tru's family has known forever. He's the father of one of our friends, a kid we went to school with. Skip. He's in Truman's year. And Truman knew about . . .

you know. About his mother and this man. He wouldn't tell me how he found out. And I don't know what, if anything, he planned to do about it. Maybe nothing. You have to understand, his father . . . I don't even know if he really blames his mother. But then Skip had a party one night, when his parents were supposed to be out late."

Sparrow stopped at a red light, rolled down her window, lit another cigarette. A million little details from this summer were tumbling through my mind. Tru's vague responses to my questions about home and coming out. The look on his face when he took a call or a text from his parents. Skip and his dad that day at the police station in Tru's story. *Gatsby* and its affairs.

When the light turned green, Sparrow started talking again.

"They came home early. Skip's parents. His father and mother. Caught Tru and Skip and all these kids drinking. Skip's Dad is, like . . . he's a hard-ass. An attorney. He flipped out. Screaming at them. Really awful stuff, belittling them. Taking it way too far."

We were almost there. I could see our turn just up ahead. Sparrow still drove slowly, like she didn't really want to get where we were going.

"This is all secondhand. From Tru. So I can't, you know, vouch for it exactly. But he told everyone. Right there. And I just know that it was bad."

Sparrow left it at that, but I could see the rest of it unfolding perfectly, all the details filled in like some scene in a movie. It was set in the drawing room of a beautiful mansion in Connecticut, with lush rugs and leather sofas and cabinets full of fine liquor. The man was in a tux, the woman in a spangled dress with shining jewelry. They were back from the symphony because she didn't feel well. There were kids everywhere, drunk and draped on furniture, then leaping up, trying to hide their cups and cans. He yelled and threatened and told them to sit their asses down in a row and they did. All of them did except for Tru.

Tru was standing up, the glass in his hand shining with some amber liquid. He would have been looking dapper in a T-shirt and jeans. And then he would have opened his mouth and done the unthinkable, letting loose what he knew, being beautiful and awful all at once. Hurting many.

He said I was the honest one. I wasn't so sure. For all his lies and his bullshit, part of me thought that the honest one was him. But a different kind of honesty. Not the cardinal kind.

Sometimes honesty was a darker thing. Maybe even selfish. Maybe even cruel.

Sparrow and Kieran sat in the car outside Siren for a minute, arguing about whether Kieran should come in, too. She said there was no way she was sneaking in more underage people after what happened earlier, and Kieran finally relented. Sparrow disappeared inside, alone. Kieran turned around to look at me, and I could tell that he thought he should ask me more about what happened with the me and the creep. I stared back at him and shook my head.

"I don't want to talk about it. Not now. Please."

"Okay, okay. I'm sorry."

He turned around and looked at his phone, mumbling something about texting Jimmy to see if Tru had reappeared. I leaned my head against the window, watching the crowds filter by. Ice-cream cones tilted in their hands. Cigarettes hung from their lips. Couples walked hand in hand. Everyone seemed to be laughing, happy, clinging to this last bit of summer, giving an extra buzz to the air. The sidewalks were packed, almost every parking space full.

And then suddenly there was our minivan, screeching head-first into the last empty spot on the block.

I jumped a little at the sight of it, but Kieran was still busy on his phone and didn't notice. Some instinct kept me quiet for a moment. I just waited and watched, sure that Tru would get out and walk toward Siren any second, and then I'd have to give a yell, make sure we stopped him.

But if I craned my neck I could see that the van's lights were still on. He hadn't moved.

I should tell Kieran. I knew that I should. But I wanted to talk to Tru, and I knew that if we confronted him now, it would be chaos, a shouting match. Sparrow and Kieran fighting with him, while I was shut out on the sidelines.

Quietly, I readied myself to run.

"I'll be right back."

I said it so fast, I doubt Kieran could even understand me, and then I was out of the car, not even bothering to shut the door, just racing down the sidewalk. I reached the van, opened the passenger side, leaped onto the seat, and shut myself in with a slam.

Tru looked only mildly surprised to see me.

"I keep forgetting I'm not in Connecticut anymore. I really need to keep this thing locked. God knows who might get inside."

"What are you doing here?"

"Well, the party at the Mack's was really kind of a drag. I thought maybe I'd come back here and listen to more half-assed karaoke. Or finish kicking someone's ass. You know, whatever."

Before I could respond to that, Tru clicked his tongue and said, "Oh my."

He was looking down the sidewalk, watching Kieran sprint toward the car. The engine was still running, so it only took him a second to throw the van in reverse and speed off down the road. He was driving way too fast, almost clipping the bumpers of the cars on our right.

"Where the hell are we going?"

"Right now, just away from your brother. And Sparrow, I presume. I didn't see her, but I'm sure she's rounding out the little Hardy Boys crew that's on the hunt for me. How mad is she? She used my full name, so that's never a good sign. Did she smoke a million cigarettes on the drive over? That's another one of her tells."

I buckled my seat belt, at a loss for words. A few quick turns and we were out of the neighborhood and heading south, where things quickly got dingier, dirtier. We stayed quiet for a few minutes, while outside my window, the city deteriorated, happy little row houses turning into busted-up row houses turning into abandoned row houses, their windows bricked over with crumbling mortar. A siren wailed.

"We should go home," I said quietly. "Before we get in trouble. So we can still go to Prettyboy tomorrow."

He scoffed.

"Oh, right. Our little adventure. I know it's a big deal and all, but I'm a little distracted at the moment. You know, preparing to go home and start my senior year. Everyone loves senior year! So many memories to make."

I couldn't even picture Tru sitting at a desk, taking quizzes or whatever—and when I thought about it a little harder, I realized more fully what it would mean, to be back with all those kids he'd known forever.

"But . . . are you really going back to the same school?" I asked. "Even after everything?"

He shot me a look, taking in the fact that I knew. He ran a hand through his hair.

"Oh yes. I'm going back to the same school. With Skip and all my buddies. Richard insisted, which—I have to give it to him— is an amazing power move. Mom and I will be holed up in the house together, and he's gotten a place in the city, it sounds like. I'm sure that legal moves are imminent. So you'll have to pardon me if I'm not really focused on our big swim. Frankly, I don't think Jeremy will want to join, so I may just bow out completely."

That brought back the image of Jeremy at the party, on the verge of tears, while Tru blew out the door like nothing had happened, nothing at all. Then I was angry. Really angry.

"You shouldn't have done that to Jeremy."

I wanted to tell him that it was cruel, but I couldn't quite form the stark edges of the word. Then he looked at me so hard I almost flinched.

"Jeremy? That's why you're mad at me? *For Jeremy?*"

I clenched my jaw. I wouldn't let this go.

"It's hard for him! He probably never kissed anyone before, and then you…you embarrassed him. You made him uncomfortable."

Tru ran a red light as I gripped the seat. Horns blared in our wake.

"And what do you think life is like for me, back home? Just gorgeous young gay men everywhere I look? What exactly do you think my options are? Perhaps you don't realize this, but my school is almost exclusively populated by the future presidents of the Ivy League's douchiest frats."

That wasn't something I'd ever thought about, and I tried to process it, but there was too much going on. I couldn't think straight.

"I didn't know." My voice was small and bruised. "What about prom? What about Andy?"

"Andy? *Andy?* Andy is fifty pounds overweight. He's a fairy. He's a freak."

He looked over at me then, and his eyes were empty. Nothing there at all. Tears pricked at the corners of my own.

"Oh Jesus, Frannie. C'mon."

But I couldn't help it. They spilled over.

"Still," I said. "You shouldn't have done that to him. It was wrong."

"You feel sorry for Jeremy because you feel *like* Jeremy," he said.

"You're quiet and you're shy and you're always afraid of what people will think. You don't want me to be mean to Jeremy because you don't want me to be mean to you."

The tears just kept falling, and I couldn't make them stop.

"You lied to me," I said. "About why you were here."

He jerked back at that, just the slightest bit.

"Yeah, well, sorry. You came up with that story, not me."

"But why? Why did you let me believe it?"

"I don't know, all right? I don't fucking know. Maybe because you're not my bestest friend who I tell all my secrets to? Maybe because if you felt bad for me, it was easier to make you do what I wanted? Take your pick."

He came to a screeching stop at a stop sign, and we both flew forward, hitting hard against our seat belts. He slammed again on the gas, drove faster than ever, passing cars when there was barely room. The windows were still up, and it was hot and miserable inside the van.

"Screw you." My voice was a whisper, but it was angry. "You didn't even care that I was always nice to you, that I wanted to be your friend from the beginning. I was always here for you. I accepted you."

As soon as I said those last words they felt wrong, but it was too late. They were hanging there between us. He slowed down a little. He leaned his left arm against the door, while the fingers of his right hand rested more lightly on the wheel. His body had lost all its tension, but somehow that scared me more. He was lounging there like a panther, lazy before the pounce.

"Accepted me? Yes, you always accepted me. Your fag cousin. How big of you. How wonderful that I came to Baltimore, so you could throw me a pride parade and feel really good about yourself."

My face went crimson, and I almost screamed at him, told him that he wasn't being fair. But at the same time, I knew that somewhere in that accusation was an inkling of truth.

I wanted to curl up, to hide my face in my hands, but I couldn't do that. Not yet. I had to stop this, stop him, before something bad happened. I looked out the window to see where we were. Somewhere in the middle of the city, still heading south. I searched for a sign on one of the cross streets we were passing, but then I realized I didn't need any signs.

Shining just ahead of us in the night was a soft pink glow. Now blue. Now yellow. The twin hearts sending out their wordless message over the city. We were almost to the train station. Another minute and we'd be there.

"Well, look at that," he said. "Back to where we started."

He chuckled a little, and the hollowness of it scared me more than anything yet.

"Please," I said. "Can we just go home?"

"My god, Frannie. All right. You are entirely too concerned about your curfew, you know that? I thought you'd loosened up a little."

He yanked the wheel to the left, turning at the last possible second into the drop-off lane, the whole van leaning to the side, wheels screaming as we skidded, bumped, rebalanced.

"We'll turn around right now," he said.

He directed us to the roundabout, the one that looped the base of the sculpture. The man and woman towered overhead. Tonight they didn't look like art or a stupid joke either. They looked like a pair of monsters set to terrorize the city. Tru drove us around the circle but didn't drive out of it. He went around again.

And again.

"Tru," I said quietly, hoping to snap him out of whatever this was.

Instead, he sped up.

We went around. And around. Faster and faster.

Someone honked, but still, we whipped around endlessly, to the point that I was dizzy and I knew Tru must be, too. I grabbed the door with one hand, my seat belt with the other.

"Stop it, Tru! You're going to hurt us!"

"Well, it's just me being a dick again, right?"

And still we went around. Around. I could feel the van starting to lean, really lean. My heart was a hummingbird, thrumming in my chest.

"JUST STOP! I'VE HAD A SHITTY FUCKING NIGHT, AND I NEED YOU TO STOP!"

For a second he kept us flying, but then he exhaled sharply. He eased up on the gas, gently pushed on the brakes. We were still moving around the circle, but at least we were going more slowly. I waited for my pulse to stop careening.

But Tru didn't quite have control.

The front tires were where he wanted them, but the back swung out like we were doing a doughnut. I yelped as he tugged on the wheel, trying hard to correct us, to get the van back on track. He whispered, "*Shit, shit, shit,*" just under his breath, knuckles white as he strained to get everything in line, trying to slow us down just gently enough that we wouldn't spin out.

And he did it. We eased to a stop. We were at a slightly awkward angle, the front of the car facing the sculpture, but we were okay. I could hear both of us breathing.

I was about to punch him in the shoulder and shriek at him, but when I turned to do it, I saw a security guard running right toward us. Tru saw him, too.

Again he said, "Shit, shit, shit."

Tru threw his arm over the back of my seat, turning to look over his shoulder. He just needed to back up a couple of feet, and we'd be positioned to fly out of there. He hit the gas.

He hit the gas before he put the car in reverse.

He hit the gas, and we hopped right up onto the base of the sculpture.

TWENTY-FIVE

The security guard was screaming.

A pale old man with a scraggly beard, he yanked open Tru's door, sputtering and red-faced, shouting something about the police being on their way. He grabbed Tru's arm, as if he were going to physically pull him from the car, but Tru jerked free of him with a violent motion, turning a hard gaze on his face.

"Don't. Touch me. We're getting out."

The guard staggered backward, and Tru swung the door wide with a shove, jumping out. I quietly opened mine, stepping awkwardly out of the tilted van. With a small rush of relief, I realized it was really just on the curb, not touching any part of the sculpture itself. No damage. Not even tire marks on the asphalt. Even the van looked fine.

With an angry sweep of his arm, the guard ordered us toward

the sidewalk in front of the station. It was so late that there weren't many people around, just a few onlookers, whose eyes I avoided. The guard muttered the whole time as we walked, then yelled at us to sit on the curb. I slumped right down, hunching over into a semifetal position, letting my hair fall down around my face.

When I finally chanced a look at Tru, he was leaning back on his palms, face open to the night. He was looking up, toward the glowing hearts.

As the guard continued to pace behind us, I said something to Tru, as quietly as I could.

"Text Kieran. Tell him to cut Siren out of the story. Just say we all went to the party, and then you and I left with the car."

Tru didn't say anything, but he did ease his phone halfway out of his pocket, and I was pretty sure he was doing what I'd asked.

"They're going to breathalyze you," I said gently, warningly.

For a moment, he said nothing. He tucked the phone away, looking up again at the intertwined figures. Then he finally spoke.

"Different bartender tonight at Siren. Wouldn't serve me. Never got a chance to have a drink at the party. Guess it's my lucky day. Now please, for god's sake, let me sit here in silence."

That's when I realized that despite the casual pose, his face looked defeated in a way I'd never seen before. This wasn't the frustration he'd shown at the edge of Prettyboy or the raw collapse after he'd sung. He just looked . . . tired.

As for me, I was a mess. I was mad at Tru, but I was mad at myself, too. Not until just now, as we screamed at each other in the car, did I start to realize the mistakes I'd made, the depth of them.

I'd told myself a story about who Tru was, a story that made him into both a certain kind of victim and the sort of hero I needed. It was a story that fit my view of the world. A story that made me feel good about myself. A story that I leaned on to help me break free. But it wasn't the truth. The truth was far more complicated. Tru was far more complicated.

I couldn't quite look him in the face, so I just shifted my eyes from my shoes over to his. The black Converse he'd worn the first day here.

This was a moment when I needed to say something meaningful. I searched for some words that would ease the pain of our fight but also let him know that he was kind of a shit. I wanted to tell him that he was still my friend.

But I couldn't think of anything, and then came the thunder of a siren.

The cops were already here.

There were two officers, both young, one a smirk-faced white guy who seemed to be trying not to laugh, the other a black woman who was much more businesslike. She couldn't have been older than twenty-five or so, but she was looking at the two of us the way a mother would look at her unruly children.

I met her eyes and felt more ashamed than ever.

For a couple of minutes they just walked around a bit and talked to each other. They went over to the van and gave it a look. My eyes kept moving to their guns, their handcuffs. Staticky messages burst from their radios, making me jump.

Finally, they came to stand in front of us. They recorded our names, our addresses, asked what our relationship was. They took Tru's license and kept it tucked away.

The woman asked for Mom's number and walked away to call her. She kept her back to us, and I was actually glad that I couldn't quite hear what she was saying. Imagining my mother's face was bad enough without any words to go along with it.

After they had finished with the near-hysterical guard and ushered him back inside, the two of them came to stand in the pickup lane, looking down at us. They both seemed weighed down with too much equipment, their belts creaking and shifting as they moved.

The woman asked us to stand up, and we did.

"Would you like to tell me what happened?"

I assumed that Tru had a story ready, some beautiful lie that would put all the other lies to shame. A lie of redemption, a lie to save us.

The seconds ticked by, and he said nothing.

"You were driving," Smirky said, pointing his pen at Tru, notebook waiting in the other hand. "So why don't you tell us?"

Tru had been looking up at the sculpture again, but now he cast his eyes back down. He folded his hands and spoke simply. Not the bullshit polite way he had. Just calm, emotionless.

"There's no good reason for what I was doing. We were just driving, not headed anywhere, and we were out past our curfew.

We needed to head home, so I came in here. To turn around. But then I drove around the sculpture a few times. I thought I was being funny. But I went way too fast."

The woman cop gave him a raised eyebrow, and it was a thing to behold. Nothing else moved on her face. It almost put Tru's to shame.

"That's it? You just decided to have a little Indy 500 around... this thing?" She waved her finger behind her, pointing at it without bothering to look.

"I know," Tru said. "It sounds stupid. It was stupid. We just... Frannie and I . . . We have a little joke. About the sculpture. I guess that's why I did it."

"A little joke?" she asked.

Smirky put his hands on his belt and turned to look up at the two figures, stretched into the sky.

"Isn't the whole statue kind of a joke?" he asked.

The lady cop shot him a look, and he went back to scribbling in his notebook. She stared at Tru a moment more, then looked at me, assessing.

"And you? You look pretty embarrassed, and that makes me think you must be a nice young lady who knows better. Do you have anything to add?"

"No," I said, but it caught in my throat. I coughed and tried again. "It's exactly what he said. That's what happened. And I'm very, very sorry."

For a few minutes, they ignored us, talking to each other, making a call or two. Not long after a cab pulled up and out walked

Mom. Still looking nice in her black dress and big jewelry, but her face . . . her face was a twisted mess of fear and anger.

They breathalyzed Tru, and it came back at zero.

They called and checked for anything on his record. Nothing at all. Not even a speeding ticket. Mom stepped to the side with the female cop, speaking quietly just out of our hearing.

In that moment while we were alone, back to sitting on the curb, Tru spoke to me, softly enough that no one else could hear.

"I came up with a slightly different story. I told Kieran we'd go with this version: I went to The Mack's house tonight with the twins. But then I took the van and ditched them. I was really upset about something. I came home, and I was a mess. I talked to Richard on the phone, and I seemed even worse. I went to take off and you came with me, to be with me or talk to me or whatever."

He sighed.

"It's not the best, I know. But let's just go with it. I think it will work. It makes me the only real bad guy tonight, so consider it my little mea culpa. That way we can say good-bye on nice, neutral terms. Wipe this summer from our memories, go back to ignoring each other like our mothers do."

I didn't know what to say. I couldn't tell if he was still mad at me, or if maybe he'd stopped caring at all. I didn't want either one to be true.

Tru shifted his weight, trying to sit more comfortably on the curb.

"Mea culpa? That was Latin, you know. So I learned a little something this summer after all."

A classic Tru joke, only this time it was stripped of its fire. He didn't even look at me to see if I had a reaction.

The cop was back in front of us now, arms crossed. She looked at Tru.

"You don't want to hurt yourself, and you definitely don't want to hurt somebody else. Trust me. You won't be laughing at your 'little jokes' when something like that happens."

Then she looked at me.

"And you. When you get in a car with somebody, you put your life in their hands. Don't ever forget that."

Smirky took charge of easing the van off the curb and setting it right, just to be extra careful that nothing happened.

And like that, they let us go.

We drove home in complete silence. When we walked in the door, Kieran was waiting in the living room, in the dark. He shot up off the couch and looked at us.

"Upstairs," Mom told him. "Now."

He didn't hesitate, and I tried to follow him, but Mom ordered me onto the couch and told me to wait. Then she went into the backyard with Tru.

For a moment I slipped to the edge of the kitchen and spied on them. They stood just outside the door, beneath the glow of the light, bugs buzzing around them. Tru's head was down, but Mom kept looking right at him while she spoke.

I went back to the living room and sat alone in the dark, not bothering to turn on any lights. I didn't want to think about what Mom was saying to Tru or what she was going to say to me, so I tried to distract myself with thoughts of Devon. As I had a million times over the past week, I relived the kiss, every moment of it, from me running down the path to the magic appearance of the horses. Like one of my old fantasies, but this time it was real life. It ran through my mind again and again, blocking—if only for a few minutes—the memory of everything that had happened after. The man at Siren. The fight with Tru. The look on my mother's face when she got out of the cab.

The front door rattled, and I jumped.

It was only Jimmy.

He slunk inside rubbing his head, looking slightly tipsy. His ride sped off with screeching tires. He looked at me, then looked at the time on the glow of his phone.

"I am in so much trouble."

"Nope," I said. "It's your lucky day. Or night, I guess. Mom's out back. If you go upstairs now, you're saved."

He looked around, confused.

"Why the hell is she in the backyard? Why are you sitting here in the dark?"

I didn't know where to begin. Instead, I asked who his little blonde friend from the party was.

"Some new chick. *Candy*. Seriously, Candy."

"Yeah," I said, "that's kind of a bad name."

"It's kind of a stripper name. Do you think she liked me?"

I tilted my head, tried to remember her body language.

"Yes," I said. "I think so."

He did a stupid dance, pumping his fists and shaking his hips. I tried not to laugh, but couldn't help it.

"Oh, so you think I'm funny, too? Am I as funny as your best friend, *Truman*?"

"You're an ass," I said, but my voice was light.

He paused, swayed, considered.

"Oh, I'm a huge ass," he said. "Sometimes I don't know what's wrong with me."

Then he made for the stairs, tiptoeing up, doing an exaggerated *shhhhh* motion with his finger. I almost laughed again, but I felt my face crumple a little as I did. He paused where he was, squinting at me.

"Hey," he said. "Is everything, like, okay around here? And what the hell is going on between Tru and Jeremy Bell?"

Just then the back door creaked open, and I shooed him away. He hurried up the last of the stairs as Mom came back into the living room, and Tru disappeared to the basement.

She sat next to me on the couch, in the dark. For a minute we seemed to have achieved some state of equilibrium, a perfect silence. As long as I didn't speak, she wouldn't speak, and eventually I could run to my room and hide until the world ended.

"Do you understand how busy and tired and worried I am right now?" she finally said.

I didn't trust my voice, so I just nodded while she watched me.

"No, Frannie," she said. "You actually don't. You can't

understand at your age, I'm sorry to say. But I'd like for you to imagine it the best that you can. And I want you to promise me that you will not add more grief to my life."

"I promise," I said, and the words were soaked in tears.

If I had escaped upstairs just then, I think she would have let me go. But I didn't want that to be it. It seemed like just this week we had finally started talking, and I didn't want to stop.

"I'm really, really sorry. And I know you must be mad at Tru. But I just think he was upset. About stuff at home."

My words seemed to echo in the air between us. Mom began to nervously move her bracelet up and down her arm. She was never good at staying angry, and already I could feel some of the heat of tonight receding from her.

"I imagine you're right," she said. "I don't know how much he's told you about everything. But things are bad. Debbie and Richard are separating. Officially."

A sinking started in my chest, landed in my stomach. I said nothing.

"I know you're not a kid anymore, I know that, but still. I'd rather not go into all of the details, at least not right now. I'm hoping..."

She let that thought die. Again she was methodically moving the bracelet up and down, up and down.

"Everybody has a different cross to bear. That's something to remember. I know it doesn't feel like it right now, but we don't have it so bad. Not really."

There was so much I wanted to say to her, but I could only manage one brief mumble.

"Tru really likes you, Mom."

A smile did break across her face then, but it was the saddest smile I could imagine. A smile that thought it wasn't worth a thing.

I hugged her, and she held me tight, almost too tight. I stayed there for a minute, and then asked if I could go to bed. She released me.

I crept up the stairs and into my room. The twins were murmuring behind their door, and I quickly shut mine. I crawled into bed, where I tried to stop picturing the sculpture, its twin figures rising defiantly against the sky, shining and glowing, Tru and me run aground at their feet. Instead, I thought back to the night he arrived, when we'd stared up at the heart, and I'd made him smile. With a joke that he still remembered.

And that's when I had a brilliant thought, much too late. When we sat on the curb and I couldn't find any words, I knew now what I should have said.

Very subtle way to say good-bye.

He would have loved that, absolutely loved it, I was sure. It would have broken the tension, started a mend to our rift. But of course it didn't help me now, alone here in my room.

At the beginning of the summer, I felt like I was always ten steps behind. Now I was only two.

When I woke in the morning it was early. I crept downstairs but no one was around. I poured myself a glass of water, stared out the kitchen window as I slowly drank. I knew Tru might still be sleeping, but I couldn't wait. I needed to see him.

The steps to the basement creaked like crazy as I descended. His door was open a crack, and I knocked quietly, then waited. Nothing. I knocked again, then peeked inside.

No Tru. The air seemed unusually still. The bed was neatly made.

I rushed back upstairs, just as the front door opened. It was Mom, alone.

I started to get a bad feeling. My face buckled in confusion.

"Oh, honey," she said. "Debbie wanted him home right away. I had to put him on an early train."

At first I could only stare at her, not willing to believe it.

He had left without telling me good-bye.

TWENTY-SIX

At noon, I heard Dad come through the front door. He ducked into the kitchen and found me, Mom, and the twins in the kitchen, leaning against the fridge and the counters, eating a lunch of thrown-together sandwiches. His face, neck, and arms had deepened to a rich brown red—not quite a tan, not quite a sunburn. I cringed, waiting for him to explode, but I kept forgetting that, according to Tru's version of events, we'd barely done anything wrong.

He didn't even look at the boys or me, only at Mom.

"I should have been here," he said, without even a hello. His duffel bag slumped to the floor.

My mother's smile was tight, but her eyes shone with something like love. Or maybe just relief.

"We're fine," she said. "The van is fine. Poor Tru . . . I think he'll be fine, too."

Jimmy threw his arms up into the air. "Seriously? I'm going to run the car into a trillion-dollar piece of art and see if anybody says, *Poor Jimmy*."

Dad told him to shut up. Kieran told him to get his crap out of the room and back down to the basement. Mom told Kieran not to say *crap*.

And so it began, the chorus of bickering, everyone bumping into one another, grabbing the last of this or that while someone else loudly complained, all of them trying to navigate the small space without causing a collision. And me—I stood there and said nothing at all. The fight with Tru, the way he'd left, all of it had bruised me, and I was trying very hard not to prod around and test for damage. Not yet, at least. But there in the kitchen, with him gone, I felt my old nervousness and quietness threatening to return, ready to wrap me up like a blanket.

I wasn't going to let it.

Tru had gotten me out into the world, but now that he was gone, I had to keep the door open. I wouldn't go back to the way things had been.

I couldn't go to the jump-off like we'd planned, not after last night. Mom and Dad seemed okay, but I was sure they'd be on the alert, wary of more trouble. So what, then? It's not like I could go on a date with Devon—he hadn't asked, first of all, and besides, nobody went on dates. And I couldn't just hang out with him and the band, or him and P.J. None of that felt right. I needed girls, I realized, but I didn't have any.

Or maybe I did. I did have some girls. If I was willing to call them.

And I had vodka.

Grabbing the phone, I went up to my room and called Devon. I said that Tru was gone, breathlessly explaining why—an abbreviated version, at least. As I told the story, he just kept saying, "Holy shit," over and over again until I got to the end.

When I told him how the cops let us go, he responded at first with a pause.

"I can't believe they let you go," he finally said, with a short, hard laugh. "Or maybe I *can* believe it."

His voice sounded odd, but I rushed on, because I was actually getting a little thrill from telling this story, my first encounter with the police.

"I know—when it was happening, I was totally freaked out. I thought we were screwed. But I guess they just saw us as dumb kids or whatever. I don't know, maybe cops don't really have time to bother kids. They probably just like to scare them."

Another heavy pause. "Some kids they have plenty of time to bother. Some kids they do more than scare."

"What do you mean?"

"What do I mean?"

For a few beats, I sat there dumbfounded. I genuinely didn't understand. But then I did.

He meant if it were him, it wouldn't have been that easy.

"Oh." This was all that I could come up with, and it hung there in the air between us.

"So you know what I'm saying?" he asked.

Completely mortified, I tried to think how to answer, how to save myself. I thought maybe I should try to be funny.

"Yeah. I mean, I do. I know what you're saying. This, ah, wouldn't be a good situation to try Black Guy, White Guy, I guess."

This time, though, Devon wasn't laughing. I mumbled a practically inaudible "Sorry." Then like a total moron, I kept talking, trying to make things better.

"Actually, one of the cops was black. She was, ah, she was kind of nice, I think. I mean, she wasn't nice, she was mad or whatever, but . . . she seemed like a good cop."

At first he said nothing. Then he cleared his throat.

"Yeah, you'd think that would matter, if the cops are black, but it doesn't always matter. Which . . . it makes these kinds of things even more screwed up."

And with that I was out of things to say. I was still so freaking clueless sometimes. First Tru, now this. It was like I knew just enough now to realize that I knew almost nothing. I wanted to hang up the phone and go hide in some dark corner of my closet. That would have been the easiest thing to do.

But now there was a question burning in my mind, and I thought it was better to ask it.

"Have the cops ever bothered you before?"

I heard him shifting around on the other end of the line, and when his voice came back, it was softer than before.

"Actually, no. My friends, some of them can tell you stories. But I've been lucky. Part of that is because I'm careful. My mom has seriously *drilled* that that kind of shit into me, because she worries. A lot. She comes out and watches me lock my phone in the glove compartment before I can leave the driveway."

"In the glove compartment? You mean so you can't text?"

He laughed a little. "Yeah. She's crazy. Plus if I wrecked her precious hybrid she'd kill me."

I could feel a purposeful change in his voice: he wanted to get away from this conversation. He was trying to sound light.

"So, ah, what's going on with tonight?" he asked.

I took a breath and plunged ahead, pretending like everything was fine. I told him then that I couldn't go to the jump-off, not after everything, not with my parents on edge. And even though I was now nervous as hell, I asked if he and P.J. and Winston and Tara wanted to come to my neighborhood instead, to hang out in the park across the street and have a drink. He said yes, and relief rushed through my body like a physical force. As we hung up, I closed my eyes, told myself that everything might still be okay.

After that, I called Mary Beth, asked if she wanted to bring the girls and meet in the park. I said that I had boys. And vodka. She said yes, too.

Finally, I asked Kieran if he and Sparrow wanted to come, even though it was just a bunch of dumb younger kids, doing nothing much. He smiled at me kind of sadly and said no thanks. He told me he had wanted to hang out with Sparrow that night, but she'd passed. She didn't think it was a good idea.

"You should call her again," I said. "Maybe she'll change her mind."

My voice wavered a bit when I said it, though. We both sensed, I think, that the fleeting spark between them had passed, or been extinguished, perhaps, by one bad night.

Mary Beth, Dawn, and Marissa met me at our house after dinner. I told Mom we were going to sit in the park for a bit, just until it started to get dark, then we were walking down the block, to meet Devon and the other guys for ice cream or maybe something from the coffee place. She looked a little suspicious, but I reminded her that those shops only stayed open until ten. We'd be back by ten fifteen.

She gave me her cell phone. She told me to be good. She told us that we were not to stay in the park after dark, not under any circumstances. She eyed the red dress she had given me, looking at my legs. I scuttled away to grab a few iced teas, and then we hurried out the door, across the street, and down the hill.

The park was still mostly empty from the heat. Mary Beth and Dawn couldn't stop giggling. Marissa was quiet and nervous. We walked quickly to the bridge, slipping into the white cavern. This was the first time I'd passed this way in a few weeks. Looking at the walls, I searched for the summer's new graffiti, but couldn't separate it from the old—the confessions mingled with the anger, woven in with the declarations of love.

I told them to wait there, while I went to get the vodka. Popping out the other end of the tunnel into the fading sunshine, I picked my way through the overgrown grass and weeds. My hands dove into the sumac and pulled out the red handle. Trying to keep from getting too dirty, I dug into the ground just enough to open the lid and lift out the bottle.

I was ready to rush back to the girls, but as the vodka lay heavy in my hands, I paused. I realized now how silly my initial plan seemed, the idea that I could have won Tru over with this, that it would be the key to our friendship. Clearly he'd been able to find booze and pot just fine without me . . . and becoming his friend was a lot more complicated than some lame little bribe.

All summer, I'd been saving this for some epic, perfect night with Tru. But this afternoon, when I'd made the plans to finally drink it, I'd forgotten all that. It wasn't some magic token to a better summer. It wasn't a secret weapon to impress people.

It was just a bottle of cheap vodka. Something to share with my friends.

Moving more slowly now, I tiptoed out of the overgrowth, slipped under the bridge again, where right away I heard the girls murmuring. They had their backs to me as I approached, and they were whispering to one another in a strange way, like maybe something was wrong. As I come up behind them, they looked toward me for only a second, then turned their focus back out to the open field of the park.

I realized they were watching Devon, who was jogging quickly toward us.

Devon. As soon as I saw him, his easy stride, his smile visible even from here, I wanted desperately for everything to be okay. I wanted not to be so stupid; I wanted us to be able to talk. I wanted a second kiss, an even better kiss than the first.

From my stance behind the girls, I raised both arms, waving big and wide, smiling back at him.

"Frannie, why is that sketchy guy coming down here?" asked Marissa. "Should we leave?"

Her words hit me like a blow.

"I have, like, tons of shit in my purse," Mary Beth said. "My iPad, my new phone."

They turned back to look at me, wide-eyed and nervous, and only then did they see my frozen pose, arms still raised in the air, calling Devon to us.

As I lowered them to my side, comprehension flooded their faces. They looked embarrassed.

But not, I thought, embarrassed enough.

"Oh, shit," Marissa said. "Sorry. I mean, I didn't know. We didn't know."

I had no idea how to respond, and I couldn't have anyway— Devon was almost here. As he approached, I took in every detail of him. The skinny jeans, the David Bowie T-shirt, the perfectly white sneakers. His big eyes shined, his hair was twisty, as it had been since the day I met him. I still thought he looked like he belonged on a college brochure. He didn't look *sketchy*.

Except that he did. To the girls.

He arrived at my side, and I did my best to smile as he grabbed my wrist, gave me a kiss on the cheek that felt more friendly than anything else. He pulled his cell out of his pocket.

"We came in way at the other end, at the top of the path? Everybody else is by the creek—I just came to find you." His thumbs flew over the keys, and when he was finished, he shoved the phone away, gave his most charming smile to the girls. "Hey there. I'm Devon."

He shook all their hands as they told him their names, and I tried to read their faces, hoping to see more guilt than they had shown before, but I couldn't tell what they were thinking, what they were feeling. And now I could see P.J., Winston, and Tara were hurrying over to us, too. They came from a break in the trees, their necks craned, looking around and smiling, taking everything in. A moment later they were there beside us, everyone introducing themselves in a flurry, telling me thanks for the vodka.

Meanwhile I could barely think straight, could barely form a word. All I could do was replay what the girls had said, again and again. I was angry at them, but I was angry at myself, too. Because I knew that a couple of months ago, I might have reacted exactly the same. Even now, I cringed to admit this, but I'd probably be edgy, too, having the same kind of thoughts they did, if it was a black boy I didn't know. If it wasn't Devon.

I felt a little pinch on my arm. I turned and there he was, smiling. Concerned.

"You okay?"

I tried to smile back, felt myself failing. "It's been a weird couple of days."

He tilted his head, looking at me closely. We were standing a little bit apart, and he kept his voice quiet. "Look, I'm sorry about earlier. On the phone."

"No," I said. "I'm sorry. I said some stupid things."

"It's fine. I mean—I don't expect you to get it." I winced a little, and then he did, too, as if it had come out sounding worse than he'd expected. "I just mean it's hard to understand."

I looked down, nodding, because nothing had ever seemed more true to me. Everything, everyone, was so hard to understand—this summer had convinced me of that completely. Everything that Sparrow had said that day at the stadium was suddenly echoing back to me. I was hearing her words about the quiet, subtle way we view people, how insidious it can be. And I knew that she meant the way that the world looked at black boys, and I felt a little chill when I thought of the emotion in her voice, and when I thought about that the fact that she was right. The big, tragic things that happened with the cops, the little ugly judgments made by people like my friends, like me—they were all part of it. I'd spent so much of my life never bothering to think about things like that, and even now that I wanted to, it was hard to know where to begin. I was starting to understand how many little biases I had, how much they affected the way I saw people, the assumptions I made. And not just the Black Guy, White Guy kind of assumptions. There were so many others. I was starting to realize how unfair I'd been to some of the people in my life, really important people. Two months ago, I hadn't understood Kieran—not really, at least. I hadn't understood my mother either.

Or Tru.

But the fact that I'd been so mistaken and had still managed to know them better . . . that gave me hope. At least I could go try to move forward with a more open heart, whether it was in school next year or whatever came beyond. Being a nice, quiet girl wasn't enough, I knew that now. Trying to see people for who they were—once I started trying, I wasn't sure the work would ever stop. It meant looking inside, deep inside, and not always liking what was there.

I couldn't imagine a graceful way to do it—fumbling would have to be enough.

Devon had walked back closer to the others, leaving me to linger apart and alone. I almost edged away from him, closer to the girls. But instead I stepped forward, grabbed his hand lightly, pulled him back toward me.

"I just wanted to say . . . I wish that I understood better," I told him. "I want to."

His fingers gave mine a light squeeze, and this time he hung on for a moment. That touch gave me some small rush of relief, of joy, and I tried to live there, in those seconds when we were palm to palm. I tried to forget all my tangled and intricate failings.

Our hands drifted apart, and we found a place to stand in the tight circle that was forming. P.J. was busy chatting up the girls, wearing a full-on silly grin, speaking in a pretend-suave voice and tipping a pretend hat as he liked to do. They were sent into fits of happy laughter. In that moment, I added P.J. to the list of people that I hadn't seen clearly. The way he owned himself, his goofiness—it was something to admire.

We opened the vodka and mixed it into the iced teas, pouring until the bottle was bone-dry and then hiding it in a bush. Sitting on the concrete, the seven of us passed the drinks around, sipping slowly and talking softly. I couldn't forget what the girls had said, I didn't want to, but even as it hung over my head, I tried to just be here in this moment, imperfect as it might be.

Devon wanted me to tell everyone about what had happened with Tru, and so they all listened as I spun the story of his last night in Baltimore. I didn't tell everything—nothing about the man at Siren. Someday, I could talk about it, the way Tru could talk about the rock, the police station. But I wasn't there yet. I left out the part about Aunt Debbie, too, kept Tru's motivations murky. Without all that, the story had a kind of mad, pure beauty. Already, I could feel it growing and changing, becoming a legend.

Split among us all, the vodka wasn't much. Just enough to give the last light of day an extra sheen. Just enough that we had an excuse to be here together, shaping this twilight into something that mattered, something worth remembering.

That night, after I crawled under my sheets, a knock came at my door. I sat up as Mom walked in, and I was sure she was here to grill me, to ask me where I'd been tonight, if I'd stayed in the park later than I should.

But then I saw that she had something in her hand. A book.

Not just a book. A worn-out paperback with a broken spine, pages roughed. *The Great Gatsby.*

"I forgot that this was in my purse. Tru gave it to me before he left. Said he wanted you to have it."

She handed it to me with a sad smile, then turned around and left.

Tears came to my eyes as I opened it, and I was sure that he had written me a note. The inside cover and first page were full of pencil scrawls, but not for me. They were just words. Big words from the book that he'd looked up, copying down their definitions. I sat there and read through them again and again, reading them for their beauty, not for their meaning, reciting them to myself like a prayer. *Wan, garrulous, hauteur, meretricious, caterwauling, affectations.* On and on they went.

The last one made me blush: *orgastic.*

Tru still loved words, still studied them. Here they were in all their beauty. And like he said, somehow that beauty made things better.

The whole book, in fact, was covered in soft pencil scratches. Sloppy and half-finished, his thoughts were there on nearly every page—little missives that I was sure I'd never fully understand, like an excavator trying to make sense of some lost civilization.

I turned the lights off and dug out my flashlight, the one I'd used when we went camping. Under the safety of my covers, I flipped through the pages swiftly but carefully. I went two times through before I found what I was looking for: the part I'd read out loud to him that night. The part about honesty. Cardinal virtues. Underneath those sentences, he had drawn the faintest line, almost invisible. Just below that, he'd made a mark.

It could have been almost anything, perhaps just a slip of a pencil. But the longer I looked, the more I felt sure it was an *F,* drawn with some measure of tenderness.

EPILOGUE

A year would pass before I made the leap from the jump-off.

It was the end of the summer after my sophomore year. There were five of us who went in the middle of the night. We hadn't planned to do this, had come here on a whim, and we didn't have swimsuits. I was the last one to get undressed, and I noticed that the other girls, already walking toward the rope, were down to their bras. I had an extra layer tonight, a little tank top, and I left it on. It was too thin and white to be much of a shield, but I still felt better that way. Less exposed. More like me.

I took another minute folding my shirt and shorts and probably looked like I was stalling. Really I just wanted a moment alone to take this all in. The dark, the smell of water, the sound of cicadas. Our laughter, echoing. As I watched everyone else walk over toward the edge—tugging on the rope, issuing challenges, deciding who would go first—I was happy to kneel there alone, grass tickling my legs, just watching and thinking.

Right before I went to join them, I pulled my phone from my purse, sent a quick text.

At Prettyboy. About to jump.

I waited for a moment, even though I didn't necessarily expect a reply. I hadn't been in touch with Tru for a while, after all, too busy and distracted with other things. Besides, he didn't always respond, and when he did, it sometimes took a while.

But this time my phone buzzed right away.

Guess my invitation got lost in the mail? Unbelievable.

Don't tell me everyone else is there without me.

My mouth screwed into a smile. Someone called my name, and I told them I'd be just a second.

Nah. Different people. New friends from school.

A moment passed without Tru answering, so I followed up with a question.

What are you doing tonight?

The silence from him continued, so I tucked the phone back into my clothes and made a move to leave.

Then came another buzz.

In with the boyfriend. Don't worry, I'm breaking up with him before I leave. Only the most shameful and pathetic of optimists show up to college attached.

The phone gave one more little shake.

Swing high and fall fast. If you don't make it, I'll speak beautifully at your wake.

As I put my cell away, I smiled. I walked over to where every-one waited, feeling braver than I would have guessed, half-naked in the veil of the night. The ground roughed my bare feet, a night breeze chilled my skin. But none of that mattered now. Looking up at my friends, I was filled with a giddy, silly kind of love for them, all of them, but especially the one I'd lately fallen for—the boy who right now was holding the rope, inclining it in my direction.

I went and stood right next to him, looked out. Spread before us was the dark horizon of the reservoir. I took the rope from him. At first he looked surprised, but then he smiled, backing up to give me room. Before I could look down, before I could think too hard, I ran. I ran and tossed myself toward the glassy, black abyss.

There was a moment, just a moment, of suspension, when I had absolutely no control, and I could only fall, fall, fall. . . .

I hit with a hard splash, and Prettyboy was as chilled and dark and deep as I'd thought it would be. I came up for air and waved my hands to show I was safe, not sure if anyone could even see me. Whipping my legs, feverishly treading to stay above water, I heard a splash to my left. Then one to my right. Then some-one came down so close to me, I actually yelped, the impact sending a ripple of waves washing over my face. There was a pause, and then the final jumper came down with a whoop and a crash.

We called to each other, laughing, stroking over until we could see each other's faces, until we could see that all of us were okay.

The boy is looking at me. I can just barely see his expression in the dark, but it's enough that I know. I know that something's going to happen. I duck down below the water, then burst back out, brushing the hair back from my eyes.

I'm ready for anything.

ACKNOWLEDGMENTS

Thank you. . . .

To all those who were kind enough to offer advice and encouragement on early drafts, including Elisabeth Dahl, Elissa Weissman, Maggie Master, and, of course, Jennifer Fortin, an amazing writer and best friend.

To my agent, Steven Chudney, who has been such a stellar advocate for this book. From the very beginning you saw both what was good and what was missing. The chapters I added with your help are some of the best and most important.

To my editor, Andrew Harwell, who delivered brilliant insight with enthusiasm and key criticism with diplomacy. Working with you is a privilege. Thank you from me and thank you from Frannie, who was able to grow so much more with your help.

To all those who contributed at HarperCollins. From cover

design to copy editing, I've always felt I was in the very best hands. I'm thankful to everyone there who believed in a story about a quiet girl from Baltimore.

To the Rivers and Hattrup families, I am incredibly lucky to have you and forever grateful for all that you do for me. Thank you especially to my parents, who are wonderful in every way. Thank you to my mom, who made me love reading, and to my dad, who always thought it was cool that I did.

To Kevin, who, for years, remained irritatingly insistent that this book would be published. Thank you for being optimistic when I was not. Thank you for making me think and laugh every day and for helping me to build a life that's everything I could want. More important, thank you for your incredible ability to come up with fake band names. I still think the boys should have picked Thunderface.

To Nora. Being your mom changed my life in so many ways. It's made me want to do something big. It made me want to keep trying.

To Liam. In the midst of all the nerves and excitement that came with watching this book come together, you were a ray of light, putting everything in perspective.

JOIN THE

Epic Reads

COMMUNITY

THE ULTIMATE YA DESTINATION

◀ **DISCOVER** ▶
your next favorite read

◀ **MEET** ▶
new authors to love

◀ **WIN** ▶
free books

◀ **SHARE** ▶
infographics, playlists, quizzes, and more

◀ **WATCH** ▶
the latest videos

◀ **TUNE IN** ▶
to Tea Time with Team Epic Reads